THE DREAD LINE

Forge Books by Bruce DeSilva

Rogue Island
Cliff Walk
Providence Rag
A Scourge of Vipers

THE
DREAD LINE

Bruce DeSilva

A Tom Doherty Associates Book

NEW YORK

THE DREAD LINE

Copyright © 2016 by Bruce DeSilva

A Forge Book
Published by Tom Doherty Associates, LLC
175 Fifth Avenue
New York, NY 10010

www.tor-forge.com

Forge® is a registered trademark of Tom Doherty Associates, LLC.

The Library of Congress Cataloging-in-Publication Data is available upon request.

ISBN 978-0-7653-7433-2 (hardcover)
ISBN 978-1-4668-4144-4 (e-book)

Our books may be purchased in bulk for promotional, educational, or business use. Please contact your local bookseller or the Macmillan Corporate and Premium Sales Department at 1-800-221-7945, extension 5442, or by e-mail at MacmillanSpecialMarkets@macmillan.com.

First Edition: September 2016

Printed in the United States of America

0 9 8 7 6 5 4 3 2 1

For Mikaila, who came to us as a wary two-year-old
and has grown into a confident, strong-willed, open-minded,
independent, and stunningly beautiful young woman.
I can't wait to see what she does next.

AUTHOR'S NOTE

This is a work of fiction. Although a few of the characters are named after old friends, they bear scant resemblance to them. For example, the real Marcus Eliason is a retired Associated Press journalist; he is not and has never been the assistant director of player personnel for the New England Patriots. Several real people (Hello, Bill Belichick) are mentioned in passing, but only a handful of them have speaking parts, and those who do are allowed only a few sentences of fictional dialogue. My depictions of Rhode Island history and geography are as accurate as I can make them, but I have played around a bit with space and time. For example, Hopes, the newspaper bar where I drank years ago when I wrote for *The Providence Journal,* is long gone, but I enjoyed resurrecting it for this story. References to past scandals are largely factual, but the events investigated—and in some cases perpetrated—by the main characters of this novel never happened. I made them up.

THE DREAD LINE

1

He was a serial killer, but I didn't hold that against him. It was just his nature. The *way* he killed irked me some. His victims were all missing their heads. But what I couldn't abide was his habit of using my porch as a dump site.

The first corpse appeared on a cool, damp September morning. I'd just carried my second cup of coffee out the back door and settled into my Adirondack chair with the daily newspaper. As I read, I was vaguely aware of the cries of the gulls and the slap of the waves against my dock. Then something red fluttered in my peripheral vision.

Even without a head, the victim was easy to identify. A northern cardinal. Either that or a scarlet tanager, but I hadn't spotted one of those in Rhode Island in years. This killer, I thought, preferred to slaughter things that were beautiful. But his next two victims were moles. Then a wren, a starling, and a field mouse.

Like most predators, he clung to the shadows, but today I finally caught a glimpse of him as he fled down my porch steps. A big tabby with a torn left ear and a matted coat. People on the island take care of their pets, so this one had to be a stray. Or maybe it was feral. He'd left me his latest victim, a full-grown rabbit.

Cat the Ripper was escalating.

I didn't figure I'd be able catch him, and reforming him was out of the question, but perhaps I could nudge him into choosing another disposal site. It was time to get a dog.

I was on my laptop, checking out the offerings from the Animal Rescue League of Southern Rhode Island, when Johnny Rivers belted out "Secret Agent Man," my ringtone for Bruce Mc-Cracken, the boss man at McCracken & Associates Confidential Investigative Services. "Associates" was an exaggeration because I was the only one—and I was part-time.

"You busy?" he asked.

"I am."

"With what?"

"Shopping for a dog."

"Yeah? I got an ex-con pal who needs a new home for his two-year-old Rottweiler."

"Why?"

"Says he's getting too aggressive."

"No thanks," I said.

"Don't tell me you want a damned punt dog."

"What's a punt dog?"

"A little shit you can dropkick fifty yards."

"Oh, *hell* no," I said. "I want a pooch big enough to knock me down when I come home. But I'd prefer one without a record."

"I don't think Bandit's bitten anybody yet."

"Maybe so, but with a name like that, he's destined for a life of crime."

"Speaking of crime," McCracken said, "we've been retained to look into a major one."

"Oh?"

"Seems somebody knocked over the Pell Savings and Trust branch on the island."

"When was this?"

"Three weeks ago."

"What? How come I haven't heard about it?"

"Because armed robbery is bad for business," he said. "The bank's trying to keep it under wraps."

"They *did* call the police, right?"

"Oh, sure."

"And?"

"And they're not happy with the lack of progress from the, quote, hick Jamestown PD."

"Bank robbery is a federal crime," I said. "Isn't the FBI involved?"

"An agent from the Providence office took a report, but you know how it is these days. If it's not terrorism, the feds aren't much interested."

"How much did the bank lose?"

"I don't have any details," he said. "Mildred Carson, the branch manager, wants a face-to-face."

"Did you say *Mildred*?"

"I did."

"There are still people named Mildred?"

"At least one, anyway. So can you handle this or not?"

"Gonna reimburse me for mileage?"

"Mulligan, you *live* in Jamestown."

"So?"

"So the whole damn island is only one mile wide."

"Yeah," I said, "but it's nine miles long."

Jamestown, population 5,405 in winter and about twice that in summer, is the lone municipality on the island of Conanicut, which basks like a harbor seal at the entrance to Narragansett Bay. I was keeping house this year in a five-room cottage situated on two acres of meadow along the island's north shore, just a ten-minute drive from Newport's mansions and forty-five minutes south of McCracken's office in downtown Providence. I'd bought the place last spring, about nine months after I lost my job as a reporter for the dying *Providence Dispatch*. The little house needed work, but it was a step up from my old digs in a squalid Providence triple-decker.

My new job with McCracken seldom paid enough to meet the mortgage, and the loose change I picked up freelancing for *The Ocean State Rag*, a local news Web site, barely covered my cigar and Irish whiskey habits. But for the first time in my forty-five years of life, I had a little money left at the end of the month. Before he retired to Florida last year, my old friend Dominic "Whoosh" Zerilli had taken pity on me and made me a silent partner in his bookmaking racket.

After two decades as an investigative reporter for Rhode Island's biggest newspaper, it felt odd to be living above the poverty line. It felt even odder to be a lawbreaker. But the way I saw it, I wasn't breaking any important ones.

2

Mildred Carson sat behind a glass-top desk in an office the size of a motel bathroom. I put her at thirty-five years old, with watery blue eyes and a Viking helmet of straw-colored hair. A pair of eyeglasses with purple frames hung by a chain and fell between swollen breasts draped in a violet maternity dress. She looked to be about fifteen months pregnant.

"I was *expecting* Mr. McCracken," she said.

"Really? I was thinking it might be twins."

She frowned and drummed her fingers on the desk. I waited a beat for any sign of amusement. Seeing none, I added, "I am Mr. McCracken's associate."

"May I see your credentials?"

I opened my wallet, slid out my PI license, and dropped it on the desk. She put on her glasses and took half a minute to examine it.

"Mr. Mulligan," she said, "what I am about to share with you must remain strictly confidential."

"So I've been told."

She removed the glasses and took another half minute to study me. "May I count on your discretion?"

"Sure thing. Long as I can stay sober."

She arched one painted-on eyebrow. "I do hope that was another attempt at humor."

"That makes two of us," I said, and flashed a grin that could charm the bloomers off a Bible-thumper. She returned it with a scowl.

"I have no patience for banter, Mr. Mulligan. Can I trust you with this or not?"

"Your secrets are safe with me."

"Your firm came highly recommended," she said, "so perhaps I can make allowances for your lame comedy routine."

"Lame? Perhaps I should fire my writers."

The corners of her mouth twitched as if she were fighting off a smile. Maybe I was growing on her. "Then let's proceed," she said. "Where would you like me to begin?"

"As the King said to Alice, 'Begin at the beginning and go on till you come to the end. Then stop.'"

She furrowed her brow at the allusion. Then it came to her. "Lewis Carroll?"

"Yes."

"My, my. A gumshoe who reads."

"I'm full of surprises, Mrs. Carson. I can even count to ten."

She did smile this time, displaying a row of small bleached teeth. "The beginning would be quarter past nine on the morning of September eighth, when one of our most valued customers, a gentleman who lives in an estate off Highland Drive, entered the bank."

"You mean one of those mansions on the island's south shore? The ones with a view of the Castle Hill Lighthouse?"

"Yes. One of those."

"What's the gentleman's name?"

"I'd prefer not to identify him unless it becomes absolutely necessary."

I chose to let that pass for now. "So what happened next?"

"He crossed the lobby to the desk of our assistant manager, Belinda Veiga, and requested access to his safe deposit box. Miss Veiga had him sign and date the signature card, and together they stepped into the vault. They located the correct box number and inserted their keys. As Miss Veiga removed the tray, a man entered the vault, pointed a handgun at them, and ordered them to remain silent."

"Hold on," I said. "Did you witness any of this?"

"No. I am merely repeating what the gentleman and Miss Veiga related to me and to the police."

"Then if you don't mind, I'd prefer to hear Miss Veiga tell it."

Carson nodded, picked up the phone, and asked her to join us.

Belinda Veiga stood about five feet four, with black dreads that bounced on the shoulders of a pearl-gray business suit. She looked to be in her mid-twenties. Judging by her brandy-colored skin and Portuguese surname, she was among several thousand Rhode Islanders whose ancestors hailed from the Cape Verde Islands off the west coast of Africa. The woman I'd been getting naked with had taken a temporary out-of-state job this year, but that didn't mean I was in the market. Still, I glanced at Veiga's left hand out of habit. No ring. As she slid into the office's other visitor's chair and crossed her legs, I tried not to stare. I was not successful.

The bank manager handled the introductions and explained why I was there. Veiga sighed audibly.

"Tired of repeating the story?" I asked.

"Uh-huh. And tired of reliving that day."

"You must have been very frightened."

"Yes."

"I'm sorry to put you through this again Miss Veiga, but I assure you it's necessary. Can you start with when you first sensed something was amiss?"

She paused for a few seconds to gather her thoughts. "As I turned to hand the safe deposit box tray to the customer, I saw him stiffen. That's when I turned toward the vault door and saw the man with the gun."

"Did he speak?'

"Not at first. He just put a finger to his lips and went *shhhhh*."

"Can you describe him?"

"Not really. He was wearing a ski mask."

"What color was the mask?"

"Black."

"Could you tell his race?"

"White, I think."

"Eye color?"

"I don't know."

"How tall?"

"About a foot taller than me."

"Thin? Fat?"

"Not obese. Other than that, I couldn't say."

"Why not?"

"He was wearing a loose-fitting sweatshirt."

"A hoodie?"

"I didn't notice a hood."

"What color was the sweatshirt?"

"Mustard colored."

"Yellow mustard or brown mustard?"

"Brown."

"Any lettering on it?"

"I don't think so."

"What else did he have on?"

"Blue jeans, I think."

"Hard shoes? Sneakers?"

"I didn't look at his shoes."

"Any visible scars or tattoos?"

"Not that I could see."

"Rings on his fingers?"

She shrugged. "He might have been wearing gloves, but I'm not sure. It was hard to take my eyes off the gun."

"What kind of a gun was it?"

"I don't know anything about firearms."

"Was it a big hand cannon like Dirty Harry carried? Or a small one that fit neatly in his hand?"

"Small."

"A revolver or an automatic?"

She gave me a blank look.

"Mrs. Carson," I said, "could you please type 'images of handguns' into Google, click on the first listing, and show the results to Miss Veiga?"

She did, turning the computer screen so the assistant manager could see it.

"Like this one," Veiga said, pointing to a revolver. "But shorter, I think."

"Okay, then. What happened next?"

"The man told me to put the tray down on the metal table we have in the vault. Then he handed me a roll of duct tape and ordered me to bind the customer's hands."

"In front or in back?"

"He didn't say."

"So what did you do?" I asked.

"I bound them in front."

"Did the customer say anything or try to resist in any way?"

"No. I think he was even more afraid than I was. His hands were trembling."

"What did you use to cut the tape?"

"My teeth."

"And then?"

"He ordered me to put tape over the customer's eyes. When that was done, he put tape over my eyes, too."

"Did he bind your wrists?"

"No."

"Huh. . . . I wonder why."

"I have no idea."

"Perhaps he didn't consider you a threat."

"Sure," she said. "That makes sense."

"What did his voice sound like?"

"I never heard him speak normally. He just whispered."

"Then what happened?"

"I heard some rustling and clinking sounds. I assume that was him removing the contents from the box."

"And then?"

"He told us to remain in the vault and count slowly to one hundred."

"Did you?"

"Yes."

"And when you were done?"

"I peeled the tape off of my eyes. The masked man was gone."

"Along with the contents of the box?" I asked.

"Yes."

"How long would you say the whole thing lasted?"

"Maybe three or four minutes."

"What had been inside the box, Miss Veiga?"

"I never saw, but I understand the customer has provided a list to the police."

"What did you do next?"

"I rushed into the lobby to sound the alarm. Then I fetched a pair of scissors from my desk, returned to the vault, and cut the tape from the customer's hands."

"Thank you, Miss Veiga," I said. "We're done for now."

When she was gone, I asked Carson why the "gentleman" had wanted access to his safe deposit box that morning.

"He was returning a diamond and emerald necklace that he normally stores in our vault. He had taken it from his box the previous Friday afternoon so his wife could wear it to a weekend society event in Newport."

"What event would that be?"

"I don't know."

"Was there a bank guard on duty in the lobby on the morning of the robbery?"

"There was."

"Really? Most small branch offices don't have them."

"Wealthy clients who summer on the island seem to find their presence reassuring."

"The guard's name?"

"Owen McGowan."

"A retired cop?"

"Yes."

"Did he notice anything suspicious?"

"No."

"He didn't see an unauthorized person walk into the vault?"

"He wasn't watching the vault. He was at his post by the front door, keeping an eye on the teller windows."

"Because bank stickups normally happen there?"

"We'd never been robbed before," she said, "but I've been told that is the case."

"Think McGowan was hungover?"

"Why on earth would you ask that?"

"September eighth was the day after Labor Day," I said. "The holiday is one of the booziest of the year. I for one got totally wasted."

"I believe Mr. McGowan was in full command of his faculties."

"Then why do you suppose he failed to notice a man in a ski mask?"

"The gunman didn't pull it on until he stepped into the vault."

"You know this how?" I asked.

"From our surveillance cameras."

"Did they capture the guy's face as he passed through the lobby?"

"No. He knew how to turn his head to avoid them. And when he passed directly in front of one of them, he held a handkerchief over his nose as if he were fighting a cold."

"May I review the surveillance video?"

"The police have it," she said.

"Is there video from inside the vault?"

"No. There aren't any cameras there."

"Why not?"

"Safe deposit box customers expect a measure of privacy. Would you care to speak with Mr. McGowan?"

"Maybe later." I sat silently and thought for a moment.

"Doesn't this robbery strike you as awfully high-risk?"

"How so?" she asked.

"What if another employee had stepped into the vault when it was going down?"

"It's against policy for anyone else to enter the vault when a safe deposit box is being opened." She paused for a beat, then added, "I guess the robber must have known that, too."

"Maybe so," I said. "What did he manage to steal?"

"Jewelry. Very valuable pieces, as I understand it. The customer has provided a list, along with photographs of each item, to the police."

"Including the necklace the customer was returning to the box?"

"Yes," she said. "The robber removed it from the customer's suit jacket pocket."

"Interesting. That suggests he knew it was there."

"So it would seem," she said.

"And the customer's name?'

"Why?"

"Obviously I need to talk to him."

"I'm not at liberty," she said, "but I can ask if he would be willing to meet with you."

"Could you call him now, please?"

"If you would step out for a moment," she said.

So I did, taking a seat in one of the visitor's chairs in the bank lobby.

It felt good to finally have an interesting case. Until now, my work for McCracken had consisted of delivering summonses in civil suits, investigating employee pilfering at a Walmart, doing background checks on a handful of Raytheon Company job applicants, and tracking down a couple of sad sacks who were delinquent on their child support payments. I was still reveling in my good fortune when Mrs. Carson stepped out of the office and tapped me on the shoulder.

"I'm sorry," she said. "The customer declined your request for an audience."

"An *audience*? Is that your word or his?"

"His."

"Who the hell does he think he is, Prince Charles?"

3

Mister Ed, my year-old metallic-blue Ford Mustang, taunted me whenever I flouted Rhode Island tradition and obeyed the speed limit. He was doing it now, his 420-horsepower five-liter V-8 neighing "Chicken!" as I dawdled across Narragansett Bay's west passage on the majestic Jamestown Verrazzano Bridge. I cranked up the volume on the sound system and let B. B. King's guitar drown him out. I was as big a scofflaw as anyone, but with the top down on this fine fall afternoon, I saw no reason to hurry.

When the bridge disappeared in my rearview mirror, I swerved south on Tower Hill Road and headed for Curtis Corner in the sleepy village of Peace Dale. It was more than a year since I'd been down this way, and I was surprised by what I found. Judging by the look of its new home, the Animal Rescue League of Southern Rhode Island had found some generous benefactors.

I pushed through the front door and strolled past a wall of glass. Behind it, a space larger than my sitting room was crawling with cats. A few other felines peeked out from the bars of wire cages, perhaps because they were recovering from injuries, perhaps because they were bad-tempered.

Just ahead, a young woman in a peasant blouse, her auburn

hair pulled back in a ponytail, sat behind a receptionist's desk. She rose to greet me.

"Good morning, sir," she said. "I'm Tracy O'Malley, the shelter manager. Is this your first visit to our new facility?"

"It is."

"Impressed?"

"I am. It's swankier than the Atlantic House hotel."

She laughed. "The building is six thousand square feet. We have individual kennels for dogs, a quarantine area, a community meeting room, a food preparation space, offices on the second floor, and a grassy, fenced yard where dogs can socialize outside. Oh, and I believe you've seen our cat playroom."

"Sweet," I said. "How much did all this cost?"

"One point eight million."

I whistled. "How'd you manage to pay for all this, Ms. O'Malley?"

"Oh, please. Call me Tracy. About a third of the money was bequeathed to us in the will of a local animal lover. The rest came from a fund-raising campaign."

I raised an eyebrow.

"When it comes to homeless animals," she said, "people can be very giving. Would you like a tour?"

"What I'd like," I said, "is to find a good dog."

She beamed and said, "Please come with me."

We turned and entered a large airy space lined with windows on the right and a long row of roomy wire dog kennels on the left. The occupants started yipping.

Tracy stood near the doorway and watched me as I strolled slowly past the kennels. About a third of the dogs appeared to be purebreds. A few were pups, but most looked full-grown. Only the golden retriever was an old-timer, the hair around his muzzle geezer-white. They all looked healthy and well cared for. The ASPCA wouldn't be shooting any of those mournful animal cruelty TV commercials here, I thought.

When I got to the end of the line, I turned back and squatted beside a kennel that caged a well-muscled mutt who looked vaguely like a German shepherd.

"Hello, girl," I said.

She whined, wagged her tail, and pressed her muzzle against the wire.

I talked quietly to her for a while, then moved to a cage that held a huge dog with a large head and a barrel chest. He was mostly black with a white blaze, chest, and paws and with rust-colored markings on his legs and along the sides of his mouth. Before I could squat, he reared up on his hind legs, braced front paws the size of oven mitts on the wire, and stared into my eyes.

"Who's *this* guy, Tracy?"

"That's Brady," she said. "He's a Berner. A Bernese mountain dog. We don't often get one of those here."

"Named after Tom Brady?"

"Could be. He already had the name when we got him."

"Hi, Brady," I said. He stuck a tongue that Kiss's lead singer would envy through the wire and tried to lick me.

"I take it you want a big dog," she said.

"I do."

"Then you should also take a look at Rondo."

"Named after Rajon Rondo?"

"Yeah. I stuck him with that. I'm a big Celtics fan, and I was really mad when they traded him to the Mavericks."

"He doesn't look very big," I said as I squatted in front of his kennel.

"He will be. Probably bigger than the Berner. He's only ten weeks old. Just look at the size of those paws."

She unlatched the kennel door and reached for him. Rondo retreated a couple of steps and yapped at her. After a moment, he cautiously approached the door and stuck his head out. He was mostly black with a white blaze, a white chest and legs, a shawl of black-and-white mottling across the shoulders, and an amoeba-shaped patch of white on his rump.

"What kind of dog is he?" I asked.

"He's a mixed breed."

"A mix of what?"

"If I had to guess, I'd say his mother was a Newfoundland and his father was a brontosaurus."

Rondo was venturing out of the cage now. I noticed that he had another splash of white at the tip of his tail. He looked up at me with a goofy grin and wagged that tail with enough torque to bash a baseball over Fenway Park's green monster. Then he crawled into my lap and pressed his muzzle against my chest.

"A marriage made in heaven?" Tracy asked.

"Except for one thing," I said.

"What?"

"A huge stray tabby has been leaving his kills on my porch. I'm looking for a dog who can discourage him, but until Rondo gets bigger, he's just going to look like prey."

Tracy folded her arms across her chest and gave me a stern look. "Is that the only reason you want a dog?"

"Of course not. I've been wanting to get one ever since I moved into a house on Jamestown last April."

"You want the Berner, then?"

"I'm thinking on it."

"He's a beautiful boy," she said. "The George Clooney of dogs. Why don't you take him for a walk in the yard, see how you get along?"

So I did. I promptly discovered that Brady knew how to come, sit, and stay and that he loved playing tug-of-war with a pull toy made of rope. When he exhausted me with his pulling, I decided to teach him how to high-five. He mastered it in less than ten minutes. The whole time we were together, his eyes rarely left mine.

Nearly an hour passed before Tracy ventured out to see how we were doing.

"How old is he?" I asked.

"Six months and a few days."

"So he's going to get bigger?"

"Oh, sure. He weighs about seventy-five pounds now. When he's full grown at eighteen months, he should be a good hundred and twenty. Maybe more."

"I want him," I said as I led the big guy inside. "I'll take good care of him, Tracy. I promise."

"We'll see," she said.

She put Brady back inside his kennel, led me upstairs to her office, and handed me a form containing fifteen personal questions designed to determine my fitness as a pet owner.

"I just want a dog," I said. "I'm not trying to adopt a baby."

She laughed as if she thought I was kidding. "After you fill this out," she said, "I'd like to pay a visit to your home to make sure it's suitable for such a large animal."

"Okay," I said, and got to work on the form.

When I was done, she gave it a quick once-over. "You're a private detective?" she asked. "Really?"

"Really."

"Normally, we require a donation of a hundred and fifty dollars for a purebred dog," she said, "but if you're willing to look into something for us, I could waive the fee."

"Look into what?"

"Please come with me," she said.

I followed her downstairs to the quarantine area, where she opened a wire crate and coaxed its occupant out onto the floor.

"Oh, God," I said.

She was about the size of a collie, her body wrapped in a bright yellow bandage and her head encased in a plastic cone to stop her from tearing the dressing off.

"What happened to her?" I asked.

"Somebody doused her with a flammable liquid and set her on fire."

"How bad is it?"

"She has second- and third-degree burns over thirty percent of her body," she said. "And she lost her left eye."

"Will she live?"

"Too early to say."

"Where and when did this happen, Tracy?"

"Last Thursday at Fort Wetherill State Park in Jamestown. She'd be dead already if she hadn't dashed into the surf to douse the flames. A passerby found her whimpering on the rocks and brought her here."

"Who the hell would do something like this?"

"That," she said, "is what I'm hoping you can find out."

"Aren't the police looking into it?"

"Yes, but it doesn't seem to be a high priority for them."

I took out my cell phone and snapped a photo of the victim. "Okay, then," I said. "I'll see what I can do."

"And Mr. Mulligan?"

"Yes?"

"She's the third one on the island since late August. The other two didn't make it."

I knelt on the floor and looked into the wounded dog's one good eye. "What's her name?" I asked.

"We're calling her Crispy."

I raised an eyebrow at that.

"When you deal with this kind of viciousness," Tracy said, "a little black humor helps get you through the day."

"If I remember correctly," I said, "you can get two years in prison and be fined up to a thousand dollars for animal cruelty in Rhode Island."

"Yes, but the creeps usually get off with a two-hundred-dollar fine."

I looked down at the broken dog as she struggled to wag her tail. "That," I said, "isn't nearly enough."

4

"Jamestown PD. Officer Clark speaking."

"Good morning, Officer. Is Chief Ragsdale in?"

"Who's asking?"

"My name is Mulligan. I'm a private detective."

"Does he know you?"

"We're old friends," I lied.

"He's not in his office right now, but I can take a message."

"Know where I can find him?"

"I imagine he's having lunch at the usual place."

"What place would that be?"

"If he's a friend of yours, you wouldn't have to ask."

"I said *old* friend. It's been a while since I got in touch."

"Try the Narragansett Café," he said. "The chef, Mike Watson, serves the best burgers in the state."

"Okay, thanks."

I drove to the island's quaint three-block commercial strip on Narragansett Avenue, parked in front of the barn-red café, and pushed through the front door. To my right, a half dozen people sat on stools arranged around a large, oblong bar. By the back wall, two middle-aged women were playing eight ball on a green felt pool table. To my left, a dozen diners hunched over rude wooden tables laden with crab cakes, burgers, and fries. Behind them, an empty bandstand.

The dark wood-paneled walls were plastered with posters trumpeting the virtues of the Tim Taylor Blues Band, Big Cat Blues, Sarah and the Tall Boys, and a bunch of other acts I'd never heard of. A dry-erase board listed coming attractions. Roomful of Blues, my favorite New England band, was scheduled for Saturday night.

My eyes roamed over the clientele. All wore civilian clothes, mostly shorts and cargo pants, but only one, a tall lanky dude in a Hawaiian shirt, had a semi-auto strapped to his hip. He clutched a cheeseburger in one big red hand and a half-full glass of beer in the other.

I wandered over to the bar and studied the logos on the tap handles: Blue Moon, Buzzards Bay, and Samuel Adams. "A Sam Adams draft, please," I said. "And a glass of whatever Chief Ragsdale is having."

The bartender drew my beer, filled another glass with Blue Moon, and stuck an orange slice on the rim. I tossed twelve bucks on the bar, wound my way between the diners, and clunked the drinks on the table where the chief was eating alone.

"Mind if I join you?"

He turned his steel-gray eyes on me, then glanced around the room. "There's plenty of empty stools at the bar, bud."

"True," I said, "but I'm in a mood for conversation."

"That's what bartenders are for."

"What's the barkeep's name?"

"Lyle."

"Hey, Lyle," I shouted. "Heard anything about the armed robbery at the Pell Savings and Trust?"

The murmuring from the diners faded, and all eyes turned toward me.

"Jesus!" Ragsdale said. "Shut the hell up and sit your ass down."

So I did.

The chief drained his beer, reached for the fresh one I'd

bought him, and gave me a hard look. "Who the hell are you, and how do you know about the incident at the bank?"

"Love the shirt," I said. "Is that standard issue at the Jamestown PD?"

"I asked you a question, bud. And keep your voice down."

I opened my wallet, slid out my PI license, and tossed it on the table. He glanced at it, not bothering to pick it up.

"Huh. . . . Who hired you?"

"The bank manager."

"Why?'

"Apparently she's not satisfied with the progress of your investigation."

"Me neither," he said.

"So you're nowhere on this?"

"Didn't say *that*."

"What can you tell me?"

"Not a damn thing till I have you checked out."

I nodded.

Ragsdale slid a cell phone from his shirt pocket and hit speed dial. "Clark? It's the chief. Got a few minutes to run a check for me? . . . The name is Liam S. A. Mulligan. Claims he's an operative for McCracken and Associates, some PI outfit up in Providence. . . . Oh, he told you that, did he? . . . Hell, no. I just met the asshole. Ring me back when you've got something."

He ended the call, scowled at me, went back to his burger, and munched in silence. After five minutes or so, I returned to the bar and ordered us both another round. By the time I got back to the table, the chief had downed the first beer I'd bought him and hauled himself to his feet.

"Clark says you check out," he said. "Meet me at the station in thirty minutes."

I sat down and took my time with the Sam Adams. When it was gone, I tried a sip of the Blue Moon, got up, and walked out, leaving the fruity wheat beer on the table.

. . .

Ragsdale leaned back in his fake-leather office chair and thunked his sky-blue Converse All Stars on his desk blotter. The only other items on the desk were a laptop, a family photo, and a Spanish cedar humidor.

"So?" I said.

"So I'm trying to decide whether you're gonna be helpful or just another pain in my ass."

I slipped a San Cristóbal de la Habana from my shirt pocket and placed it on the desk. He reached for it, studied the gold-and-brown cigar band, and raised an eyebrow.

"Damn," he said. "Been a long time since I smoked a Cuban. Where do you get these?"

"Sorry, Chief. I never betray a source."

"Good to know. What do you need from me?"

"For starters, a peek at the incident report and witness statements."

He opened a drawer, extracted a file, and slid it across the desk. "Take a seat in the hall, look it over, and bring it back when you're done."

So that's what I did. The paperwork told me nothing I didn't already know. The list of stolen items was not in the file, and the name of the victim had been redacted with a black marker.

"Questions?" Ragsdale asked as I reentered his office.

"Who's the victim?"

"A filthy-rich dude who values his privacy."

"I already gathered that."

"The bank manager wouldn't give you the name?"

"Nope."

"Neither will I," he said.

"The guy must have a lot of pull around here."

"He does."

"Got any leads?"

"Nothing solid."

"How much is the stolen jewelry worth?"

"Do I look like a fucking appraiser to you?"

"I'm told you have photos. Can I get a look at them?"

"No can do."

"Come on, Chief. Give me *something* to go on."

"Why should I?"

"Because I'm good at what I do—and because some of the people who talk to me would never spill anything to a cop."

Ragsdale took a moment to think that over. Then he nodded, fished a cigar cutter from his shirt pocket, and clipped the tip from the Cuban.

"Tell you what," he said. "I'm gonna step outside and have me a smoke. It's a big cigar, so I won't be back for a good forty-five minutes. While I'm gone, don't you go peeking at what I've got in my top right-hand desk drawer."

"I wouldn't dream of it."

He rose, tossed me a conspiratorial grin, and shut the door on his way out.

I sat behind the desk, opened the drawer, and found an unsealed, letter-size envelope. Inside was a flash drive. I slid it into one of the laptop's USB ports and flipped through twenty-six color photos of what appeared to be very expensive pieces of women's jewelry. I inserted the thumb drive I carry on my key ring into the computer and copied the files. Then I rummaged through the chief's humidor, extracted a Perdomo torpedo, and notched the tip with my cutter.

I set fire to it, put my feet up on the desk, and blew a smoke ring at the ceiling. I'd smoked the cigar down to the band by the time the chief came through the door.

"What the hell do you think you're doing, Mulligan? Don't you know there's a state law against smoking in public buildings?"

"Must have slipped my mind."

"Toss me another San Cristóbal, and maybe I'll let it slide."

"Sorry, Chief. I don't have any more on me."

"Then get your bony ass out of my chair."

As he reclaimed his seat, I plopped into the visitor's chair across from his desk. He glared at me and raised an eyebrow.

"Something *else* I can help you with?"

"There is. What can you tell me about a dog named Crispy?"

5

Next morning, I scraped a headless gull from my porch, dropped it into a plastic grocery bag, and tossed it into my trash can. Then I settled into my Adirondack with the morning's second cup of coffee and watched a tanker plow its way through the chop toward the Port of Providence.

I was idly wondering what the tabby was doing with the all those heads when the intercom buzzed. Someone was seeking admittance at the electronic gate I'd had installed at the top of my driveway. The rich aren't the only ones who value their privacy. Bookmakers do, too.

Going off the grid is next to impossible in our interconnected world, but I wasn't about to make it easy for strangers to nose around in my business. I used the detective agency as my mailing address, registered my car under the company name, made most purchases with cash, and stuck to untraceable prepaid cell phones. According to the Jamestown tax rolls, my cottage was owned by a shell corporation with no paper trail leading back to me. I'd told only a handful of people where I lived.

I entered the kitchen, tapped the call button on the wireless intercom, ascertained the name of the visitor, and punched the remote to open the gate. I closed it a moment later when I heard tires crunch on my long crushed-stone drive. I'd just stepped back outside when a red Mazda CX-5 braked to a stop behind my Mustang, and Tracy, the woman from the animal shelter, climbed out.

As I skipped down the porch steps to greet her, she gave me a wave, opened the rear hatch, and let Brady leap out. The big guy raised his nose and sniffed the air. Then he bounded off at full gallop, scattering a covey of quail in the meadow of saw grass and wildflowers I left unmowed in the long stretch between the street and the house.

"Good morning, Mr. Mulligan."

"Drop the 'mister,' and just call me Mulligan."

"Not Liam?"

"Never."

"But why? It's a lovely name."

"Bad memories," I said. "I was named after my grandfather, a Providence policeman who was shot dead on the job."

"Oh! I'm so sorry."

"It was a long time ago, Tracy."

As we climbed the stairs to the porch, Brady barked. He sounded joyful.

"Let's let him run for a while," she said. "He didn't have much chance to do that at the shelter."

"Can I get you a cup of coffee?"

"No, thank you. Do you mind if I have a look around?"

Before I could answer, she opened the screen door and stepped into the kitchen. I sat back in the porch chair and let her prowl the house. It was a good ten minutes before she returned.

"I noticed your gun case," she said, a note of disapproval in her voice. "Two handguns and a shotgun. Do you hunt?"

"Only humans."

"Well, then," she said. "This is certainly a fine place for a big dog, but I do have a concern. The property is fenced on three sides, but there's no barrier between the house and the water."

As if to make her point, Brady tore around the corner of the house and dashed down the steep grade to my dock, where the twenty-six-foot Sundowner I'd picked up secondhand was tied up. He stared into the water for a moment and then plunged in.

"I doubt the big guy's going to drown, Tracy."

"Of course not. But he could come out of the water half a mile from here."

"Brady, come!" I shouted. He paddled to shore, shook himself, climbed onto the porch, and sat on my feet, soaking my Reeboks.

I plucked the cell phone from my pocket and placed a call. "Eddie? It's Mulligan. Yeah, the electric gate is working fine, but I've got another job. Can you run about two hundred feet of chain link across the back of my property between the house and the water? And I'll need a gate big enough to tow my boat through. Sometime next month would be great. Thanks."

"Okay, then," Tracy said. "You've got yourself a dog."

"Thank you."

"What about Crispy? Have you made any progress?"

"The police chief showed me what he has on the three dog burnings, but it isn't much," I said. "Apparently no one saw anything."

"Is he going to do something about it?"

"Not much he can do unless a witness comes forward the next time somebody torches a pooch. Chief Ragsdale is mad as hell about this, Tracy. He likes dogs. Has two Border collies of his own. But you were right. It's not a high priority for him."

"Is there anything *you* can do?"

"No guarantees, but I'm going to look into it."

"How?"

"Creeps who torture animals are usually teenagers," I said. "When they get older and wiser, most of them stop because they're afraid of getting caught."

"What about the ones who don't stop?"

"Some of them graduate to human prey."

"Jesus!"

"Yeah."

"How does knowing that help us?"

"Maybe I can get some of the kids around town to talk to me. One of them might have heard something."

"Forgive me for being blunt," she said, "but are you really going to do this, or are you just trying to get out of paying the hundred and fifty dollars for Brady?"

I opened my wallet and drew out three hundred in cash. "Here," I said. "Use this to help pay Crispy's vet bills."

When she was gone, Johnny Rivers heralded a call from Mc-Cracken.

"Morning, boss."

"Any progress on the bank heist?"

"A little," I said, and filled him in. "The gunman knew how to avoid the security cameras, so he must have spent some time casing the place."

"Or had an accomplice do it for him," he said. "Be good if you could wrap this one up quick, because we just landed a major client."

"And who would that be?"

"The New England Patriots."

"Really? What do they want?"

"Don't know yet. A couple of front-office types are coming down for a meet early Monday afternoon. Can you make it?"

"Wouldn't miss it."

After we finished up, I sat at my desk and printed the color photos I'd downloaded from Ragsdale's computer. Then I carried my laptop out to the porch and did an online search for society events held in Newport the weekend before the bank heist.

I found only one, a fund-raising soiree for the Newport Preservation Society. It had been held at the Breakers, the seventy-room monument to bad taste and conspicuous consumption that New York Central Railroad chairman Cornelius Vanderbilt II erected in the 1890s.

Attendees and the organization's official photographer had posted a lot of photos. As I flipped through them, Brady climbed onto the porch and rested his head in my lap. It took me nearly a half hour to find what I was looking for.

6

"I *directed* that bitch not to give you my name," Ellington Cargill said.

"Directed? Unless you own Pell Savings and Trust, Mildred Carson doesn't work for you."

"It's not currently among my holdings," Cargill said, "but perhaps I should arrange a hostile takeover so I can have the pleasure of discharging her."

"Don't bother," I said. "I didn't get your name from her."

"From that bumbler Ragsdale, then?"

"Not him, either."

He reached for the beaded pitcher of martinis on the bamboo table beside his Lake Erie–size swimming pool and refilled his stemmed glass. He didn't offer me a drink. He hadn't offered me a chair, either, but that hadn't deterred me from claiming the seat across from him. I grabbed the pitcher and helped myself, even though I didn't care for martinis.

"Impudent bastard," he said.

"It's genetic. I come from a long line of impudent bastards."

"So if not Carson or Ragsdale, who?"

"Does it matter?"

"It does to me," he said.

"A couple of days before the robbery, your wife wore the diamond and emerald necklace to the Newport Preservation Society fund-raiser. I spotted it in a photo of the event posted on the organization's Web site."

"Ah. . . . But wait a minute. How could you have identified the necklace as one of the stolen items?"

"Private-eye trade secret."

"So you're not going to tell me?"

"No."

Neither of us was making a good first impression.

I loathed Cargill even before I met him, my opinion colored by what I'd learned by researching him on the Internet. He'd inherited a hundred million dollars from his oil baron father and parlayed it into two billion by mastering the sort of financial manipulations that had crashed the economy at the close of the George W. Bush administration. Despite the head start he'd had in life, he imagined himself a self-made man. The Jamestown house was one of five he shared with his third wife, a Brazilian-born supermodel twenty years his junior. In a recent CNBC interview, he'd ridiculed concerns about America's growing income gap, branded the poor as lazy and not deserving of help, and proclaimed that calls for higher taxes on the rich were the moral equivalent of the Holocaust.

In a just world, Cargill would have looked like Charles Montgomery Burns, the hideous skeletal billionaire from *The Simpsons*. Instead, he bore a disconcerting resemblance to that tall, smug Hollywood liberal, Alec Baldwin.

Earlier that afternoon, I'd filled Brady's water bowl, locked him in the house, driven to Cargill's mansion on Highland Drive, and parked on the street near his gated driveway. I climbed out and pushed the buzzer at the gate, but there was no response. As I turned to leave, the gate rolled open, and a black Ferrari convertible with a young man behind the wheel burst out. As the gate began to close, I slipped onto the grounds, admiring the distinctive shriek of the Italian car's monstrous engine as it sped away.

I hiked eighty yards up the paving-stone drive, climbed the steps to a massive front door that would have looked at home on Westminster Abbey, and rang the bell. A liveried butler opened the door, informed me that Mr. Cargill was not receiving visitors, and ordered me to remove myself from the premises. Instead, I strolled around to the back and found Cargill drinking by the pool, a woman I took to be his trophy wife sunning topless on a nearby chaise in the warmth of a day that felt more like late August than early October.

The woman spotted me, removed her sunglasses, and gave me the once-over, not bothering to cover herself. Her husband followed her gaze, startled, and pulled himself to his feet.

"Who are you, and how the hell did you get in here?"

"My name is Mulligan. I'm a private detective. The bank hired me to investigate the jewelry robbery."

"Get out."

"As soon as you answer a few questions."

"Yuri," Cargill shouted, "please remove this intruder."

That's when I noticed him, a tall, well-muscled young man in a beige Italian suit dozing in the shade of a dogwood tree. He roused himself, glided to his feet, swaggered over, and clamped his right hand on my shoulder. I stomped on his instep, grabbed his right wrist, and twisted his arm behind his back. Then I bulled him to the pool, tossed him in the deep end, and seated myself at Cargill's table.

"Impressive," Cargill said.

"Not really. My resistance took him by surprise."

Yuri was hauling himself from the pool now. I'd humiliated him in front of his boss, and the scowl on his face said he intended to do something about it.

"Get out, Yuri," Cargill said. "You're fired."

Yuri squeezed pool water from his dirty-blond ponytail and took a step toward us.

"Out," Cargill said.

The hired muscle hesitated, then lowered his head and trudged off.

"A bit harsh," I said, "don't you think?"

"Not at all. I don't pay bodyguards to be taken by surprise."

"Bodyguards? You mean you have more than one?"

"Of course." He smirked and added, "Doesn't everyone?"

We were sitting across the table now, sipping martinis and taking measure of each other.

"It would be in your interest to talk to me," I said. "I'm your best chance of getting the jewelry back."

"I don't much care about that."

"You don't?"

"No. The items have no sentimental value, and they are fully insured. I can't tolerate someone stealing from me, however. I want that son of a bitch behind bars."

"Well, then, I'm your best chance for making that happen, too."

"I doubt that. My chief of security is on it. He's a former treasury agent. He knows what he's doing."

"Is he from Rhode Island?"

"No."

"Then he doesn't know the players here. I've got a huge head start on him."

Cargill pursed his lips, thinking it over. "His name is Ford Crowder," he said. "Give me your card, and I'll have him give you a call. Perhaps the two of you can put your heads together."

"What about the insurance company? They stand to lose a lot of money from this, so they must have their own investigator working the case."

"I'll have him call you as well. Are we done?"

I shook my head. "Who knew you'd be going to the bank that morning to access your safe deposit box?"

"My wife, Fabiola, of course. And my son, Alexander."

"How old is Alexander?"

"Twenty."

"Was that him behind the wheel of the Ferrari that screeched out of your driveway a few minutes ago?"

"Yes."

"Could anyone else have known?"

"I don't believe so."

"What about the household staff?"

He paused to consider that.

"I suppose it's possible one or two of them could have over-heard Fabiola and me discussing it."

"How many people are we talking about?"

"Seven."

"I'd like their names."

"Ask Crowder."

"What about members of your security staff?"

"I didn't inform them of my plans."

"Did you take any of them with you to the bank that morning?"

"Yuri drove me."

"But he didn't accompany you into the bank?"

"I had him wait in the car."

If Belinda Veiga's description was accurate, the bodyguard was about same height as the robber. "When you finished telling your story to the police and returned to the car," I said, "was Yuri by any chance wearing a brown sweatshirt?"

"Certainly not. I require my personal staff to be properly attired."

After the robbery, when Cargill was busy with the police, Yuri would have had plenty of time to ditch a sweatshirt and jeans and climb back into a suit. But what about before the robbery? Could he have changed into a sweatshirt and jeans and made it into the bank in time to pull the job?

Maybe.

I thanked Cargill for his cooperation, left my martini

unfinished on the table, and hiked back to the street. When I got there, the Mustang's taillights were shattered. I hoped the vandalism had slaked Yuri's thirst for revenge. I'd be no match for him in a fair fight.

7

Over the next few days, I left Brady home alone for hours while I worked the case. Each time I returned, he hurled himself at me, licking my face and whining as if he'd been afraid that he was never going to see me again. I could tell he was lonely. On Saturday I rose at dawn, intending to give him a lot of attention.

I let the big guy out to do his business, filled his food and water dishes, and carried them to the porch. As soon as I stepped outside, I saw them, Brady and the big tabby nose to nose down by the waterline, their coats shimmering in the golden morning light. Brady's tail wagged as if he were eager to play with a new friend. The cat, something dead gripped in his jaws, hissed and arched his back.

"Brady, no!" I shouted. But I was too late.

The tabby raked its claws across Brady's face. The big dog howled, turned tail, and dashed for the porch. He clambered up the steps and cowered behind my back. The cat stood stock still, studying us. I knelt and took Brady's head in my hands. Blood seeped from a four-inch gash. The claws had just missed his left eye.

I led him inside, washed the wound, and dabbed it with hydrogen peroxide. When that was done, I stepped back onto the porch. Brady hesitated at the door and then cautiously followed me out. The cat was gone now, but he'd deposited the headless corpse of a chipmunk in Brady's water dish.

My plan to deter Cat the Ripper was not working.

After breakfast, Brady and I went for a run, five laps around the perimeter of the property. Brady was jaunty, his momentary fright seemingly forgotten. Then I showered, dressed, took the newspaper out to the porch to enjoy the unseasonably warm weather, and waited for company to arrive.

At nine o'clock, my cell played the opening riff of "Who Are You," by the Who, my ringtone for unknown callers.

"Mulligan."

"It's Ford Crowder. I hear you been waitin' on my call."

"I have."

"I'm fixin' to have a sit-down with the insurance investigator on Monday. Y'all might want to sit in." His accent suggested Kentucky, or maybe West Virginia.

"Can't do Monday," I said. "Can we make it Tuesday instead?"

"Half past ten Tuesday mornin'. Village Hearth Bakery on Watson Avenue."

"I'll be there," I said, and he clicked off.

A few minutes later, a red Toyota Tundra rolled down my drive, and Joseph DeLucca, one of only two people I trusted with the keypad code for my gate, jumped out with a brown paper bag in his fist. He climbed the porch, gave me a fist bump, and dropped the bag in my lap.

"Feels overweight," I said.

"Yeah. Eight grand this month."

"It's supposed to be only six."

"We had a big September," he said, "what with the baseball playoffs, college football, and the start of the NFL season. Figured you oughta share the wealth."

"You didn't have to do that."

"I know."

When I first met him six years ago, Joseph had been unemployed. Since then, he'd found temporary work as a mall cop and a strip-club bouncer. But recently he'd found his calling running the day to day for me from the back room of Zerilli's Market on Hope Street in Providence. Our deal was that he'd keep whatever was left of the bookmaking profits after expenses, which included payoffs to the cops; a taste for the local mob boss, Giuseppe Arena; and the six grand a month for me. My role was to wire half of the monthly take to my old friend Zerilli's bank account in the Caymans and deal with any trouble that might arise. So far, there hadn't been any. The arrangement put Joseph's cut at more than double mine. Since he was doing all of the work and taking most of the risk, it seemed only fair.

"Coffee?" I asked.

"Beer."

"Of course. What was I thinking?"

I took the paper bag inside, deposited the bundle of hundred-dollar bills in my floor safe, fetched a coffee for myself and a beer for Joseph, and rejoined him.

Brady followed me out and immediately took a liking to Joseph. Before I knew it, the two of them were rolling around on the porch, growling and play-fighting like litter mates. After ten minutes of this, Joseph pulled himself to his feet, brushed a bushel of dog hair from his size triple-X Boston Celtics game jersey, and said, "Beautiful day, ain't it."

"Want to take the boat out? Could be our last chance till spring."

"Fuck, yeah."

He helped me stock an ice chest, Narragansett for him and Killian's Irish Red for me. As I loaded it onto the boat, Brady leaped aboard. I let Joseph take the helm as we chugged north toward Bristol, Brady sniffing the salt air and barking at the swooping gulls.

We chatted about sports—who the Red Sox might chase on

the free agent market, the Patriots' chances of making it to the Super Bowl again, and Danny Ainge's struggle to rebuild the Celtics' roster.

"Any problems at the store?" I finally asked as we cruised along the east coast of Prudence Island.

"Not really. One of my regulars is on the hook for eight grand, but I ain't worried. He's good for it."

"You sure?"

"Yeah. I mean, he ain't got it now, but he will soon as he gets drafted."

"Drafted? Who are we talking about?"

"Conner Bowditch."

"*The* Conner Bowditch."

"Uh-huh."

"Jesus! What's he been betting on?"

"Last winter, basketball and hockey. Since then, mostly baseball."

"No football?"

"No."

"You sure he hasn't bet on any Boston College football games?"

"Fuck, no. If he tried betting on his own team, I wouldn't have let him."

"Good thinking. . . . Could he be laying bets with anyone else?"

"No idea."

"Maybe you should cut him off."

"Naw. He's the best defensive tackle in the country. Gonna be one of the first five players taken in the NFL draft next spring. That means a four-year deal for at least eighteen mill. And probably a twelve-million-dollar signing bonus."

"Next spring? He's just a junior, right?"

"Yeah, but the word is he's gonna declare for the draft a year early."

"Okay, then. I trust your judgment."

I took the wheel on the way back, Joseph too blitzed on 'Gansett to be trusted. When we got home, I poured coffee into him, sobering him up for his drive home to Providence.

Once Joseph was gone, I fed the dog and chowed down on some leftover Chinese takeout. Then Brady and I sat together and watched the sun go down. As the moon rose over the bay, I locked him inside and drove the Mustang to the Narragansett Café.

Roomful of Blues was already a couple of songs into the first set when I pushed through the door, squeezed into the packed house, and ordered my first Sam Adams. I was on my third when I spotted Belinda Veiga.

She was wearing a tight blue dress and sipping a cocktail at a two-top she shared with a tall, ruggedly handsome twenty-something who sported a short auburn beard. Ellington Cargill's son, Alexander, was standing over them, his face contorted in anger.

I considered making my way over there to eavesdrop, but I would have needed the Patriots' offensive line to clear a path through the crowd. Besides, the music was too loud for me to hear anything anyway.

When the band took a break between sets, I slipped outside for a short smoke. I'd just set fire to a stubby Arturo Fuente Perfecto when Veiga came out and poked a cigarette between her lips. I whipped out my Colibri and gave her a light.

"Great band, huh?" she said.

"You bet."

"I'm loving that lead singer."

"Phil Pemberton," I said. "Roomful has been tearing it up since he joined them a couple of years ago."

"How's the investigation going?"

"Slow."

"Learn anything new?"

"A little."

"Like what?"

"Nothing I'm ready to talk about."

"Come on. You can tell me."

"There's not much to tell, Belinda."

"Oh. . . . Okay."

"Was that Alexander Cargill I saw standing at your table a few minutes ago?"

"You noticed that, huh?"

"I did. Looked to me like he was mad about something."

"That jerk's been hitting on me all night," she said. "I finally told him to fuck off, and he didn't take it well."

"Most young women would have leaped at the chance."

"Because his daddy's rich?"

"Of course."

"Yeah," she said, stringing the word out. "That's why I let him take me out a couple of times last summer."

"It didn't work out?"

She shook her head, those dreads bouncing on her bare shoulders. "Money's nice, but it can't buy a personality. And he's shorter than me even when I'm wearing flats. Money can't fix that, either."

"I suppose not."

"I prefer tall men. How come *you* haven't asked me to dance?"

"I thought you were with the guy with the red beard."

"Dmitry? He's just a friend."

That sounded like another Russian name, a rarity in Rhode Island. Did Yuri and Dmitry know each other?

"I *was* tempted." I said. "But I'm not in the market. I've got a steady."

"Oh, really? Then how come you're alone tonight?"

"She's a visiting law professor at the University of Chicago this year," I said. "I won't see her again till Christmas break."

Belinda tossed me a stern look. "There's not something else going on here, is there?"

"Like what?"

"Like maybe you've got something against colored girls."

"Far from it," I said. I fished out my wallet and showed her a photo of Yolanda.

"So I'm your type, then." Her lips curled in a mischievous smile. "I won't rat you out to your girlfriend. I promise."

"This place is too crowded for dancing," I said.

"Come on. We'll make it work." She grabbed my hand and tugged me inside.

As Roomful began its second set, Belinda stood in front of me and moved to the rhythm, her ass rotating against my groin. I told myself that getting close to Belinda might help with the investigation. I knew it was a lame excuse, but it was the best I could do on short notice.

Later, as Pemberton crooned a sexy ballad, Belinda draped her arms around my neck. I caught Cargill and Dmitry staring at us. Judging by the looks on their faces, neither of them liked what they saw.

As usual, Pemberton closed the last set with Sam Cooke's classic "A Change Is Gonna Come," his voice dripping soul. As the band packed up, Belinda planted a wet kiss on my lips and insisted that I take her home with me. She was a fine-looking woman, but she was no match for Yolanda. Nobody was.

I drove home alone and spent a few minutes cuddling with Brady. Then I crawled into bed with my cell phone and checked the time. It wasn't midnight yet in Chicago.

"Hi, baby." The warmth in her voice sent a ripple straight through me.

"Hi, Yolanda."

"Where you been? I tried calling earlier."

"Roomful was playing a little club on the island."

"Damn! Wish I'd been there with you."

"Me too."

"Who'd you go with?"

I told her everything—except the part about the kiss.

.   .   .

On Sunday, I dropped the Mustang at Art's Auto Body and took a cab to Barry's Auto Group in Newport. There, I checked out the sports utility vehicles and made a deal for a black five-year-old all-wheel-drive RAV4 with seventy thousand miles on the odometer. A second car was a luxury, but I figured Brady would be growing out of the Mustang before long. The manager let me drive the car off the lot with dealer plates and promised to call when the paperwork went through.

On the way home, I stopped off at a hardware store and bought a kid's lever-action Daisy air rifle. I didn't relish the thought of hurting an animal, not even by stinging it with non-lethal BBs, but Cat the Ripper had no such qualms. I wasn't about to let him maul my new pal again.

8

"That's one hell of a disguise," McCracken said. "I almost didn't recognize you."

"What are you talking about?"

"I've never seen you in a suit before."

"Just bought it last week," I said. "First one I ever owned."

"No shit?"

"No shit."

"Hoping to make a good impression on our new client?"

"I was worried they might not take me seriously unless I look the part."

"Yeah," he said. "That's why I wore Armani today."

I was seated in a leather visitor's chair in front of McCracken's glass slab of a desk on the fourteenth floor of the Turks Head Building in downtown Providence. Behind him, high windows looked down on a neighborhood of restored colonial homes nestled just across the shit-brown ribbon of the Providence River.

Shortly after one o'clock, Sharise, McCracken's secretary, buzzed to alert us that the representatives from the New England Patriots had arrived.

"Show them in," McCracken said.

The door swung open, and a fiftyish bruiser with a shaved head and a gray handlebar mustache strutted in. He was trailed by a slim, somewhat younger man who wore his hair in a brush cut. Both sported New England Patriots T-shirts under unzipped Patriots warm-up jackets. It was apparent that our sartorial splendor was wasted on them.

The bruiser introduced himself as Marcus Eliason, the assistant director of player personnel. The younger man was Ellis Cruze, the team's chief of security.

Sharise stuck her head in the door and asked if she could get us anything. "Coffee," Eliason barked. "We both take it black." Sharise raised an eyebrow. She was not accustomed to being barked at.

Our guests took a moment to admire the framed, autographed photos that lined the off-white office walls. Action shots of Ernie DiGregorio, John Thompson, Jimmy Walker, Marvin Barnes, Johnny Egan, Lenny Wilkens, and a half dozen more basketball legends from Providence College, where McCracken and I had been undergrads half a lifetime ago. Then they settled into the tan calfskin couch. As McCracken and I took easy chairs opposite them, Sharise popped in, curtly delivered the coffee, and departed, shutting the door firmly behind her.

"So how can we be of assistance?" McCracken said.

"Are you football fans?" Eliason asked.

"We both are," I said.

"Then you must be aware of the character problems the NFL has been dealing with the last few years."

"Of course," McCracken said. "Adrian Peterson's child abuse case. Domestic violence charges against Greg Hardy and Ray Rice. Assault charges against T. J. Ward and Pacman Jones. LeGarrette Blount's and Kellen Winslow Jr.'s drug cases. The gun charge against Aldon Smith. Michael Vick's dog-fighting conviction. To say nothing of the three murder charges against your former tight end, Aaron Hernandez."

"Those would be some of the highlights," Eliason said.

"The league has been getting a bad rap on this," Cruze said. "Fewer than three percent of all professional football players ever get arrested. They're much less likely than the average American male to get into legal trouble."

"But we aren't trying to minimize this," Eliason broke in. "Incidents like these damage the NFL brand. And when teams are forced to suspend players for off-field behavior, on-field performance suffers."

"Not to mention the havoc it wreaks with my fantasy football team," McCracken said. "How can we help?"

"In previous years," Eliason said, "the Patriots have relied on our scouting department to conduct background checks on all of the players on our draft board."

"The NFL security department helps, too," Cruze said. "Every year, they provide all thirty-two teams with investigative reports on two thousand draft-eligible players."

"But clearly, some red flags have been missed," Eliason said. "This year, we've decided to hire professional investigators to supplement our research. What we'd like you to do is run a thorough background check on one particular player we've got our eye on."

And then it dawned on me. "Conner Bowditch," I said.

Eliason's eyes widened in surprise. "How'd you know?"

"He's the only Rhode Island kid likely to be taken high in the draft."

"I guess you *do* know football," Eliason said. "Looks like we came to the right place."

"Our corporate rate is twenty-two hundred a day plus expenses," McCracken said. "And we'll need a thirty-thousand-dollar retainer to get started."

Cruze nodded and pulled out a checkbook.

"Our scouting department has compiled a preliminary report on Bowditch," Eliason said. "I'll FedEx it to you, but there's not much in it. As far as we can tell, the kid's a choirboy."

"He's not," I said. "He's into a Providence bookie for eight grand."

Eliason and Cruze exchanged glances.

"You know this how?" Cruze asked.

"I figured you'd be asking about Bowditch," I lied, "so I've already done some digging."

"Your information is solid?" Eliason asked.

"It is."

"What's the kid been betting on?" Cruze asked.

"Hockey, basketball, and baseball."

"Not football?" Eliason asked.

"Not in Providence," I said, "but we should make inquiries in Massachusetts. And I think we ought to see if the kid's made any trips to Las Vegas."

"Agreed," Cruze said. He paused and added, "Can you find out if he's been placing bets online?"

"Sure, if we can access his credit card records and hack into his personal computer," McCracken said.

"Can you?"

"Not legally."

Cruze and Eliason exchanged glances again.

"The New England Patriots," Cruze said, "cannot officially condone the violation of any state or federal statutes."

"Of course you can't," McCracken said.

"Do we understand each other?" Cruze asked.

McCracken nodded.

"Well then," Eliason said. "As I'm sure you know, damned near everybody bets on sports now and then, so this isn't necessarily a deal breaker. But if you turn up evidence that he's bet on any of the Boston College games he played in, that would be a different story."

"Understood," McCracken said.

"We need you to stay on this until draft day," Eliason said. "In fact, keep looking for red flags—about gambling or anything else—right up until the dreadline, when the Patriots go on the clock."

"*Dread* line?" I said.

"A slip of the tongue, but it's apt," Eliason said. "You wouldn't believe the pressure we're under preparing for draft day every year."

"One thing I don't get," I said.

"What's that?" Eliason asked.

"Bowditch projects as one of the top five players in the draft. With your win-loss record, you won't be picking anywhere near that high."

Eliason paused to consider how much he should tell us. "The kid's a monster—a cross between J. J. Watt and Ndamukong Suh. Coach Belichick is considering trading up for him."

"I see."

"I assume I don't need to tell you how crucial it is that you don't reveal that to anyone," Cruze said. "And that you conduct your investigation in strict confidence."

"How are we supposed to do that?" McCracken asked. "As soon as we start making inquiries about the kid, other teams are bound to hear about it."

"We have no problem with *that*," Cruze said. "Every team will be doing due diligence on him as a matter of routine. But anything you learn that could give the Patriots an edge on draft day must remain secret."

"Especially from the Jets," I said.

"Yeah," Eliason said. "Belichick hates the fucking Jets."

When they were gone, McCracken went to his bar, clinked ice into two glasses, and returned with a Johnny Walker Black for him and a Locke's single malt for me.

"I assume you got the dope on Bowditch from Joseph," he said.

"A logical deduction, Sherlock."

"Good work. You impressed the hell out of them."

"Thanks. But twenty-two hundred a day? That's nearly twice our normal rate."

"If I asked for less, they'd figured it was all we were worth."

"How do you want to handle this?" I asked.

"You've still got the bank heist to deal with, so I'll take the lead. I'll nose around Vegas for a few days and then head up to Boston to check in with the Massachusetts cops, drop in on the local bookies, and see what I can learn from Bowditch's coaches and teammates."

"What should I do?

"Talk to the Rhode Island State Police and the cops in Providence and Newport. Find out if the kid's gotten into any scrapes that didn't make the papers. Then chat up his high school friends and coaches to see where that leads us."

"What about the online betting angle?"

"For that," McCracken said, "I need to know what credit cards he carries and get a look at his phone and his computer hard drive."

"Okay," I said. "Let me see what I can do about that."

But first, I had to attend to another piece of business.

"We're going to run the story whether you comment on it or not," my old friend, Edward Anthony Mason III, barked into his desk phone as I strode into his office. Mason, son of *The Providence Dispatch*'s former publisher, was the owner and managing editor of *The Ocean State Rag*, an online news site that had recently surpassed the newspaper in both readership and advertising revenue. "Okay, Mayor. It's your funeral," he said, and hung up.

"Big story?" I asked.

"Another city hall no-show jobs scandal."

"Is that news? Be more surprising if there wasn't one."

"It'll have to do until we come up with something better. Got anything for me?"

"I do. There was an armed holdup at the Pell bank branch in Jamestown back on September eighth, and both the bank and the local PD have been keeping it under wraps."

"Why would they do that?"

I ran it down for him.

"So you're telling me Ellington Cargill will be apoplectic if we name him?"

"You bet."

"Then be sure to work that asshole's name into the first paragraph."

I found a vacant desk in the newsroom and spent a half hour banging out the story. Then I downloaded the insurance photos of the stolen jewelry into the Web site's computer system. Publishing them might make the swag harder to fence.

When I was done, I bought a cup of weak coffee from the office vending machine and drank it while I waited for Mason to read the copy. About fifteen minutes later, he waved me into his office.

"Just one question," he said. "What's the stolen jewelry worth?"

"I don't know."

"Can you find out?"

"Maybe tomorrow. I've got a morning meeting with Cargill's chief of security and an investigator for the insurance company that's on the hook for the loss."

"Any chance we'll get scooped if I hold the story for a day?"

"I don't think so."

"Okay, then."

"One more thing," I said. "Can you leave my byline off this one?"

"Why?'

"The bank hired McCracken to investigate the robbery, and he put me on it. If people know I wrote the story, my sources will dry up. And the bank will probably fire us."

"I see," Mason said. "I guess I'll have to give you a pen name. . . . How about Richard Harding Davis?"

"Love it."

Davis was a swashbuckling reporter who got famous covering the Spanish American War for Joseph Pulitzer's *New York*

Herald. Teddy Roosevelt even made him an honorary member of the Rough Riders. But in the hundred and eighteen years since, his star had faded and blinked out. Mason and I might have been the only people in Rhode Island who remembered his name.

9

Tuesday morning, I was sitting on the porch before sunrise with the Daisy air rifle across my lap. In the eerie glow of a false dawn, the tabby materialized at the waterline. He prowled through the wet sand and then turned toward the house. I waited until he was no more than fifteen feet away and slowly raised the gun.

The cat caught the movement and froze. I snapped off a shot, then fired two more BBs in quick succession. Cat the Ripper never flinched. He just tossed his head, turned, and slinked away into the shadows.

I always was a lousy shot.

I sat there in the gloom, thinking things over. I was working as a private detective, freelancing for a news Web site, and supervising an illegal bookmaking racket. I was trying to solve a jewelry robbery, investigating one of the country's best college football players, and hoping to prevent the next dog burning. I'd annoyed one of the richest men in America and pissed off his thug of an ex-bodyguard. I was resisting the advances of a sexy bank employee and sorely missing the woman I loved. I'd taken on the responsibility of raising a dog and was carrying on a vendetta against a stray cat.

Perhaps I had too much on my plate. It took a while to find

the autographed Manny Ramirez Red Sox jersey, but as soon as I did, I clipped a leash on Brady's collar and led him to the RAV4.

Fifty minutes later, the sun slipped over the horizon and lit up the top of Pastor's Rest Monument, an obelisk that marked the final resting place of Providence's leading nineteenth-century ministers. Using it as my guide, I led Brady a hundred yards through Swan Point Cemetery, passing the graves of thriller writer H. P. Lovecraft, Civil War hero Major Sullivan Ballou, and legendary mobster Ruggerio "the Blind Pig" Bruccola.

We circled a row of rhododendrons and knelt in the grass beside a headstone. I replaced the dead flowers with fresh ones and ran my hand over the letters carved in the granite. I knew who was buried there, but I needed my fingers to say her name.

ROSELLA ISABELLE MORELLI.
FIRST WOMAN BATTALION CHIEF OF THE
PROVIDENCE FIRE DEPARTMENT.
BELOVED DAUGHTER. FAITHFUL FRIEND.
TRUE HERO.
FEBRUARY 12, 1968—AUGUST 27, 2008.

Rosie and I had been best friends and confidants since kindergarten. The crash that took her life as she raced to a house fire one foggy night had changed many things, but it could never change that.

I draped the Ramirez jersey over her gravestone, just as I did every time I visited. Rosie had been Manny's most devoted fan. She was gone before the Sox traded him to Dodgers, before he was suspended for using performance-enhancing drugs. But I never saw the need to bring any of that up. I wrapped my arms around the stone and gave her a hug. Brady, ever sensitive to my mood, whimpered and rested his head in my lap.

"It's a beautiful morning, Rosie. The sun is just coming up.

A yellow tug is churning up the Seekonk River. The flock of Canada geese that made such a racket the last time I was here must have reached the winter feeding grounds on Chesapeake by now, but a dozen stragglers are honking and picking through the grass. . . .

"I want you to meet my new pal, Brady. He's only been with me for a few weeks, but he's already got my heart. I've been telling him what's going on with me, but it's hard to know what he's thinking. I could use some advice. . . .

"Yeah, I guess you're right. I need to prioritize. . . . Let's see. The Patriots are the most important client. But, dammit, the bank robbery is the most intriguing case. . . . Cat the Ripper? He's just a nuisance. But the dog burnings? *That's* what's really got me pissed off. . . . I guess I should start with the bank. See if maybe I can knock one thing off the list."

Once she'd helped me sort that out, I plucked the jersey from her stone shoulders and led Brady through the graveyard to our car.

10

Shortly after ten thirty that morning, I tied Brady's leash to a parking meter, walked into the Village Hearth Bakery, bought a coffee at the counter, and looked the place over. Only two people inside the popular island breakfast spot were wearing suits and ties. I took a seat at their table, one facing the window so I could keep an eye on Brady, and introduced myself.

Ford Crowder, Cargill's security chief, stretched a big mitt across the table and shook my hand. Harvey Booth, the insurance investigator, offered a wrinkled left, explaining that the arthritis in his right was killing him.

"We over-ordered on the pastry," Booth said, "so help yourself."

I selected a scone and said, "Can you two run down what you've got so far?"

"Well," Crowder said, "as I was just tellin' Harvey here, it seems clear the perp knew Cargill was goin' to the bank that mornin'. Must've known why, too. I've been tryin' to dope out where he got his information."

"Who have you talked to?" I asked.

"First off, the household staff—three maids, the butler, the valet, the cook, the chauffeur, and the gardener."

"That's eight people," I said. "Cargill told me there were seven."

Crowder shrugged. "Man like him don't take much notice of the help 'less one of 'em spills a drink or misses a spot washin' the limo. Then he throws a conniption fit—like Sean Penn whenever some shutterbug has the nerve to snap his picture."

"What did you learn?" I asked.

"Not a damned thing."

"Can you give me their names?"

"Why? You want to take a run at 'em?"

"Couldn't hurt," I said.

"Okay, then. I'll text you the list."

"What about Cargill's bodyguards?" I asked.

"Yuri Bukov's the only one he brung with him to the island." Crowder smiled and added, "I hear tell you all met."

"He invited me to dance," I said, "but we haven't been formally introduced."

"According to Belinda Veiga's vague description, Bukov is the about same height as the perp," Booth said. "Of course, so's about three percent of the male population of the United States."

"What did he have to say for himself?" I asked.

"Claims to be clueless," Crowder said. "The way he tells it, he got a tad fretful when Cargill took so long inside the bank. More so when a couple of Jamestown police cars pulled up. But Cargill had told him to stay in the car, and Bukov's the sort who follows orders."

"Ex-military?" I asked.

"Nah," Crowder said. "Just too freakin' simpleminded to think for himself."

"He's Russian?" I asked.

"Wasn't born there, but his granddaddy was."

"Any Russian Mafia connections?" Booth asked.

"I vetted him myself," Crowder said, "and I never come across anything to suggest that."

"Is he still on the island?" I asked.

Crowder cracked a smile. "Worried he might come gunnin' for ya?"

"The thought has crossed my mind."

"I s'pose he still could be hangin' around," Crowder said, "but nobody's seen hide nor hair of him since you got his ass fired."

"What about Fabiola and Alexander?" Booth asked.

"Both of 'em swear they never spoke of the bank run to anybody outside the family," Crowder said.

"What do you know about Fabiola?" I asked.

"Laid eyes on her yet?"

"Oh, yeah."

Crowder grinned. "She's as hot as a goat's butt in a pepper patch, but don't let that fool ya. That lady's one sharp cookie. She was one of the world's top runway models when she roped and tied Cargill about five years ago. Before the marriage, she had a net worth of three hundred and fifty mil, and since then she's been spending *his* money. Don't strike me as a gal who'd need to steal her own jewelry for the insurance money."

A goat's butt in a pepper patch? Crowder's shit-kicker slang was starting to sound like an act.

"What about Alexander?" I asked.

"He's a polecat," Crowder said. "Snorts blow. Screws high-priced call girls. Trashes hotel rooms. Gets into drunken night-club brawls, and always gets the worst of 'em. The little shit's already crashed two European sports cars. If he was my kid, he'd be doin' time, but his daddy always buys him out of trouble."

"Think he's wild enough to help somebody steal his step-mother's jewelry?" I asked.

"Don't seem likely," Crowder said. "His daddy's got him on a pitiful allowance—just twenty-five grand a month. But he gets control of a big fat trust fund soon as he turns twenty-one."

"How big?" I asked.

"Four hundred million, the way I heard it. Hard to picture him being fool enough to risk that."

"Which brings us back to Bukov or one of the household staff," Booth said.

"That's how I see it," Crowder said.

"What was the stolen jewelry worth?" I asked.

"It's insured for six point three million," Booth said. "Of course, anybody trying to fence it will have to settle for about twenty percent of that."

"Suppose you had the goods," I said. "How would you dispose of them?"

"Half of the pieces are unique designs," Booth said. "Unless you wanted to get caught, you'd have to break them up, melt down the settings for the gold and platinum, and reset the stones. The other half were bought over the counter at Harry Winston, Van Cleef, and Chopard. There are dozens, maybe hundreds, of pieces just like them, so you probably could get away with selling them out of a pawn shop or on eBay. Happens all the time."

"How would you know which ones were unique?" I asked.

"A fence who specializes in rare jewelry could figure it out," Booth said.

"How many fences like that are there?"

"In the U.S., we've identified a couple of dozen, but there are sure to be others we don't know about."

"Any of them local?"

"The closest one is Max Barber up in Boston."

"Have you had a chat with him?" I asked.

"I have," Booth said. "Gave him photos of the stolen jewelry, asked him to be on the lookout, and promised him fifteen percent of the insured amount if he helps with recovery."

"Did you make the same offer to the others?"

"The ones we know of, yeah."

"Does this ever work?"

"More often than you might think."

"Have you talked to Carmine Grasso?" I asked.

"Who's that?"

"The go-to guy in Rhode Island for disposing of stolen goods."

"Does he have the expertise to handle something like this?" Booth asked.

"He deals mostly in pilfered electronics and hijacked liquor," I said. "But there are a lot of jewelers in Rhode Island, Harvey. Expertise can be bought."

"Guess I should pay him a visit, then. See what the man has to say."

"I know Carmine," I said. "Why don't you leave that to me?"

"Okay," Booth said. "That makes sense."

"I'll need photos of the stolen jewelry, then." Booth and Crowder didn't know I already had them, and for now I wanted to keep it that way.

"Have to clear that with my supervisor," Booth said. "If he's okay with it, I'll e-mail them to you when I get back to the office tomorrow."

"Sounds like a plan," Crowder said. "Are we done?"

"One last thing," I said. "What if *I* recover the stolen jewelry?"

"If you can pull that off," Booth said, "you'll get a fat check and our everlasting gratitude."

Crowder raised one bushy eyebrow. "Got a lead you're not telling us about, pardner?"

"No. Just thought I'd ask."

I was still wondering if Bukov and Belinda's friend Dmitry knew each other, but their shared ethnicity wasn't much to go on. The fact that Belinda Veiga and Alexander Cargill were acquainted was intriguing, too, but it was hardly surprising. She was a fox and he was a hound dog, so they were bound to run into each other on the small island.

I decided to keep those thoughts to myself.

I thanked Booth and Crowder for their cooperation, walked out of the breakfast spot, fetched Brady, and pulled out my cell phone.

"*Ocean State Rag,* Mason speaking."

"I've got that figure for you, and it's a big one."

"I'm waiting."

"Six point three million."

He whistled. "You sure?"

"That's what they were insured for."

"Okay. The story will be online within the hour. Have you got anything else for me?"

"Some nut's been setting dogs on fire on the island. Could you use a few graphs on that?"

"Are you kidding? Readers eat up animal stories. How many dogs are we talking about?"

"Three so far."

"When can I have it?"

"I'll try to get it to you by tomorrow," I said, and clicked off.

I drove Brady to Petco in Middletown and blew a hundred and seventy bucks on two twenty-four-pound bags of premium dog food, five bags of treats, and assorted doggie toys.

Afterward, I drove back to Jamestown and parked beside the Beavertail Lighthouse. I grabbed my laptop from the backseat, logged on to *The Ocean State Rag* site, and saw that my story was online, along with the photos of the stolen jewelry.

Then I scanned a couple of skateboarding sites and familiarized myself with the lingo. When that was done, Brady and I sat together on the shore and watched the surf beat on the rocks. A half hour later, I drove home and played tug-of-war with my pal until it was time for school to let out.

11

The Jamestown Skate Park was located behind the Lawn Avenue School. Most of the teens carving and grinding around the mega-ramp were boys. A coven of girls lined the edge, some of them cheering, others making snide remarks. I sidled over and struck up a conversation.

"The skinny dude in the blue helmet is sick," I said. "That was an awesome laser flip."

"That's Frankie," one of the girls said. "I've seen him do it better." She was pimply and overweight, the only girl at the park who didn't look like she needed to be force-fed cheeseburgers through a tube. "Look, he's gonna try it again."

I turned in time to see Frankie flip in the air, bail, and land hard on the concrete surface. He grimaced and clutched his knee. The other boys whizzed by and laughed at him.

"Poser!" one of them shouted.

Frankie smirked, bounced up, and got back on his board.

"Who's the top gun around here?" I asked.

"That would be Buster," one of the skinny girls said. "He ain't here today 'cause he got detention. . . . So which one is your kid?"

"I don't have a kid. Just a dog."

"Then what are you doing here? You some kinda perv?"

"I'm on a case."

"You a cop?"

"I'm a private detective."

The girls exchanged glances.

"What kind of case?" the heavy girl asked.

"Somebody's been grabbing dogs off the street and setting them on fire. I've been hired to find out who and put a stop to it."

"Yeah?" one of the skinny girls said. "I ain't heard nothin' about that."

I slid my cell phone out of my pants and showed her the photo of Crispy.

"Oh, *hell*, no," she said.

"I'm afraid so. There have been three attacks already. This little pooch is the only one that survived."

A short wraith with blue hair slid a vape pipe out of her mouth and said, "Lemme see that."

I handed her the phone, and the others crowed around for a look.

"Jesus," blue hair said. "Whoever's doing this needs an ass kicking."

"Any idea who it could be?" I asked.

They all shook their heads.

"You sure? Maybe one of you heard somebody talking."

Nothing.

"How many of you have dogs?" I asked.

They all did.

"Better keep a close eye on them." I handed out my business cards and added, "If you do hear anything, I'd appreciate it if you'd give me a call."

The heavy girl had my phone in her hand now, her thumb flying across the keyboard.

"What are you doing?" I asked.

"Posting Crispy's photo on my Facebook page. Maybe somebody out there knows something."

"What's your name?"

"Clara."

"Clara what?"

"Clara Martin."

"How old are you?"

"Sixteen."

"That was good thinking, Clara. Thanks. If something comes of it, you know how to find me."

It was dusk by the time I got home, climbed the porch steps, and heard Brady yipping on the other side of door. When I opened it, he lunged at me, whimpering and rubbing his head against my legs. Behind him, my sitting room floor was covered with mounds of something white and fluffy.

Brady had ripped my sofa cushions to shreds.

After I cleaned up, I took the big guy on our daily run around the property. Then I logged on to Facebook and found that two dozen of Clara's friends had already commented on the news about Crispy. None of them had anything helpful to offer, but most of them had "shared" her posting on their own pages.

I'd been scooped by a sixteen-year-old girl, but I batted out my dog-burnings story anyway. Then I e-mailed it to Mason, included the photo of Crispy, and asked him to preserve my cover on the island by running it under the Davis pen name.

When that was done, I researched destructive dogs online and learned that sofa demolition was usually caused by separation anxiety. No doubt about it. When I left him at home, best pal got lonely.

Next morning, I was jolted awake by a sharp jab in the ribs. I rolled over and looked directly into two moist brown eyes. Sometime during the night, Brady had abandoned his spot at the foot of my bed and climbed in with me.

I dug my fingers into the fur at the nape of his neck and nuzzled him. The closeness was comforting, but once Yolanda returned from Chicago, Brady and I would need to renegotiate the sleeping the arrangements.

I got up to shower and was toweling off when my cell phone rang.

"Hello?"

"Mornin', Mr. Davis."

"Sorry," I said. "Wrong number."

"I don't think so, pardner."

"Crowder?"

"Uh-huh."

"What's up?"

"Ellington Cargill's in a lather about that little story of yours in *The Ocean State Rag.*"

"*My* story? I didn't have anything to do with it."

"Aw, sure you did. You *wrote* the dang thing."

"You're mistaken. Didn't you see the byline? My name's not Richard Harding Davis."

"Yeah? Well, I looked up your Mr. Davis. Turns out he was a hotshot scribbler back in the 1890s. He'd be more'n a hundred and fifty years old by now, so I can't quite buy the notion that he's still workin' a beat."

"That does seem unlikely."

"I went ahead and looked you up, too," Crowder said. "Found out you've done a little freelancing for that Web site from time to time. I'm disappointed in you, Mulligan. Would've figured you'd be better at covering your tracks."

"If it was me, how'd they get the photos of the jewelry? Booth hasn't sent them to me yet."

"I was just askin' him about that. He said I should tell you they'll be comin' your way this morning."

"So?"

"So I figure you must of got 'em from Ragsdale."

"I suppose you talked to him, too."

"Yep. The chief claims he never heard of you. Can't say I found him all that convincing."

I didn't have anything to say to that.

"But what the hell," Crowder said. "Publishing the photos wasn't a bad move. Makes it harder to fence the merchandise."

"You and I are okay, then?"

"I'll let this one slide 'cause I still think you might be of some use. If Cargill knew what you done, he'd order me to freeze you out, so I'm gonna go ahead and blame the leak on Ragsdale."

"Okay, then."

"Keep me in the loop from now on, Mulligan. I don't want any more damned surprises."

12

Brass Balls, Carmine Grasso's pawnshop, was located on Allens Avenue in a Providence neighborhood of tank farms, salvage yards, medical supply companies, strip clubs, and abandoned warehouses. I parked the recently repaired Mustang at the curb, clipped a leash to Brady's collar, and led him to the front door. We passed under three dangling brass balls, the traditional pawnbroker symbol, and stepped inside.

The place was empty except for a lanky young guy with a shaved head and sleeve tattoos who slouched behind a glass case filled with smartphones and computer tablets.

"Hey, dude," he said. "No dogs allowed in here."

"He's a seeing-eye dog."

"Yeah? You don't look blind to me."

"Then I guess he must be really good at his job."

"Come on, man. I don't want no trouble."

"Then don't start something you can't finish. Just pick up the phone and tell your boss Mulligan's here to see him."

He shrugged, grabbed the phone, and mumbled into it. Then he hung up and said, "You can go right on back."

I led Brady past a wall display of electric guitars, pushed through a swinging door, and entered a high-ceilinged warehouse. Brady surged forward. I pulled him back as a forklift carrying cases of Crown Royal chugged past. Then I walked him down an aisle stacked with boxes of liquor, flat-screen TVs, and laptop computers. Judging by appearances, the stolen-goods racket was booming.

At the end of the aisle, a refrigerator in a blue suit stood guard in front of a frosted-glass door.

"Hey, Mulligan," he said. "What's with the dog?"

"Last time I left him home alone, he tore up my couch, so I decided to bring him along today."

"You carrying?"

"No."

"The boss says I gotta check."

I raised my arms, and he patted me down. Then he opened the door and ushered us inside.

Except for the fact that it had been built inside a warehouse and had no windows, Grasso's office was something a captain of industry would covet. Expensive leather chairs, a well-stocked bar, a Persian rug, and framed Ansel Adams prints on the walls. He rose from behind his huge ebony desk to shake my hand.

"Who's your friend?"

"My new pal Brady."

Grasso rubbed the dog behind the ears, pointed me to a visitor's chair, and plopped back down behind the desk. I told Brady to sit and dropped a hand on his shoulder.

"So how's business?" Grasso asked.

"Good. September was a strong month. October's shaping up even better."

"The kid you got running the book still working out?"

"He's no kid, Carmine. He's nearly forty."

"Since I turned sixty-five, you all look like kids to me."

"Joseph's doing great. I got no complaints."

"So to what do I owe the honor?" he asked.

"I'm wondering if you've heard anything about the Jamestown jewelry heist."

"All I know is what I saw on the news."

"It was quite a haul," I said.

"So they say. . . . You got?"

"Of course not."

"Too bad. For a second there, I thought maybe you been branching out."

"Armed robbery's not my style."

"So you come to me about this why?"

"I'm trying to get a line on who does have it," I said.

"And you figured whoever stole it might seek me out?"

"The thought crossed my mind."

"If they had, you think I would tell you?"

"You might if I made it worth your while."

"What's your interest in this, Mulligan?"

"You know I do some work on the side for McCracken, right?"

"Yeah. I heard something about that."

"The bank hired us to investigate the robbery."

"And you come to me for help?"

"I come to you with an offer. You heard that the loot is insured for six point three million, right?"

"I'm with you so far."

"The insurance company will pay fifteen percent of that to anyone who recovers the goods. That's nine hundred and forty-five thousand dollars just for making a phone call, Carmine."

"No questions asked?"

"That's right."

"I'll put some feelers out, see if anything turns up. If it does, maybe I give you a call. Or maybe I don't."

13

Providence's two biggest high schools, Classical and Central, share a large plot of land on the edge of the city's downtown. Each serves over a thousand students. Classical grooms kids for four-year colleges. Central prepares them for the rigors of technical training, nail school, burger flipping, or the unemployment line. Both of the high schools usually have decent football teams. The Central team is called the Knights. The Classical team is absurdly dubbed the Purples.

Steve Shroyer, Classical's head coach, had packed on a few pounds since his playing days as a fullback at the University of Rhode Island. As he waddled across the empty practice field in a purple Classical High hoodie, he resembled an enormous grape.

"You Mulligan?" he asked.

"I am. Thanks for agreeing to see me."

"What's this about?"

"I've been hired to conduct a background investigation on one of your former players."

"Which one?"

"Conner Bowditch."

He nodded. "What kind of dog is that?"

"A Bernese mountain dog."

"Purebred?"

"He is."

Shroyer got down on one knee and ruffled Brady's coat. "How ya doing, big fella?" Then he rose and asked, "What's his name?"

"Brady."

"For Tom Brady?"

"He had the name when I got him, but it's a good bet. Half the dogs in Rhode Island are named after Boston sports heroes."

"Got a five-year-old Rottweiler myself. His name is Gronk."

"After Rob Gronkowski?"

"Yeah, but if I had it to do over again, I'd name him Conner. Best athlete I ever coached. Come on. We can talk in my office."

"Mind if I bring Brady? I don't want to leave him in the car."

"Okay by me."

As we strode down an empty corridor lined with student lockers, a janitor emerged from a classroom carrying a wastebasket. "Excuse me, sir," he said, "but dogs aren't allowed in the school."

Shroyer waved him off. "Making an exception for this guy, Hank. He's built like a middle linebacker, so I'm trying to recruit him."

The coach's office, located just off the locker room, was lined with framed photos of his team in action. Plastic cases holding footballs signed by Classical teams dating back decades were stacked waist-high along one wall. The oak desk was bare except for a photo of canine Gronk and a folder containing the game plan for Saturday's contest against Ponaganset. As Shroyer seated himself behind his desk, his office chair shrieked in agony. I settled into a visitor's chair across from him and told Brady to sit.

"Scouts from a dozen NFL teams already showed up here to ask me about Bowditch," Shroyer said. "Which one sent you?"

"The Patriots."

"Why you instead of somebody from their scouting department?"

"Their screwup with Adrian Hernandez has made them skittish. They figure a professional investigator is better equipped than a football scout to find any skeletons Bowditch might have in his closet."

"Well, there aren't any."

"Tell me about him."

"During his four years here, Conner was very focused—and not just on football. The kid was a leader both on and off the field. Team captain. Senior class president. National Honor Society. Active in Students Against Drunk Driving. Volunteered to tutor kids struggling with physics and calculus. Graduated fourth in his class, just a hair short of valedictorian."

"He must have had a lot of scholarship offers."

"Oh, hell yeah. All the top football schools recruited him. Alabama, Florida State, Auburn, LSU, Baylor, Ohio State, Oregon, Mississippi State, Notre Dame, TCU. You name it."

"Why'd he choose Boston College?"

"He wanted to play big-time college football, but he also wanted to stay close to home. Only schools he considered seriously were UConn and B.C."

"He ever get into any trouble?"

"Never."

"Substance abuse?"

"Absolutely not."

"Gambling problems?"

"Not that I ever heard."

"Did he get into scrapes with anybody?"

"A few shoving matches after the whistle, sure, but nothing serious."

"Never anything off the field?"

"No."

"Who were his friends?"

"Most everybody liked Conner," he said, "but the kid he was closest to was Ricky Santos."

"Another football player?"

"No. Ricky wasn't built for that. He played trombone in the school marching band. Poor little guy became a target when he came out of the closet toward the end of his junior year. The usual shit. Name calling. Bullying. Conner stepped in and made the assholes back off. That's the kind of friend he was. The kind of man he is."

"Is Ricky still in town?"

"Why?"

"I'd like to talk with him."

"He's enrolled as a film student at Rhode Island School of Design."

The friendship made me wonder if Bowditch might be gay. "Was Conner popular with the girls?"

"Had to beat them off with a stick."

"Anybody special?"

"Meghan Falco. Class secretary and a member of the cheerleading squad. They dated on and off through high school, went to the senior prom together."

"Know where I can find her?"

"She's a biology major at URI. Last I heard, she and Conner had gotten engaged."

Really? Mister Perfect was going to marry his high school sweetheart? By the time I left Shroyer's office, he'd all but convinced me that I was investigating Saint Conner of Classical.

The following evening, I was watching the third quarter of the Celtics-Knicks game, chomping a pepperoni pizza and tossing the crusts to Brady when the cell phone played my ringtone for McCracken.

"Evening, boss. Still in Vegas?"

"Caught the red-eye home early this morning."

"Learn anything?"

"No, but I need you tonight."

"Where are you?"

"At Rhode Island Hospital getting my broken wrist set."

"Aw, hell. What happened?"

"I'll fill you in when you get here. And Mulligan?"

"Yeah?"

"Bring a gun."

14

I floored the Mustang on I-95, made it to Providence in forty minutes, burst into the hospital, and found McCracken in the emergency department waiting room. He was slouched in a molded plastic chair, a gauze bandage taped to his forehead and his right arm in a cast.

"Are you okay?"

"Fuck, no. I need a drink."

"Have they finished patching you up?"

"A couple of minutes ago, yeah. Let's get the hell out of here. I'll meet you at Hopes in ten minutes."

"Sure you're okay to drive?"

"I'll manage."

Hopes, the local press hangout, was nearly empty when I pushed through the door. Just a couple of alkies smoking cigarettes and pitching woo to their boilermakers at the scarred mahogany bar. I strode across the grimy linoleum, bought two bottles of Killian's, and carried them to a table in back. A couple of minutes later, McCracken came in, walked gingerly toward me through the dim light, and slumped into a wobbly wooden chair.

"You okay?"

"Wrist's still numb from the junk they shot into it, but my head hurts like a bastard." He thumbed a plastic bottle from his pants pocket and dropped it on the table. "Mind opening this for me?'

I shook two Vicodin tablets into his left palm. He swallowed them and washed them down with a swig of beer.

"The doc warned me not to mix these with alcohol," he said, "but I hear they work better this way."

"You probably heard it from me."

"Did you remember to come strapped?"

I unzipped my jacket and gave him a peek at the Walther in my shoulder holster. "So, tell me. Who do you want me to shoot?"

"Soon as I find out who they are, I'll let you know."

"What happened?"

"After my plane landed, I went home, caught a few z's, and then dropped by the office. Sharise had already left for the day, so I stepped into my inner office and snapped on the light. First thing I noticed was that my file drawers had been rifled, papers thrown all over the floor. Second thing I noticed was two mugs with pistols sitting on the couch."

"Anybody we know?"

"Never seen them before."

"Descriptions?"

"Looked enough alike to be brothers. Both of them six-two, two-twenty. Shaved heads. Brown eyes a little too close together. Purple Phoenix Suns T-shirts under dark brown Wind-breakers. Blue jeans. Black Nikes. One clean shaven, the other with a dickish porn mustache."

"What were they carrying?"

"Both had compact nine millimeter semi-autos. Looked like maybe the Ruger LCP."

"A woman's gun," I said.

"Yeah. Would have told them that, but I didn't want to make them mad."

"How'd they get in?"

"Must have picked the lock. Gonna have a high-end electronic lock installed next week, so remind me to give you the key code."

"What did they want?"

"First off, they asked if I had a good time in Las Vegas. I told them Andrew Dice Clay's show at the Hard Rock was awesome but that I'd lost three hundred bucks at a Golden Nugget craps table."

"You went to see Andrew Dice Clay?"

"Of course not. He sucks."

"Then what happened?"

"They asked why I was investigating Conner Bowditch."

"And you said?"

"I said, 'Who's Conner Bowditch?'"

"How'd that go over?"

"They forced me to sit, duct-taped my arms and legs to my desk chair, and hurled questions. Who was I working for? Why had I gone to Las Vegas? Who had I talked to there? I told them I'd love to help them out, but that I was bound by client confidentiality."

"And then?"

"The clean-shaven one, who did most of the talking, gave me an appraising look. Said the two of them could get rough with me but that he figured it probably wouldn't do any good. I told him it probably wouldn't do me any good either. He seemed to think that was pretty funny. Tell you what, he said. I don't need to know what you're doing as long as you quit doing it. Stop and there's ten grand in it for you. But if you don't, you're in for more of this. Then he pulled a blackjack out of his Windbreaker and slammed it down on my wrist. I *heard* the bone crack."

"That when he clubbed you in the head?"

"He didn't. He just cut me loose with a pocket knife and said they'd be keeping an eye on me. Then the two of them walked out the door."

"So why the bandage on your brow?"

"It's embarrassing."

"Tell me."

"The duct tape must have cut off the circulation to my feet. When I got up, I stumbled and whacked my noggin on the corner of the desk."

I suppressed a chuckle. "When you try to pick up women with your story about facing down a couple of thugs, you might want to leave that part out."

That's when a tall stranger with a shaved head pushed through the front door and took a slow look around. I slid my hand into my jacket and rested it on the Walther.

"What's wrong?" McCracken said.

"The guy who just came in. Don't turn around. Use the bar mirror to check him out."

"Nope. Not one of them."

I relaxed, went to the bar, and fetched us another round.

"The two guys," I said as I settled back across from him. "You said they wore Phoenix Suns T-shirts?"

"Yeah. Purple T-shirts under brown Windbreakers. What kind of an asshole dresses like that?"

"Think they could *be* from Phoenix?"

"Nah. They're too pale to have spent any time in the sun. Their accent was pure Boston."

I sipped my beer and thought for a moment. "Does it seem odd to you that we're getting pushback on Bowditch?"

"It does," he said. "So far, we haven't turned up anything. And if we do find some dirt, who's it gonna hurt?"

"Just him," I said.

"You think *he* sicced the thugs on me?"

"Can you think of anybody else with a reason?"

He took a pull from my beer and rubbed his jaw. "I got nothing. But how would the kid even know we've been looking at him?"

I pulled out my phone, punched in some digits, and put it on speaker.

"Shroyer residence."

"Good evening, Coach. It's Mulligan."

"What can I do for you?"

"I was wondering if you've got a number for Bowditch. I want to give him a courtesy call, let him know my firm's been hired to do a background check on him."

"He already knows. I mentioned it to him on the phone yesterday. Him and me, we're still close. He calls me about every week."

"Okay, but I'd like to give him a call anyway."

Shroyer rattled off Bowditch's cell number. I thanked him and hung up.

"Well," McCracken said, "it looks like Mister Perfect is trying to cover up some seriously bad shit."

15

Thanksgiving is a day for family, but I didn't have much of one left. My parents and grandparents were dead, and I hadn't been on speaking terms with my brother for years. That left my sister, Meg, who'd invited me to spend the holiday at the New Hampshire farmhouse she shares with her wife and their adopted daughter. But today they were snowed in, the roads impassable.

I didn't like turkey anyway.

Joseph DeLucca had less family than I did, meaning none at all. He arrived shortly before noon toting my monthly share of the gambling proceeds and a last-minute feast he'd assembled: Four bakery pies—pumpkin for me and apple for him. Six large pizzas—two with pepperoni for me and four with bacon, meat-balls, sausage, anchovies, onions, and mushrooms for him. And two cases of beer—Killian's Irish Red for me and Narragansett for him. He also brought a sixteen-ounce sirloin for Brady.

"Heard from Bowditch lately?" I asked as we loaded the beer into the fridge.

"He rang me up Tuesday to place bets on three of this week-end's basketball games."

"Big bets?"

"Nah. Just twenty bucks per."

"He's still not gambling on B.C. games?"

"Not with me."

We each grabbed a beer and a pizza and carried them into the sitting room, where the day's first football game was under way on my forty-two-inch flat-screen.

"Uh. . . . Mulligan?"

"Yeah?"

"Where's the fuckin' couch?"

"The dog ate it."

"Oh."

Without further comment, he squatted on some cushions I'd shoved against the wall. Not wanting to be rude by taking the only chair, I flopped down beside him.

All that afternoon and evening, Joseph's cell phone rang a dozen times an hour, gamblers calling to lay down last-minute bets on the weekend's college and pro football games. Mine rang once, around eleven P.M. I excused myself and took it into the bedroom.

"Happy Thanksgiving, Yolanda."

"Happy turkey day to you, too, baby." Her voice had smoke in it. "The storm in northern New England made the news out here. Did you make it to your sister's okay?"

"Afraid not. Three feet fell in Nashua, she's lost power, and the streets in her neighborhood still haven't been plowed."

"Oh, darn. I hope you're not spending the day alone."

"Do hookers count?"

"Most of the ones I know can't."

"You know some hookers?"

"Remember where I grew up? Of course I do. Well, back then I did. So who's there really?"

"My friend Joseph."

"Hope he didn't bring the food."

"He did."

"Oh-oh. Double cheeseburgers and fries?"

"Of course not. It's Thanksgiving."

"What, then?"

"Scads of pizza and a couple of cases of beer."

"Ha! That explains why you're slurring."

"I am?"

"Uh-huh."

"He also brought a nice sirloin."

"Mmm. That's more like it."

"Yeah. Brady gobbled it so fast you'd think the big guy had never seen food before."

"You gave the steak to your dog?"

"And the pizza crusts, too. Brady's crazy for them."

"How's the weather there?"

"Cold and blustery. We're supposed to get rain overnight. How's your mom?"

"Better. The meds have finally got her blood pressure under control. I wanted to take her to Michael Jordan's for dinner, but she insisted on cooking a turkey with all the fixin's."

"For just the two of you?"

"Uh-huh. Did it up right, too. Linen napkins, candles on the table. And, man, can she cook. By the time I leave here, I'm gonna be so fat that none of my clothes will fit. Good thing I've got a month to diet before I come home. Otherwise, my ass would be so big that you wouldn't love me anymore."

"No chance of that, baby."

When I returned to the sitting room, I found Joseph passed out on the floor cushions. I snapped off the TV, picked the empties off the floor, and flopped into bed with Brady.

I was dreaming about making love to Yolanda when Jimmy Cagney's voice startled me awake: "You'll never take me alive, copper!" He kept snarling that defiant line from his 1931 movie, *The Public Enemy*. Still groggy, I needed a moment to recognize it as my ringtone for law enforcement sources.

I glanced out the window and saw that it was still dark. Brady stirred, raised his head, and looked at me. Then he sighed and went back to sleep. I threw off the covers and groped the bedside table for my cell. By the time I found it, it had gone to voice mail. The message from Chief Ragsdale was brief:

"North Road where it cuts through the Marsh Meadows Wildlife Preserve. Wake up, Mulligan. You're going to want to see this."

I staggered into the sitting room in my skivvies, roused Joseph, and asked him to keep an eye on Brady—and to feed him if I didn't return by midmorning. The weather had turned during the night, the temperature dropping into the thirties. I pulled on jeans, running shoes, and a hooded sweatshirt and bolted out the door into a cold, steady sleet.

Five minutes later, I spotted the pulsing light bar of a Jamestown police cruiser that was parked at the side of the road. I pulled in behind it and looked around. Off to my left, flashlight beams crisscrossed in the reeds. I set off in that direction, my Reeboks sinking into the spongy earth.

"Mulligan?"

"Yeah."

"We're over here. And watch your step."

I smelled it before I saw it, the stench of burned hair and flesh. Forty yards in, I found Ragsdale and one of his patrolmen standing over the remains of a medium-size dog.

The chief shoved something in my hand and then shined his flashlight on it. A singed collar. Hanging from it were a dog license and a red metal heart engraved with the pet's name and the address of the folks who owned him. They'd named him Casper. I looked at the body again, wondering if he might once have been white.

"How'd you find him?"

"Somebody saw the flames and anonymously called it in."

"Told the family yet?" I asked.

"No. They phoned the station yesterday evening, just after supper time, to report that he'd gone missing. News about the dog burnings is all over town now, so they were scared as hell. I'm gonna let them enjoy their breakfast before I break the news."

I checked my wrist and found that I'd left my watch at home. "What time is it now?"

"A little past five."

"You done here?" I asked.

"If Patrolman Martin can carry the remains back to the patrol car."

"I got it covered," the patrolman said.

"I think we should talk, Chief," I said. "Want to grab some breakfast?"

"Nothing on the island is open this early."

"I know a place. I'll drive you."

Ten minutes later, we pulled into a lot on Broadway in Newport and sat in the car waiting for Dunkin' Donuts to open. At five thirty, we pushed through the door, ordered coffee and breakfast sandwiches, and carried them to a booth next to a streaked plate glass window. Ragsdale took off his drenched jacket and hat and dropped them on the seat. I grabbed a handful of napkins to mop my hair. Outside, the street was nearly deserted. The sleet was falling harder now.

"You got a dog, Mulligan?"

"I do."

I pulled out my cell phone and showed him a photo of Brady. He took out his and showed me a picture of his Border collies.

"What are their names?" I asked.

"Spade and Archer."

"For the detectives in *The Maltese Falcon*," I said.

"Yeah. They're only two years old, but they're such a big part of the family now that it's hard to remember what our life was like without them."

"I know just what you mean."

"If somebody did this to one of them," Ragsdale said, "I'd shoot the fucker in the head and bury him in the swamp."

"I'd help you dig the grave."

We sat in silence for a minute or two, munching our sandwiches. Mine tasted like ashes.

"Find any evidence at the scene?" I asked.

Ragsdale dipped his hand into the front pocket of his jacket, pulled out a clear plastic evidence bag, and tossed it on the table. Inside was a blue-and-yellow Ronson lighter fluid can.

"I'll dust it for prints when I get back to the station. The rain probably washed them away, but there's always a chance we could get lucky."

"Any footprints or tire tracks?"

"I told Martin to go back and take another look after daylight, but chances are the bad weather has washed that away, too."

Ragsdale went back to the counter for another round of coffees. When he returned, I changed the subject.

"Anything new on the jewelry robbery?"

"I got nothing. You?"

"I don't have any answers," I said. "But I have some new questions."

"Such as?"

"What do you make of Ford Crowder?"

"If you're thinking he could be a suspect, forget it. He wasn't even in the state when the robbery went down."

"You sure about that?"

"He was in Brazil reviewing security at offshore oil rigs owned by one of Cargill's companies. Something about him bothering you?"

"It's probably nothing. His shit-kicker act just rubs me the wrong way."

"What rubs me the wrong way is Cargill's son," Ragsdale said.

"Any particular reason?"

"Belinda Veiga let him take her on a couple of dates last summer, and since then he can't seem to leave the poor girl alone."

"What's he doing, exactly?"

"Keeps calling her, texting her pictures of his dick, sending flowers to her office," he said. "And she thinks he's been driving by her apartment late at night."

"Thinks?"

"She hasn't actually seen him, but that car of his makes a distinctive sound. No question about the rest of it, though. The calls and texts came from his phone; and Emily, the clerk at the Secret Garden, says the jerk gave her a standing order to send Belinda flowers twice a week."

"That sounds like stalking."

"Oh, I don't know. Seems to me he's just a spoiled brat who never learned how to take no for an answer. I'm not ready to make an arrest just yet, and I hope it doesn't come to that. I'd hate to have to deal with his daddy's army of high-priced lawyers again."

"*Again?*"

"Hell, there's always something with that fucking kid. Bar brawls, drunk and disorderly, public urination, DUI. It's been going on ever since the family built their estate on Highland Drive six years ago and started spending summers here."

"Think he's dangerous?"

"Only when he's behind the wheel."

"I'm not so sure," I said. "I saw him hitting on Belinda at the Narragansett Café the night Roomful of Blues played there. When she turned him down, he balled his fists and his face contorted with rage."

Ragsdale sighed. "What are you thinking, Mulligan?"

"I'm thinking you should refer her to a lawyer. Maybe she can get a restraining order."

"Okay. I guess maybe it's time for that."

"I'm surprised Alexander is still in town," I said. "I thought the Cargills would have taken off for one of their palaces in the tropics by now."

"They have, but Alexander stayed behind, probably because of his obsession with Veiga."

"No question Richie Rich is a jerk," I said, "but it's still hard to imagine him having a reason to steal his stepmother's jewelry."

"I agree."

"Have you questioned the household staff?"

"Of course. Didn't get me anywhere."

"Crowder grilled them, too. I've been thinking of taking a run at them myself, but it would probably just be a waste of time."

"Which leaves Yuri Bukov as the only plausible suspect," Ragsdale said.

"Plausible because he had opportunity?"

"And because he appears to have skipped town."

"Any idea where he is?" I asked.

"No. You?"

"No."

I picked up my coffee and drank, taking a moment to decide whether I should share a wild hunch with the chief.

"That same night at the Narragansett Café, Veiga was sitting with a young red-bearded guy. When I asked her about him, she said his name was Dmitry and that he was just a friend."

"So?"

"Probably nothing, but Dmitry and Yuri are both Russian names. Makes me wonder if they might be acquainted."

"Wouldn't surprise me any. It's a small island."

"What do you know about Dmitry?"

"His full name is Dmitry Souza. Manages a boat rental shop on Conanicus Avenue."

"Souza? That's Portuguese."

"His mother's Portuguese. His father was Russian."

"Is the father still in the picture?"

"No. He was long gone before his son was born."

"Does Dmitry have a record?"

"No."

"You sure?'

"I've known him all his life. He's a good kid, Mulligan. I can't see him getting involved in anything like this."

My vague suspicion about Dmitry was sounding like a dead end.

"What about the loot?" I asked. "Has any of it hit the market yet?"

"Have you talked to Booth about that?"

"Not for a couple of weeks."

"I touched base with him yesterday," Ragsdale said. "A few suspicious jewelry listings turned up on eBay, but he ran them down and confirmed they were being sold by their rightful owners." He drained his coffee, shrugged his jacket on, and plopped his damp hat on his head. "I'm not ready to give up on this one, Mulligan, but if I've learned anything in my five years as chief, it's this. Some mysteries don't have solutions."

"Like Jimmy Hoffa," I said.

"And Amelia Earhart."

"Time to notify Casper's family?"

He sighed. "No use putting it off any longer."

"Want me to tag along?"

"You don't have to do that."

"I know how hard these things can be, Chief. I think maybe you could use some company."

On the drive over, neither of us wanted to talk about it.

"Hey, Chief?"

"Yeah?"

"Do you by any chance know Conner Bowditch, the Providence kid who plays for Boston College?"

"Know *of* him."

"Ever hear of him getting into trouble down here?"

"Last summer, he was involved in a disturbance at the Narragansett Café, but the show was over by the time my officers arrived on the scene. The way the witnesses told it, some local kid started ragging on him. You know how it is when you're a football star. There's always some punk who wants to test his manhood out on you. Conner stayed cool and let the bouncer handle it."

"Good for him."

"Why are you asking about Bowditch?"

"Sorry, Chief, but that's confidential."

The Newcomb family lived in a modest ranch-style house that squatted on a couple of rock-strewn acres in the island's unfashionable interior. As we drove up the muddy, unpaved drive, I could see that the outbuildings were in good repair but that the house needed painting. As we climbed from the car and dashed through the rain toward the front door, I thought I heard sheep bleating.

Ragsdale rang the bell. A woman opened the door, took one look at the grim look on the chief's face, and burst into tears. Her first words: "How do I tell the children?"

Casper, it turned out, was both a beloved family pet and a working dog who guarded the Newcombs' two dozen sheep from the island's thriving coyote population. Carole Newcomb asked us what she could do to keep the grim details of the dog's death from her three preteen kids. Ragsdale told her that she couldn't. Within hours, the news would be all over Facebook.

16

Joseph hadn't just fed Brady. He'd taken the dog for a walk, washed the dishes, wiped down the kitchen counters, swept the floors, and hauled out the trash. He'd even removed the day's headless corpse from my porch. Joseph always made a mess, but unlike Cat the Ripper, he could be counted on to clean up after himself. I invited him to hang around for a couple more days so we could take in the rest of the holiday-weekend football games together.

On Saturday, we put the B.C.-Syracuse game on to watch Bowditch do his thing and were shocked to see him repeatedly mauled by opposing offensive linemen.

"What the fuck?" Joseph said. "Think he's got an injury he's been keeping secret?"

"Either that or his head isn't in it today."

The game was in the fourth quarter when McCracken called.

"I went on a beer run a few minutes ago," he said, "and somebody followed me to the liquor store and back. A silver Hummer with Rhode Island plates. It's parked on my street now, a couple of houses down."

"A Hummer? Stupid car for a tail job. Too easy to spot."

"Yeah."

"Think it's the same guys who roughed you up?"

"Seems likely."

"How do you want to handle this, boss?"

"Take a run up here and call when you get close. I'll take my car out. They'll follow me, and you'll follow them. I'll lead us into Haines Park in East Providence, where we can box them in on a deserted road."

"And if they turn out to be the guys who roughed you up?"

"We return the favor."

"We could," I said, "but if we do, we're not going to learn anything."

"Got a better idea?"

"Yeah. You shake the tail, and I'll follow them. Maybe they'll lead me to the person who sent them."

"I thought we figured they must be working for Bowditch."

"Most likely they are, but there could be some moving parts to this thing that we haven't gotten a glimpse of yet."

"Okay, we'll try it your way."

"But let's wait till dark," I said. "They won't be expecting a tail, so I might be able to get away with it, but it'll be easier once the sun goes down."

"Makes sense."

"Oh, and Joseph's here, so I'll bring him along. With your arm in a sling, we could use the extra muscle."

"Is he armed?"

"I'll lend him my Kel-Tec."

"Can he shoot?"

"Better than me."

"Mulligan, Stevie Wonder shoots better than you."

Just past eight P.M., I switched off the RAV4's headlights and turned onto McCracken's street in the little bayside town of Warren. Fifty yards dead ahead, the silhouette of a Hummer was backlit by a streetlight. I pulled to the curb, called Mc-Cracken, and asked him to keep the line open.

A minute later he moseyed out his front door, slid into his

silver Acura, and backed out of his driveway. The Hummer gave him a block-long head start and then pulled away from the curb. I waited until the little caravan made a left turn before I snapped on my headlights and followed.

"Can you see how many people are in the car?" McCracken asked.

"Give me a second," I said, and drew within twenty yards of the Hummer. "Two guys wearing ball caps." Then I fell back about forty yards.

We cut through several suburban streets, picked up route 114 north, and crossed the little bridge over the Barrington River. About ten minutes later, we turned east on County Road in Riverside, drove a couple of miles, and cut north on Willett Avenue. From there, it took McCracken less than five minutes to shake the tail in a confusing maze of residential streets.

"What are they doing now?" McCracken asked.

"They just turned around and are heading east on County Road. . . . Hold on. They just turned south on the Wampanoag Trail."

"Sounds like they're backtracking to my place."

Sure enough, fifteen minutes later they turned onto McCracken's street, parked a few houses down, and turned off the lights.

"What do you think they're up to?" McCracken asked.

"Waiting for you to come home. Why don't you find a place to hang out for a few hours until they give it up? Then we'll see where they go."

"Okay. I'll have a couple of brews at Lucky's on Warren Avenue and wait for your call."

We were still sitting in the dark a half hour later when I heard the unmistakable pssst of a beer can opening.

"Go slow with that stuff, Joseph. I'll need you to be sharp if we decide to confront these guys."

"You didn't say that to McCracken."

"Unlike you, he doesn't need to be told."

"Can you turn on the radio? Maybe we can catch one of the West Coast games on ESPN."

"Bad idea," I said. "Sound really carries on cold, overcast nights."

"But I'm fuckin' bored."

"Why don't you take a nap?"

A few minutes later, he began to snore.

I sat in the dark and watched the Hummer. Nothing stirred. I was getting cold now, but I didn't dare start the engine to run the heater. After a couple of hours, I woke Joseph, asked him to take the next watch, and caught a little shut-eye myself.

A poke in the ribs jolted me awake.

"They're moving," Joseph said.

I glanced at my watch. Just past two P.M. I cranked the ignition and handed my phone to Joseph. "Call McCracken, and put him on speaker."

Fifteen minutes later, snow began to fall as we cruised north through East Providence on the winding Wampanoag Trail, the Barrington River a black ribbon off to our right.

"We're heading in your direction," Joseph told McCracken. "Sit tight."

Except for some long-haul truckers, there were few vehicles on the road. I gave the Hummer a sixty-yard lead as we crossed the Washington Bridge over the Providence River. The city's skyscrapers were barely visible through the thickening storm.

"We just turned south on I-95," Joseph said.

"Got it," McCracken said. "I'm on the way."

As we crawled down the slick interstate, I lost control on the treacherous Thurbers Avenue curve and narrowly missed bouncing off the Jersey barrier. We passed through Cranston, took the airport exit in Warwick, and turned south on the Post Road commercial strip.

There, the Hummer pulled into the parking lot of a shabby

two-story motel with an ancient sign that boasted FREE TV IN EVERY ROOM. As I rolled by, two tall men in brown Windbreakers climbed out and trudged up the stairs toward a second-floor room.

"Only two other cars in the lot," Joseph said. "And the lights are out in the office."

"Perfect."

I continued three blocks south and turned into the parking lot of a closed convenience store. Ten minutes later, McCracken pulled in beside us and lowered his window.

"So now what?" he asked.

"We give them time to get undressed and go to bed, and then we bust in on them."

17

A half hour later, we turned back north, parked both cars in front of a liquor store thirty yards south of the motel, and trudged through the snow. As we reached the motel, a rusted Toyota Celica drove into the lot, and two teenagers in jeans and parkas got out.

"Recognize them?"

"No," McCracken said.

"I do," Joseph said. "Couple of rent-a-boys who go in for rough trade."

"You know this how?" I asked.

"They bet football."

The boys started up the stairs to the second floor, where light glowed through the shades in only one room. Sleep apparently wasn't in our prey's immediate plans. We followed the boys up, stopped them at the top of the landing, and showed them our guns.

"How old are you two?" McCracken asked.

"Nineteen," the taller one said.

"Liar. You're not even shaving yet."

"You cops?"

"No," McCracken said. "It's your lucky day."

"You the guys who called us?"

"Not that lucky," McCracken said.

"So what do you want with us?"

"We want you to knock on the door and let the occupants get a good look at you through the peephole," McCracken said. "When the door opens, turn tail and run like hell."

"Why?"

"You don't want to know."

The boys exchanged looks. "Okay. I guess we can do that."

We took our positions: Joseph to the right of the door, me to the left, and McCracken, his gun arm in a sling and his pistol in his left, just behind me. I gave the boys a nod, and one of them knocked.

Inside, someone switched off the TV.

"Who is it?"

"Carl and Anton."

The door swung open. The boys bolted. Joseph and I burst in, leading with our guns, McCracken following close behind. The man who'd opened the door stumbled backward, tripped over a tear in the threadbare carpet, and fell to the floor. The other guy was sprawled on the bed, his face draining of color. Both were naked except for their boxer shorts. They stared at our guns and didn't say anything.

"Prostitution is a misdemeanor in Rhode Island," McCracken said, "but soliciting underage boys for sex is attempted rape. That can get you hard time."

The one with the porn mustache pulled himself off the floor and sat on the bed beside his partner. "You're not cops," he said.

"No, but we can have them here in five minutes."

"Busting in on us with guns is a crime, too," the clean-shaven one said, "so I'm betting you don't want to do that."

"Oh, I'm pretty sure my friends at the Warwick PD would overlook our indiscretion in exchange for a sex-crime bust," McCracken said. "But why don't we have a chat first? Perhaps we can come to an understanding."

"We got nothing to say to you assholes," porn mustache said.

McCracken grinned, raised his pistol, and whacked him across the bridge of his nose.

"Want I should tune up the other one?" Joseph asked.

"Maybe later," McCracken said.

I walked into the bathroom, found a damp towel, and tossed it to porn mustache. He caught it and pressed it against his gushing honker.

"What are your names?" McCracken asked.

Nothing.

"Why have you been tailing me?"

Nothing.

"Who hired you?"

Still nothing.

"Was it Bowditch?"

The clean-shaven one emitted a mirthless laugh. "Man, you got no fuckin' idea who you're dealing with."

"So tell me."

Silence.

As McCracken hurled more questions, I tossed the room. In the bedside-table drawer, two loaded Ruger LCP pistols and two boxes of ammunition.

"Got permits for those?" McCracken asked.

Silence.

I scooped their wallets from the bureau top and rifled through them. "Don't see any," I said. "Looks like maybe we've got another felony."

I slid Massachusetts drivers' licenses from the wallets, looked them over, and tucked them into my pants pocket. Porn mustache's name is Romeo Vacca, and the other one is Dante Vacca. They live at the same address in Somerville, Massachusetts."

"You two look a lot alike," McCracken said. "Are you brothers?"

No answer.

I grabbed their cell phones from the bureau and tucked them in my jacket pockets. Then I opened the closet and pulled out a sawed-off double-barrel Ithaca shotgun.

"Another felony," McCracken said. "That illegal gun is worth ten years' federal time."

I finished my search, found nothing else of interest, and snatched the keys to the Hummer from the bureau top.

"I'm gonna toss the car," I said, and went out the door.

In the glove compartment, rental papers from Avis. In the back, greasy takeout food cartons, a dozen crushed Pabst Blue Ribbon empties, a stash of gay child-porn magazines, two boxes of shotgun shells, and another sawed-off Ithaca.

I returned to the room in time to see Joseph looming over Dante Vacca, whose nose now resembled his brother's. "Want me to put a slug in his kneecap?" Joseph asked. "Maybe that'll get the fucker to open up a little."

McCracken shook his head. "This isn't getting us anywhere. I think we're done here."

I nodded and gathered up their weapons.

"We can always get more guns," Dante Vacca said. "You three ain't seen the last of us."

"Yes we have," McCracken said. "More guns won't do you any good if you can't shoot."

Taking the cue, Joseph pounced on the bed, sat on Dante, grabbed his right wrist, and bent his trigger finger back until the bone snapped. Then he did the same thing to Romeo.

"What if they're left-handed?" McCracken said.

Joseph grinned and repeated the procedure, which was accompanied by a lot of shrieking.

I'd never seen McCracken condone such violence. Guess he was still miffed about that broken wrist. Given the Vaccas' taste in sex partners, I didn't have a problem with it.

Outside, I locked the Vaccas' firearms in the back of the Hummer and stuffed their car keys in my pocket. As we headed for our cars, I pulled out my burner phone, punched in the number for the Warwick PD, asked for the duty officer, and told him where he could find the Vaccas.

"They're a couple of strong-arm types from Somerville, Massachusetts. They're in possession of child-porn magazines, two illegal sawed-off shotguns, and a pair of handguns they don't appear to have permits for. You'll find it all stashed in a rented Hummer that's parked in the lot. And if you can track down two teenage prostitutes named Carl and Anton, you can probably add attempted child rape to the list of charges."

"May I have your name, sir?"

"Afraid not," I said, and hung up.

Fifteen minutes later, we were sitting in a booth at the twenty-four-hour IHOP on Pleasant Valley Parkway in Providence while the kitchen whipped up our orders. Country-fried steak and eggs for McCracken and me. And for Joseph, the egg, ham, and cheese omelet; the chocolate chip pancakes; and two sides of sausage. As we waited, McCracken and I sipped coffee. Joseph guzzled a can of 'Gansett from a paper bag.

"So now what?" I asked as the waitress slapped our plates on the table.

"Now I run the punks' names through my sources at the Boston PD and the Massachusetts State Police," McCracken said. "Maybe that gets us something. Maybe it doesn't. You go through their cell phones and find out who they've been talking to."

"What do you want me to do?" Joseph asked.

"Nothing," I said. "We'll call if we need you."

McCracken and I were halfway through our meals when Joseph shoveled in his last forkful and looked longingly at the empty plates. For a moment, I thought he was going to lick them. Instead, he got up, went out to the Mustang, and returned with another can of beer.

"Maybe we made a mistake taking the Vaccas off the board," I said.

"How so?" McCracken asked.

"With them, we knew who to watch out for. Whoever sent them is going to send somebody else now."

"And it probably wasn't Bowditch," McCracken said.

"That's what I'm thinking. He's a college kid with a gambling jones. I doubt he's got the cash to hire a couple of pros, and guys like the Vaccas don't work on credit."

"Remember what Dante Vacca said?" Joseph asked.

"That we've got no fuckin' idea who we're dealing with," McCracken said.

"Yeah," I said. "Guess we better find out."

"For our sake and Bowditch's," McCracken said. "Looks like the kid's gotten himself into some serious trouble."

After we finished our meals, McCracken and I lingered over second cups of coffee while Joseph polished off two more cans of 'Gansett. When I drained my cup, I called the Warwick PD again.

"Did you grab the Vaccas?"

"We found the Hummer, and all the stuff you told us about was inside. But the two guys had bolted. Even left some of their clothes behind."

"Aw, shit."

He asked for my name again, and I hung up.

18

When I finally got home that morning, I found more bad news. Brady had disemboweled my easy chair. I cleaned up the mess, tore off my shoes, jumped into bed with my clothes on, and fell right to sleep.

It was well past noon when Brady woke me by dropping his food bowl on my head. I hugged him, apologized for the late breakfast, and fed him. After he gobbled it down, I let him out into a cold, sunny day, the trees bending under a load of wet show. I tugged on my Timberlands and joined him.

The Bernese mountain dog breed originated in Switzerland, so it came as no surprise that Brady loved snow. He flopped on his back and rolled in it. Then he burrowed into a drift, disappeared, and popped out on the other side. I tossed snowballs at him. He leaped and caught them in his jaws.

After an hour of this, my feet were frozen, so I tried to coax Brady to come in with me. He tossed me a look that said I had to be kidding and plunged back into a snowdrift. I went inside alone and made a cup of coffee.

Then I put Etta James on the sound system, turned the volume down low, sat at the kitchen table with the Vaccas' cell phones, and dialed the numbers on their recent-calls list. The first was answered by a male voice.

"Romeo?"

"Yeah."

"Don't tell me you need more toys already."

" 'Fraid so."

"What's wrong with the ones I sold you last week?"

"Had to ditch them in a storm drain."

"You sound weird. Got a cold or something?"

"Just the sniffles."

"Fuck you. You ain't Vacca." And then he hung up.

I grabbed my laptop, looked for the number in a reverse directory, and couldn't find it. Probably an untraceable burner phone. Like bookies and tycoons, dealers who supply criminals with firearms also value their privacy.

My next call was answered by a woman.

"Dunst and Moran. How may I direct your call?"

"Uh. . . . Mr. Dunst, please."

"One moment, sir, and I'll connect you."

Two excruciating minutes of Barry Manilow crooning "Looks Like We Made It," and then: "Morris Dunst's office. How may I assist you?"

"I need a word with Mr. Dunst."

"Who may I say is calling?"

"Romeo Vacca."

"Oh. How are you, Romeo? I didn't recognize your voice. Do you have a cold or something?"

"Yeah."

"Hope you're taking something for it. "

"Bed rest and bourbon."

"Excellent choice. Mr. Dunst is in consultation with another client at the moment. Can he return your call this afternoon?"

"No thanks. I'll call back later."

After we hung up, I googled Dunst and Moran and learned that it was a small law firm with offices on Milk Street in Boston. Given Romeo Vacca's line of work, I wasn't surprised that he was on a first-name basis with his lawyer's secretary.

The next two numbers belonged to outfits that supplied male

escorts. The rest were for friends and family members. As it turned out, the number the brothers called most was their mother's.

When I was done, I called McCracken, and we filled each other in on what we'd learned.

"The Vaccas have sheets," he said. "They've both got assault and battery convictions, and Dante took a fall six years ago for possession of child pornography."

"They've done time?"

"Yeah. Short stretches in Cedar Junction. According to the Massachusetts State Police intelligence unit, they're freelancers. My guy says they work mostly for what's left of Somerville's Winter Hill Gang, the outfit made famous by Howie Winter and Stephen "the Rifleman" Flemmi. But they've also done jobs for the Angiulo mob in Boston and for one of the youth gangs warring for control of the New Bedford heroin trade."

"What kind of work?"

"Debt collection, shaking down strip club owners, persuading witnesses to keep their mouths shut. That kind of thing."

"And murder for hire?"

"Not that my guy knows of, but he wouldn't put it past them."

Shortly after we hung up, I heard scratching at the back door. When I opened it, Brady burst in looking cold but happy.

I gave him a few minutes to warm up, attached his leash, and led him to the RAV4. The snow hadn't drifted across my driveway, so the all-wheel-drive vehicle managed to churn its way to the street. I stopped there, left the gate open, and made a call to have the driveway plowed.

Fifteen minutes later, I pulled into the rescue kennel's parking lot and led Brady inside.

"Don't tell me you're bringing him back," Tracy said.

"Of course not, but I need some advice."

She listened carefully as I explained the problem.

"Well," she said, "you could always crate him when you leave the house."

"Brady would hate that," I said. "Besides, he's awfully strong. I doubt they make a crate that can hold him."

"Then if you want him to stop eating your furniture, the best solution is to get him some company."

"*Another* dog?"

"Unless you want to hire a dog sitter."

"You really think that would work?"

"Depends on how they get along. Sometimes, a dog resents it when you bring another animal into the house."

"I don't suppose you still have Rondo," I said.

Tracy laughed. "You do like them big, don't you."

"Sure do."

"Come on. Let's see how it goes when we introduce them."

When Tracy let Rondo out of his cage, I couldn't believe how much he'd grown. He was already nearly half Brady's size. After the two dogs sniffed each other's behinds, the doggie version of shaking hands, we led them outside and set them loose in the fenced yard.

Rondo crouched, growled, and launched himself at Brady, jaws snapping at the bigger dog's ears. Brady raised one massive paw and batted Rondo, sending him sprawling through the snow. Rondo scrambled to his feet and attacked again. At first, I was alarmed. Then I noticed that their tails were wagging.

Brady could have easily overpowered the big puppy, but as they continued to play-fight, it became apparent that he knew just how rough he could be without hurting his new friend. We let them go at each other for ten minutes before Tracy helped me brush the snow from their coats and load them into the back of the SUV.

When we got home, Brady led Rondo on a tour: *Here's the field where I chase quail, the oak tree where I take my morning dump, the rope toy I love to pull, the water dish I drink from.* He was displaying the same joy a child does when you give him a puppy.

When the tour was over, I sat on the porch and watched them

play-fight again. This time, they went at it for a half hour before they collapsed in a heap and fell asleep in the snow, Rondo's head resting on Brady's chest.

Over the next few days, I left them alone in the house for hours, returning each time to find what was left of my furniture intact. Brady's vandalism spree appeared to be over. I picked out a new black leather couch and matching chairs on Amazon.com and arranged for them to be delivered.

Early Thursday morning, Brady and I awoke to the sound of frantic barking. We jumped out of bed, ran into the kitchen, and found an agitated Rondo peering out the back door. I snapped on the porch light and saw the tabby dash down the porch steps.

I grabbed my air gun and threw the door open. Brady warily peered out. Rondo bolted past him, raced down the steps, and tore through the snow after the intruder. The cat leaped the new back fence just ahead of Rondo's jaws and skittered away.

I scanned the porch floor for Cat the Ripper's latest gift and spotted it in Brady's water dish. Then I went back into the kitchen to fetch a spatula and a plastic sandwich bag. I scooped the gift from the bowl and slipped it into the bag.

"An *ear?*" McCracken said.

"Yeah."

"You sure it's human?"

"I don't see how it could be anything else. Heard of anybody who's missing one?"

"Not lately. What did you do with it?"

"I put it in a baggie and stuck it under an ice tray in my freezer."

"Did you notify the police?"

"No way. If I had, they'd be crawling all over my place right now."

"And you wouldn't want that," McCracken said.

"No, I wouldn't."

"Because you've got secrets," he said.

"From everyone but you and Joseph, my love."

"Now ain't that sweet."

I killed the call, sat at my computer, and searched the online news sites that cover Rhode Island and nearby towns in Massachusetts. No news about somebody losing an ear in a bar fight or a boating accident. No reports of anyone falling overboard in the bay or getting swept away by the surf. I called the hospital contacts I'd made in my reporting days. No one had walked into any area emergency room whining about a severed ear.

I decided to keep it on ice and wait for developments.

19

Meghan Falco, Bowditch's fiancée, agreed to meet me at the 193 Coffee House on Lower College Road in the village of North Kingston, just off the University of Rhode Island campus.

The first thing she told me was that the coffeehouse's name referred to the temperature of the coffee. She also informed me that the place was a student-run cooperative and that it served only fair-trade coffee.

"What's that mean?" I asked.

"They use coffee beans certified as coming from producers who do not use child labor and who employ environmentally sustainable farming practices."

"Certified by whom?" I didn't care, but pretending I did was a way to break the ice.

The football star's girl wasn't at all what I'd expected. Average figure, turned up nose, mousy brown hair, big hazel eyes behind oversize horn-rims. She was pretty enough in a conventional schoolgirl sort of way, but no one would have mistaken her for Gisele Bündchen.

We were sitting on oak Windsor chairs, our hands clutching mugs of 193-degree coffee. A copy of *The Secret Life of Lobsters*, by Trevor Corson, rested beside her on the small round table.

"I'm going to make a wild guess here and say you're a marine biology major."

"I am."

"What do you plan to do when you graduate?"

"You mean other than see how fast I can spend Conner's money?"

"I didn't mean it like that."

"Oh. . . . Sorry about being so defensive."

"I gather the word *gold digger* has been thrown at you."

"That and worse. Got so bad I had to cancel my Twitter account."

"I'm sorry."

"To answer your question, I plan on pursuing a Ph.D. so I can teach at a university and do research on how climate change is impacting ocean currents and marine life."

"Does Conner support your ambitions?"

"Of course he does. He's not some big dumb football player, Mr. Mulligan. He plans on going back to school to finish his biochemistry degree after his playing days are over. The average NFL career lasts only three and a half years, you know."

"True, but the average career of a first-round draft pick lasts nine seasons. I looked it up."

"If Conner avoids serious injury and plays for a decade, he'll be thirty-one when he retires from the game," Meghan said. "He'll have plenty of time to finish his education."

"How did you two meet?"

"When I was six, my dad went to work as a foreman at Bowditch Construction, Conner's father's company. We were always getting invited to their big house on the East Side. Barbecues, pool parties, that sort of thing. I've known Conner nearly all my life."

"You started dating in high school?"

"Junior high if you count holding hands at soccer games and stealing a kiss under the bleachers. In high school, Conner had flings with other girls, but he always came back to me. The others chased him because he was a football star. I fell for him because he's so kind and so smart. In the fall of our senior year, he gave me his class ring to wear on a chain around my neck. We've been together ever since."

The class ring had since been supplanted by a modest diamond on her left ring finger. I figured it would be replaced with a much bigger one once Conner signed his first pro contract.

"How often do you see each other now?"

"With our class schedules and his commitment to football, it's tough—even though B.C. is just ninety minutes up the interstate. But I drive up there or he comes down here at least one weekend a month. And we Skype or talk on the phone every night."

"Has he been himself lately?"

"What do you mean?"

"Does he seem preoccupied? Worried about something?"

"Not at all. Why should he be?" A worried look crossed her face. "Mr. Mulligan, is there something you're not telling me?"

I paused to consider how much I should reveal to her and decided to give her most of it. "The background check the Patriots hired us to conduct should have been routine, but as soon as we got started, a couple of thugs from Massachusetts came to town. They broke into my boss's office, roughed him up, and told him he'd get more of the same if he persisted in looking at Conner."

"Oh, my God!"

"Do you have any idea why they did that, Meghan?"

"No."

"No idea who might have sent them?"

"No," her voice smaller now. "Do you think Conner is in some kind of trouble?"

"I'm afraid he might be."

"What kind of trouble?"

"I'm not sure. Maybe it has something to do with his gambling."

"Conner doesn't gamble."

"He does, Meghan. He owes a Providence bookie eight thousand dollars."

"I don't believe that."

"I know it for a fact."

"Jesus! Why would he keep something like that from me?"

"Perhaps he doesn't want to worry you."

"Eight thousand dollars is a lot of money. More than half of my annual tuition."

"It's peanuts compared to what he'll get when he signs his first NFL contract," I said.

"I guess. But still . . . Do you think the bookie is going to break his legs or something?"

"He won't, Meghan. He's a decent guy, actually, and he knows Conner will be good for it."

"Are you sure about that?"

"I am, but not all bookies are that patient. Is there any chance Conner could have placed bets with someone else?"

"I have no idea. Maybe I don't know him as well as I thought."

I sat quietly for a moment, giving her time to process what she'd heard.

"Please tell me he hasn't bet on B.C. games," she said.

"Just hockey, baseball, and basketball as far as I know. If that's all there is to it, his draft status probably won't be affected."

"Well, thank God for that, at least."

And then she started to cry.

"Don't take this so hard, Meghan. Every guy has secrets. Hell, I've got one I've been keeping from *my* girl."

"You do?"

"Yes, and it's a big one."

"Whatever it is, you better tell her before she hears it from somebody else."

I got up and fetched each of us another cup of coffee. When I returned to the table, Meghan's brow was furrowed in concentration.

"I'm confused," she said. "Something about this doesn't make sense."

"What do you mean?"

"If those thugs came to town because of Conner's gambling, why would they go after your boss instead of him?"

"I can't make sense of it either," I said, "and that has me worried. I'm thinking there must be something else going on with Conner that I haven't tumbled to yet."

"Like what?"

"No idea, but whatever it is, I can help. I've left several messages for him, but he hasn't returned them. Would you mind telling him that he should talk to me? And that I don't bite?"

"I will. I'll ask him to promise me that he'll call you."

"Thank you."

"But I can't be sure he'll do it, Mr. Mulligan. And if he does, you probably won't hear from him until after his last game. During the football season, Conner tries to block out all distractions."

"Except for you," I said.

"Yes. Except for me."

She fell quiet again, then asked, "Do you really think the Patriots might draft him? I know he'd love to play for Belichick."

I flashed on Cruze's warning not to reveal that the Patriots might trade up in the draft. "I doubt they'll be picking high enough to get Conner," I said, "but if they have a chance to grab him, they'd be fools not to. Of course, it also will depend on what we put in our report. Is there anyone else you think I should talk to about Conner?"

She rattled off some names, all of them in Boston. Coaches, professors, teammates, the two roommates with whom he shared an off-campus apartment.

"What about his old friends at Classical?"

"Other than me, he doesn't see them anymore."

"Oh? Did something happen? I heard he and Ricky Santos used to be tight."

"No, not really," Meghan said. "He was just a sad little queer Conner stuck up for when other kids picked on him."

Damn. Until then, I'd been starting to like her. I opened my mouth to say something, then closed it. The slur rankled, but if I called her on it, she might not be so cooperative if I needed to talk to her again.

20

The plowed streets around Jamestown's town hall were so choked with parked cars that I had to leave mine at Artillery Park and walk back on ice-slick sidewalks. As I crunched up the salted front steps and pushed through the door, a special meeting of the town council was about to get under way.

More than two hundred people, some of them waving hand-made signs reading JUSTICE FOR CASPER and PRAY FOR CRISPY, filled all the folding metal chairs. A couple dozen more lined the walls. From the looks on their faces, they were in a sour mood.

Cameras from three of Providence's broadcast TV affiliates had been set up in the aisles, and the long oak table that stretched across the dais bristled with microphones from area radio stations. The dognappings had become a big local story. I pulled out a new iPhone Mason had given me to take news video for *The Ocean State Rag.* As far as Verizon knew, the device belonged to Richard Harding Davis.

On the dais, Chief Ragsdale, Tracy O'Malley, and the town's animal control officer, Kip Shepherd, were seated beside the five members of the town council. I was surprised to see Clara Martin, the teenager I'd met at the skate park, up there, too.

At eight P.M. on the dot, First Warden Kenneth Franco gaveled the meeting to order. "Let me begin by assuring you that all of us sitting up here share your outrage about the unconscionable acts of animal cruelty that are plaguing our community. Most of us have dogs of our own." He paused, drew a deep breath, and added, "It is with deep regret that I must inform you of another incident that occurred earlier this evening."

That drew gasps and cries of "Oh, no!"

"Hamlet, George Baxter's labradoodle, was snatched from his yard sometime after five P.M. The police found him dead beside Fox Hill Pond less than an hour ago. He'd been set on fire, just like the others."

The news stunned the crowd into silence.

"Understandably, these events have aroused strong emotions, but I must request that you maintain decorum so that tonight's speakers have the opportunity to be heard."

And with that, everyone began shouting at once. In the pandemonium, I scanned the crowd, searching in vain for someone with only one ear. It took Franco several minutes to gavel the crowd to silence.

"Chief," he said, "please bring us up to date on the status of the police investigation."

"Unfortunately, we have little to go on," Ragsdale said. "We found no probative physical evidence at any of the crime scenes, and no witnesses to the abductions have come forward. If anyone has information that could assist us in the investigation, please contact my office. Meanwhile, keep your eyes open for suspicious activity and take steps to protect your animals. When you let them loose in your yards, keep a close watch on them. Don't leave them alone for a minute—not even for a short run to the grocery store."

Ragsdale then introduced the dog officer, who urged everyone to have their pets microchipped. "Unfortunately, the chip can't be used to track missing animals," he said. "It is not a GPS. However, it identifies your dog, making it more likely that a missing animal will be returned home."

Then he turned the microphone over to Clara Martin, who

announced that she had created a Facebook page under the name "Save Our Dogs."

"It's a sounding board for information about the dog abductions," she said. "Chief Ragsdale and Mr. Shepherd have promised to post frequent updates. The first post, which went up this afternoon, lists the names of local veterinarians who can insert microchips in your pets."

When she was done, Franco asked Tracy O'Malley for an update on Crispy's condition.

"Crispy is recovering and will soon be well enough to be placed with a family," she said. "Anyone interested in adopting this sweet one-eyed dog should contact me at the Animal Rescue League of Southern Rhode Island in Peace Dale."

Six people leaped to their feet and declared their eagerness to give Crispy a new home. After Tracy jotted down their names, Franco asked if anyone in the crowd would like the floor. Several dozen hands shot up.

"The chair recognizes Mr. Cargill," Franco said. Alexander, whom I hadn't spotted before, rose to his feet.

"My father and I love animals," he said. "We've got three Karelian bear dogs at our estate in Aspen and a dozen quarter horses on our farm in Montana. We are appalled by the recent events in Jamestown and are offering a twenty-thousand-dollar reward for information leading to the arrest and conviction of the person or persons responsible."

That drew the evening's first burst of applause.

"Thank you for your generosity, Mr. Cargill," Franco said. "Would anyone else like to speak? . . . The floor recognizes Marlon Jenks."

"Me and some of the boys got to talkin' at the Narragansett Café yesterday evenin'," Jenks said, "and we decided we can't keep sittin' around with our thumbs up our butts while this shit is goin' down. So we're forming a posse to patrol the streets. A dozen guys already signed up. Anybody interested in joining us, come see me at my hardware store. If enough of you sign up, we can cover twenty-four hours a day, seven days a week."

Ragsdale vigorously shook his head. "Mr. Jenks, I urge you to reconsider. Nothing good can come of this. You should leave police work to the professionals."

"Bullshit!" Jenks shouted. "That ain't gotten us nowhere so far."

"If you insist on going ahead with this," Ragsdale said, "I'm going to ask that you leave your guns at home."

"Ain't gonna happen, Chief."

And with that, everybody started shouting again.

They were still at it when I slipped out the door, skipped down the steps, and spotted Alexander Cargill muttering to Belinda Veiga on the sidewalk. She turned her back on him and started to walk away. He stretched out a hand and grabbed her shoulder.

"Get your hands off her, Alexander."

"Mind your own fucking business."

"You did a good thing tonight, kid. Don't spoil it by being a jerk."

He turned then and looked at me. That's when I noticed that he stood an inch taller than Belinda. I glanced at his shoes and saw that he was wearing lifts.

"I know you," he said. "You're that private detective."

"Then you should know better than to mess with Belinda when I'm standing here."

"Why? Are you fucking her, too?"

"He's not," Belinda said. "But he'd be a big step up from your puny ass."

"Bitch!" Alexander's face scrunched up, and for a moment I thought he was going to cry. Then he spun on his heels, stomped down the sidewalk, and climbed into a black Mercedes S-Class coupe. Apparently, he'd garaged the Ferrari for the winter and was driving one of Daddy's cars.

"Belinda," I asked, "are you okay?"

"Yeah, I'm fine."

"I heard talk you might be getting a restraining order against him."

"I did."

"Well, he just violated it. Want me to fetch Ragsdale?"

"What good would that do? His father's lawyers would spring him before the cell door slammed shut."

"At least let me walk you to your car, then."

"Thanks, Mulligan."

Her Honda Civic was parked less than a block away. As she opened the door, she turned to me.

"Could you stop by the bank tomorrow morning? We need an update on the robbery investigation."

"I'll be there. Can you give me a lift to my car so I can follow you? I want to be sure you get home safely."

"Join me for a nightcap? We can crack a new bottle of Knob Creek."

"I can't believe I'm saying this, but no."

"I can't believe it either," she said.

After seeing her home, I hustled back to my place and put Buddy Guy's "Skin Deep" on the sound system. Then I banged out Richard Harding Davis's meeting story for the Web site while Brady and Rondo sat at my feet.

21

Just past ten, I strode into Pell Savings & Trust, tossed a hearty good morning to the bank guard, and approached the manager's office. Mildred Carson wasn't in. Instead, Belinda Veiga sat behind the desk, her nose buried in what looked like a mortgage application.

"Where's Mrs. Carson?"

"On maternity leave."

"Oh. What did she have?"

"Twin baby girls, Alice and Anna."

"I should send her something. Can I have her address?"

"That would be against company policy, but if you drop the gift off here, I'll be sure that she gets it."

"She gave me her home phone number, Belinda. I can always run it through a reverse directory to find out where she lives."

"Sorry, but I still can't give it to you."

"So are you in charge here now?"

"Sort of."

"What's that mean?"

"They say I'm too inexperienced to run the branch on my own, so they're sending somebody down from Providence twice a week to check up on me. But if I don't screw up, I could be in line for a promotion."

"Good for you."

"So how about that update? From what I've heard, you must have grilled everybody on the island by now."

"Not quite," I said.

"And?"

In the office, the sexy flirt was no longer in evidence. Belinda was all business now.

"I haven't turned up any solid leads, but I do have a suspicion."

"Tell me."

"I'm thinking it was probably an inside job."

Judging by the look on her face, that shocked her.

"What makes you say that?"

"The stickup man knew a lot about bank operations. How to avoid the surveillance cameras, for example."

"Couldn't he have figured that out by, what do they call it? Casing the joint?"

"That's what I thought at first," I said, "but I've walked through the lobby several times looking at the cameras. I can sort of tell where they are pointing, but I can't be sure how much area each one covers. I can make a rough guess about how to avoid them, but I could never be sure."

"And the robber was sure?"

"Looks that way. He avoided them perfectly. I doubt he could have done that unless he, or an accomplice, had spent time studying the monitors to see what each camera picks up."

"I find it hard to believe any of my colleagues could be involved in anything like this."

"No teller with a sketchy boyfriend? Nobody having money problems?"

"The pay here sucks. All of us have money problems."

"I also think the perp knew the bank's rule against anyone entering the vault when a safe deposit box is being opened," I said. "Otherwise, he was taking a hell of a risk, and this guy doesn't strike me as the reckless type."

"Anyone with a box could have known that."

"Well, can you give me a list of the box holders? Maybe a name will leap out at me."

"No can do. That would be a violation of our privacy policy."

"Okay. I'll just keep digging to see what else I can turn up."

Belinda sighed. "You've been at this since September, Mulligan, and all you've got is a wild theory. Corporate is telling me that unless you've got something solid, they can no longer justify the expense. Just send me your final report in writing. And your bill."

I hadn't expected that. "Look, Belinda. Suppose I keep poking around on my own? If I don't figure it out, you don't have to pay me. If I do, I'll bill the bank for the hours I put in."

"Sorry, but it's still no. Ellington Cargill's security chief and an investigator for the insurance company are both still working on this. And so is Chief Ragsdale. Headquarters wants to let them take it from here."

"I understand," I said. "Thank you for your business. I'm sorry I wasn't able to accomplish more."

But I was too intrigued by the mystery to let it go. On my way out, I invited the bank guard, Owen McGowan, to meet me for dinner at the Narragansett Café.

That afternoon, I stopped in at the hardware store, introduced myself to Marlon Jenks, and asked how his vigilante committee was shaping up.

"Sorry, bud, but we can't use you. Forty-eight guys signed up this morning, which is all we need. Already had to turn six people away."

"How have you organized them?"

"Two guys to a car, four-hour shifts. Gives us four cars on the road at all times."

"Did you take the chief's advice about guns?"

"Hell, no. Half the guys are carrying pistols or shotguns. The rest are lugging crowbars or baseball bats. . . . Oh, and I equipped each car with a Kidde fire extinguisher from my stock."

When I entered the Narragansett Café that evening, Owen McGowan was already seated at a two-top, foam from a glass of Buzzards Bay coating his upper lip. I grabbed a Sam Adams at the bar and joined him.

"Dinner's on me," I said.

"Bet your ass it is."

"I hear you were on the job."

"Put in my thirty at the Newport PD."

"Doing what?"

"Two years walking a waterfront beat, four in a patrol car, the rest in the criminal investigations division."

"You were a detective?"

"That's right."

"Were you any good at it?"

"I knew my way around. I'd like to think I still do."

"Ever seen anything like the stickup at the bank?"

He grinned. "I been wondering when you'd finally get around to me."

"Want to know why it took so long?"

"If you want to tell me."

"Ragsdale let me read your witness statement."

"And there wasn't anything helpful in it," he said.

"Hell, Owen. You didn't even realize the place had been robbed until Veiga ran out of the vault and started yelling."

"Yeah. Fuckin' embarrassing."

"And I bet you've been brooding about that ever since," I said.

"Every damned day."

"And?"

"And I heard you got fired today."

"I did."

"But you can't let go of it either," he said.

"Nope."

The waitress came by to take our orders, stuffed quahogs and chicken parmesan for McGowan, clam cakes and a strip steak for me, and a refill on the beers. In the back corner, someone was setting up a drum set for the evening performance by Sally and the Tall Boys. For now, the only percussion accompanying our conversation was the click of balls on the pool table.

"I've asked Ragsdale for updates," McGowan said, "but he's shutting me out. How about filling me in on what you've got?"

"It's not much," I said, and gave him the facts, leaving out my suspicions.

When I was done, he rubbed his face and said, "None of the swag has hit the market yet?"

"Not that we've heard."

"Smart. If it was me, I'd definitely be laying low until the heat dies down."

"It *wasn't* you, was it?"

He narrowed his eyes and folded his arms across his chest. "And here I thought we were having a friendly conversation. Why in hell would you ask me a thing like that?"

"Because it smells like an inside job."

He nodded. "Smells that way to me, too."

"Got anything to go on besides your nose?"

"I might."

"I'm listening."

He grinned. "Guess you didn't notice that my glass is empty. And when I'm done with this chicken, I'm gonna have a hankering for some apple pie."

I waved the waitress over and ordered the same for both of us.

"First thing's the way the perp knew how to avoid the five surveillance cameras," McGowan said.

"That's been bothering me, too."

"Don't see how he could have done it without help."

"Me either."

"Has Ragsdale shown you the video?" he asked.

"No. Did you get a chance to look at it before it was grabbed by the police?"

He shook his head. "A few weeks ago I got to chewing on this, so I spent an hour studying the video feeds in the security office, checking out all the camera angles. The longer I watched, the surer I got that he couldn't have pulled this off unless he'd sat right there in front of those monitors and done the same damned thing."

"Do the cameras cover the security office?" I asked.

"No. Not the hallway leading to it, either."

"Too bad. Is the office kept locked?"

"Supposed to be."

"Who has keys?"

"Carson, Veiga, and Philpot."

"The head teller?"

"Yeah. The crew that takes out the trash and mops the floors after hours has keys, too."

"How many of *them* are there?"

"Two or three. Come to think of it, I suppose some of the five hundred vice presidents wasting office space in Providence could have keys. Might even be a corporate vice president for keys and locks, 'cause they got one for every other fucking thing."

"Anyone else you can think of?"

"Me, of course."

"Well," I said, "at least this narrows it down some."

"Not really. Nothing valuable is kept back there, so we've been careless with the keys. Leaving them on desktops. Stashing them in unlocked drawers. Any bank employee could have snatched one and had a copy made. Hell, a customer probably could have done it, too."

"Shit."

"'Course, to go back there and watch the monitors, you'd have to work here. Anybody else would have been noticed. Most likely, it was done after hours, somebody coming in early or working late."

"Did anyone work extra hours in the weeks before the robbery?"

"Oh, sure."

"Who?"

"Carson stayed late most nights. But everybody puts in long days from time to time."

I finished my pie, paid the check, thanked him for his time, and rose to leave.

"Hang on there, pal."

"What?"

"I got more."

I settled back in my chair and ordered us both another beer.

"When I studied the monitors, I noticed that the camera above the vault entrance, the one that would have been hardest for the perp to avoid, was tilted downward so it covered only about six feet of the approach. So I went back and looked at the video from the weeks before the robbery. Sure enough, the camera was picking up people a good twenty feet from the vault. But three days before the robbery, the angle changed."

"Is the angle controlled remotely from the security room?" I asked.

"No. To change it, you'd have to do it manually."

"Could you do that without being picked up by the camera?"

"Yeah," he said. Just stand out of camera range in the vault door, reach up, and give it a tug."

"Did you tell Ragsdale about this?"

"I did. He didn't seem to think it was important, but I kept bugging him about it. Finally he came by, looked at the camera, and noticed the bracket that holds it in place was a little loose. Said that meant the camera probably slipped on its own."

"But you don't think that's what happened," I said.

"It's too damned convenient. I think the hardware loosened when somebody yanked on the camera to change the angle."

22

The way Ricky Santos told it, Meghan Falco's claim that he and Conner Bowditch were never tight was far from the truth.

"She really told you that?" he said.

"She did."

Santos sadly shook his head.

Midafternoon, we were seated in the sunroom of Kabob and Curry, an Indian restaurant just up College Hill from the Rhode Island School of Design, where Santos was enrolled. We were both drinking Jaipur lager, an Indian brew that Santos recommended. I pretended to like it.

"What do you think he sees in her?" I asked.

"You know, I've always wondered about that. I mean, with that body of his, and with all the moolah he stands to make, he ought to be screwing movie stars and supermodels by now."

"Maybe he values intelligence more than looks," I said.

"Could be. She is a smart girl. You gotta give her that. But she never *did* like me."

"Because you're gay?"

"Yeah."

"What the hell is her problem? Is it a religious thing?"

"I don't know, man. I guess her old man's bigotry rubbed off on her."

"Think she sees you as a threat?"

"As competition for Conner?" He laughed and shook his head.

"Nothing sexual between you two? You never experimented even a little?"

"God, no. Don't get me wrong. Conner's wicked hot. I would have gone for that in a second. But he's as straight as they come."

"How long have you been friends?"

"We were tight all through high school," Santos said, and went on to confirm Coach Shroyer's account of Conner defending him from homophobic bullies—except, apparently, Meghan.

"Are you still in touch?"

"We talk on the phone a couple of times a month. Summers, when he comes home from Boston, we hang out sometimes. Conner lies to Meghan about that. Just, you know, to avoid getting into an argument."

The way he told it, Santos knew nothing about Bowditch's gambling, had no sense that he was worried about anything, and could think of no reason why he should be.

After I paid the bill, I stepped outside, scanned the student-infested sidewalks, and spotted a middle-aged brute who had wandered into the wrong movie. He was sucking on an e-cigarette and leaning against the window of Antonio's Pizza across the street. When he saw me pull out my phone and snap his picture, he turned and pretended to find something worth watching inside. I put him at six-one, two-thirty, with a Gold's Gym body that strained the seams of his trench coat. There was a telltale bulge under his left arm.

I strolled down the sidewalk, crossed Thayer Street, found Mister Ed parked unticketed at an expired meter, and got behind the wheel. Through the windshield, I watched the gym rat turn and climb into the passenger seat of a white Honda Accord.

I pulled from the curb, crawled down Thayer, made three

quick left turns, and led the Honda into a baffling web of narrow one-way streets lined with Victorian and colonial-era houses.
Once I shook the tale, I circled back to Thayer and scooted down
the Indian restaurant's driveway. There, I parked in the area
reserved for deliveries, took my Walther from the glove box,
jacked a round into the chamber, and called McCracken.

"Where are you right now?" I asked.

"In Boston doing more interviews on the Bowditch case."

"Learning anything?"

"Nothing worth mentioning. You?'

"I'm parked behind Kabob and Curry in Providence with a
pistol in my hand."

"Planning to stick up the place?"

"Maybe later. Right now, I'm waiting to make sure I shook
the tail I picked up a few minutes ago."

"Tell me."

"Two guys in a Honda Accord with Massachusetts plates."

"One of the most common cars on the road," McCracken
said. "Guess they aren't as dumb as the first two. Get a look at
them?"

"Just one. I'm texting you his picture now."

"So what are you planning to do about this?"

"Once I'm sure I've lost them, I'm heading home."

"You *could* call Joseph and give them the same treatment we
gave the last pair."

"Yeah, but what good would that do?"

"Well, listen. I might have picked up a tail myself. I noticed
it behind me when I was driving through the BC campus in
Chestnut Hill. When I pulled into the lot at state police headquarters in Framingham a few minutes ago, I saw it again. At least
I *think* it was the same car."

"But you're not sure?"

"No. If they're on me, they're good."

"Watch your ass, McCracken."

"You too."

Later, as I cruised south on I-95, I spotted an occasional white Accord in my mirror, but when I took the turnoff for the Jamestown Verrazzano Bridge, I was confident I wasn't being followed. I'd just pulled into my driveway when McCracken called back.

"According to my Massachusetts state police source, the guy in your photo is Michael "Mickey Scars" McNulty, forty-six, of Brockton, another freelance strong arm loosely affiliated with the Winter Hill Gang."

"I didn't notice any scars," I said.

"The nickname comes from the marks he leaves on other people. Got a rap sheet that includes extortion, assault, and an attempted murder rap he beat at trial."

"Swell."

"They say he usually runs with another charmer named Efrain Vargas, thirty-four, also of Brockton. Chances are, that's who was driving."

23

If the next couple of weeks had been erased from my life, I wouldn't have missed much. No likely suspects for the bank job had suggested themselves. Conner Bowditch hadn't called, and each time I dialed his cell number, it went straight to voice mail. I still hadn't found anyone who was missing an ear. And except for those rare mornings when I rose before sunup to let Rondo out, Cat the Ripper always left a fresh carcass on my porch.

> *On the first day of Christmas*
> *The tabby gave to me*
> *One headless squirrel.*

At least there hadn't been more dognappings. Either the creep had been scared off by Jenks's vigilantes or his heart was bursting with the spirit of the holidays.

When I wasn't obsessing over unsolved cases, I amused myself by studying the strengthening bond between Rondo and Brady. Whenever I let them out to explore my two snowbound acres, they rarely strayed more than five feet apart. At night, Brady no longer climbed in with me. Now, he snuggled with Rondo on the braided rug by the foot of my bed.

One morning, I locked Rondo in the house so I could drive

Brady to the vet for a routine checkup. Neither took it well. Rondo pressed his nose to the kitchen window and howled. Brady rooted himself in the driveway and refused to move. It took me five minutes to drag, push, and lift him into the back of the SUV. When we returned home an hour later, the dogs leaped at each other, yipping and crying as if they'd been afraid they were never going to see each other again.

In our absence, Rondo had tried to break out of the house. He'd ripped the molding from both outside doorjambs. He'd crushed the brass doorknobs in his jaws, chipping one of his teeth. That afternoon, I replaced the molding, installed new hardware, and vowed never to separate them again.

Although they were as close as brothers, their personalities were startlingly different. Rondo was protective and territorial, displaying his suspicion of strangers by barking incessantly at them. Brady was gregarious and affectionate with everyone he met. Rondo was eager to please, constantly studying me for clues about what he should do next. Brady was stubborn and independent, obeying commands to come or stay only when it suited him. Rondo loved to fetch, gleefully chasing tennis balls across the yard and carrying them back to me. Brady watched the balls sail over his head and tossed me a look that said, "You expect *me* to get that?"

Rondo was nearly as big as Brady now. I'd never seen anything grow so fast. I swear I could stand in the kitchen and almost *watch* him grow.

Two days before Christmas it snowed again—just a couple of inches this time, but enough to cover the yellow stains the dogs had made in the yard. I rummaged through my storage shed, found my bow saw, trudged to a cluster of four- and five-foot-tall white pines that had seeded themselves on the west side of the property, and cut down the one that was too close to a towering white maple to ever amount to much. I was dragging it toward the house when the gate at the top of my driveway rolled open and a wine-red Lexus GS pulled in.

The driver's door swung open, and Yolanda burst out. She hooted, churned across the yard on long legs, and hurled herself at me. I caught her in my arms, swung her in a circle, slipped, and toppled into the snow. Yolanda landed on top of me.

Two minutes later, she pulled her lips from mine and said, "Let's take the make-out session inside. I'm getting cold."

"Really? Because I'm getting hot."

While Yolanda fetched her suitcase from the car, I dragged the pine to the house, dropped it on the porch, and let the dogs out to greet her. Brady met Yolanda's eyes, held them, and rubbed his body against her hips. Rondo woofed at her, then glanced over his shoulder for any sign that I might want him to drive her off. Yolanda rubbed Brady behind the ears and reached out to Rondo with her other hand. He retreated a step and eyed her with suspicion.

"You told me they were big," she said, "but I had no idea."

"They're going to get bigger."

"What's it cost you to feed them?"

"Nearly enough to make the monthly payment on your Lexus."

"Seriously?"

"Yeah."

With that, we stepped inside, dashed for the bedroom, shut the door, and tore off our clothes. A few minutes later, Yolanda's cries alarmed the dogs. The door thudded as they hurled their bodies against it, trying to break it down. Lucky for me, it was a strong door.

That night we didn't talk, we never thought about dinner, and I forgot to feed Brady and Rondo. I didn't even let the boys out to do their business.

About seven o'clock the next morning, their barking woke us. I threw on a robe and I found them jitterbugging around the kitchen the way they did when the need to urinate grew urgent. As I opened the door to let them out, Yolanda drifted out of the bedroom wearing nothing at all and padded wordlessly to the bathroom.

Every time I looked at her, something caught in my throat. She was sleek and sinewy, her hair a soft explosion, all of her the hue of shadow. I couldn't explain my good fortune, but I'd finally learned not to question it. I got a pot of coffee started and joined her in the shower. I grabbed a washcloth and ran it over her skin, lingering on her backside.

"I could do this all day," I said. "There's nothing better than a wet woman."

"Any wet woman?"

"Well, yeah, but I've got a special thing for this one."

"Didn't we have this same conversation once before?"

"Move in and we can have it every morning."

Yolanda hesitated, and for just a moment I thought she was going to say yes. "Don't rush me, baby. I'm not ready to give up my own place. . . . But it makes sense to leave some of my things in your closet."

I knew I shouldn't have read too much into that, but I did anyway.

While we dressed, the dogs raised a ruckus outside. Brady yipped excitedly. Rondo's bark was low and menacing.

I'd never worried about them being snatched from the yard— not as long as the front gate was locked. A dognapper would need to vault a four-foot fence, pick up a squirming Brady, and some- how transport him to the other side while Rondo's jaws were locked on his leg. Unless, of course, he decided to risk burning them on the spot. But that wasn't his MO.

Still, whenever the boys were outside, I went to the window every few minutes to check on them.

This time, I peered out the kitchen window and saw Brady and Rondo prowling along the back fence. On the other side, the stray cat kneaded the snow with his paws. Suddenly, he sprang to the top of the fence. Brady turned tail and ran for the porch.

Rondo leaped at the cat, jaws snapping. The cat dropped something, jumped to safety, and calmly slinked away.

I walked out to the fence, picked up a headless blue jay, and wrapped it in a paper towel.

"What's that?" Yolanda asked as I entered the kitchen. So I told her about my war with Cat the Ripper—except for the part about the ear.

Afterward, I urged Yolanda to relax at the kitchen table. She scanned the news on *The Ocean State Rag* Web site and called out the headlines she thought would interest me. I rifled the fridge, found the makings for scrambled eggs and bacon, and got a pan sizzling on the stove. Brady rested his head on Yolanda's thigh, but Rondo kept his distance and eyed her suspiciously, as if he thought she might try to steal something.

"Brady's a sweetie," she said, "but I think Rondo needs diversity training."

"He just needs time to get used to you."

And sure enough, that afternoon, right after we trimmed the tree, Rondo climbed onto my new couch, laid his head in Yolanda's lap, and thumped his massive tail. I sat on the floor, leaned against her legs, and draped an arm around Brady.

And we talked. Yolanda told me how much she enjoyed teaching, how much she loathed the tedious faculty meetings, and what her favorite students were like. I filled her in on the frustrating cases I'd been working.

"I get the feeling you're leaving something out," she said.

"I don't like to worry you."

"Tell me."

So I described the run-ins McCracken and I'd had with the thugs who'd been tailing us.

"What do you know about them?" Yolanda asked.

I spilled the details about their criminal records and what I'd learned by calling the numbers on the Vaccas' cell phones.

"Back up a second," she said. "Romeo Vacca made frequent calls to *what* law firm?"

"Dunst and Moran in Boston."

"Do you know which lawyer they talked to there?"

"Morris Dunst."

"Huh. That's odd."

"In what way?"

"I don't know Dunst, but I *am* familiar with the firm. They specialize in business law. Contracts, patents, incorporations, asset protection. That sort of thing."

"Not criminal cases?"

"No."

"Well, I guess they must be branching out."

Yolanda nodded, then said, "I *am* worried about you."

"You always are."

"Because you keep giving me reasons. Those thugs. Do they know where you live?"

"I don't see how they could. Except for you, McCracken, and a couple of other people I trust, no one does. You know how careful I've been to keep this place secret."

"That's good. You need to be very careful in your line of work."

She meant detective work, but I flashed on what Meghan Falco had said about men who keep secrets from their wives and girlfriends. I needed to come clean with Yolanda about the bookmaking racket, but how could I find the words to put a positive spin on it?

That evening was Christmas Eve. After dinner, I put James Taylor's holiday album on the sound system and popped the cork on a bottle of Antonio Galloni champagne. We carried our glasses to the living room, sat on the floor next to the tree, and exchanged presents.

Yolanda gave me a case of Locke's single malt, my favorite Irish whiskey. She also gave me a Christmas sweater with the New England Patriots' logo on it that was so breathtakingly ugly that it was actually cool. After I put it on, I had her open a small box wrapped in shiny green foil paper.

"Oh, my god," she said. "It's beautiful."

"Do you know what it is?'

"You mean, other than being a silver charm bracelet?"

"I do."

"Then, no."

"It's a Victorian love token bracelet."

"It's antique?"

"It was made in the 1880s. Each of the nine charms is a Liberty-seated dime that was smoothed on one side and then hand engraved with a name, date, or symbol that meant something to the original owner. See, this one says 'Fanny,' and here's another that says 'Lilly'—probably the names of her children. This one depicts a cottage, perhaps the place she grew up in."

"And look at this one," Yolanda said. "It's a wreath with the words 'Christmas 1881' inside."

"Probably the year her husband gave it to her," I said. "It must have meant a great deal to both of them."

"And now, a hundred and twenty-five years later, you're giving it to me."

"Yes."

"Think our love will last that long?"

"Now you're just being sappy."

She punched me in the shoulder, then straddled me and planted a kiss on my lips. The smooching didn't last. Brady, who craved petting, and Rondo, a rampant kisser, wormed their way between us, demanding their share of affection.

I laughed, pulled down two red felt Christmas stockings I'd hung from the mantel, and tossed them to the dogs. Inside each was a pull toy, a new collar, a real beef bone stuffed with peanut butter, and a dozen loose Beggin' Strips that were gobbled up in seconds.

Three blissful days later, Joseph DeLucca paid us a surprise morning visit. He stomped the snow from his boots, stepped into the kitchen, and ruffled Brady's coat while Rondo circled and woofed at him.

"Good to see you again, Yolanda," Joseph said as he set a brown paper grocery bag on the kitchen table.

"Oh-oh," I thought. Or maybe I said it out loud.

"Nice to see you, too, Joseph," Yolanda said. "I was about to start a late breakfast. Did you bring us some goodies?"

"Uh. . . . Not exactly, but if you want, I could run out for something."

That's when Rondo's tail swept across the table. Two empty coffee mugs fell to the floor and shattered. The paper bag tipped over. And dozens of hundred-dollar bills sailed out.

"Aw, hell," Joseph muttered. "Sorry about that, boss."

Rondo lunged forward, snatched a mawful of bills, and bolted for the sitting room. Joseph cursed and thudded after him. For a moment, Yolanda and I stared wordlessly at each other and listened to shouts, growls, and what sounded like a lamp crashing to the floor. Then I got down on my knees, gathered the remaining bills, and returned them to the bag.

"Mulligan?"

"Um?"

"What the hell is going on here?"

I took her hand, led her to the sitting room, sat beside her on the couch, and watched Joseph pry drool-soaked bills from Rondo's jaws. Then he righted the fallen floor lamp and twisted the metal shade into a facsimile of its original shape.

"I've been waiting for the right time to tell you," I said.

"You mean she don't know?" Joseph said.

"Know what?" Yolanda said.

Joseph sadly shook his head. Then he tossed the wet bills in my lap and flopped into the recliner.

"Yolanda," I said. "Remember last year, when the Providence cops accused me of shooting somebody?"

"I do," she said. "You gave me five bucks as a retainer before telling me the story."

"Does that mean you're still my lawyer?"

"Among other things, yes I am."

"Joseph, give Yolanda a five-dollar bill."

"Don't think I got one."

"Give her this, then," I said. I scrunched one of the hundreds into a ball and threw it to him. He caught it, nodded, and tossed it into Yolanda's lap.

"Jesus, Mulligan," she said. "What have you two boys gotten yourselves into this time?"

"Joseph works for me," I said.

"Doing what?"

I sucked in a deep breath and gave her all of it.

When I was done, she sat quietly for what was probably a half a minute. To me, it felt like an hour. Finally, she narrowed her eyes and said, "Why didn't you tell me this before?"

"I was concerned about how you'd take it."

"So you let Rondo break the news?" she said. And then she laughed. A minute later, she was still giggling.

"Does this mean you're not dumping me?"

"Of course I'm not."

"Oh, thank God."

"But you should have told me earlier, baby. I can help."

Now that was a surprise. "Help how?"

"By making you legal."

"You can do that?"

"Yes, I can."

"You've got my full attention."

"Under Rhode Island's gambling laws," Yolanda said, "it's not illegal to place a bet on a sporting event. What's outlawed is operating an enterprise that accepts those bets."

"Which is what we do," Joseph said.

"Yes, but you could set up an online gambling site with an IP address in the Bahamas or the Caymans. When bettors call you or come into the store to place their bets, just tell them you're going digital and give them the Web site address."

"And that would get around the state law?" I asked.

"Absolutely."

"I don't know," Joseph said. "A lot of my regulars are old-timers. They don't know nothin' about computers."

"You can teach them."

"I don't know nothin' about computers either."

"You can learn, Joseph. It's easy."

"What about the ones that ain't got computers?" Joseph asked.

"They can log in at any public library," Yolanda said. "Or you could let them use a computer at your store."

"Then I guess I better get one," Joseph said.

"Hold on a minute," I said. "What about federal law?"

"That's more complicated," Yolanda said.

"Go on."

"First off, the Wire Act of 1961 prohibits using telegraph and telephone lines to place sports bets."

"That sounds like trouble," I said.

"Not really. Since the Internet didn't exist back then, it's not clear that the law can be applied to online gambling."

"Okay."

"Then there's the Unlawful Internet Gambling Enforcement Act of 2006," Yolanda said. "But all it does is prohibit U.S. banks from processing online sports-gambling payments."

"So how do we pay off the winners and collect from the losers?" Joseph asked.

"With prepaid cards or wire transfers that don't go through U.S. banks. I can show you. It's really easy."

"Anything else?" I asked.

"The federal Professional and Amateur Sports Protection Act of 1992 outlaws sports betting everywhere but in Nevada and three other states that were grandfathered in. But it's unclear that it can be applied to bets placed on Web sites located outside the country."

"How unclear?" I asked.

"It's never been adjudicated," Yolanda said, "but the bottom line is that no one has ever faced federal prosecution for online sports gambling."

"Well, I'll be damned," I said. "Know anyone who could set up a Web site for us?"

"No, but I can make some calls."

I rubbed my jaw and thought about it for a moment. "If we do this, I assume our profits will end up in some bank in the Caribbean. Is that going to be a problem?"

"Of course not," she said. "The foreign bank will issue you an ATM card that you can use anywhere."

"And you're telling me all this is legal?"

"As long as you pay taxes on your income."

"Well, I'll be damned."

Yolanda laughed. "Mulligan, you said that already."

24

"Speed up," Yolanda said. "You don't want me to miss my flight, do you?"

"Of course I do."

"It's only five more months, baby."

"Only?"

"I'll miss you, too," she said, and rested her hand on my thigh. I sighed and gave her Lexus a little more gas as we cruised north on Interstate 95 toward Green Airport.

"Can't you tell the dean you've got a family emergency?"

"And what emergency would that be?"

"That your man can't live without you."

"I think you'll survive."

"What will I do for sex?"

"Internet porn and hand lotion."

"It's not quite the same."

"Good to know."

I was about to reintroduce the subject of living arrangements once the semester ended, but Yolanda had something else on her mind.

"Mulligan? Tell me about the jewelry robbery again."

"What about it?"

"I'm not sure. Something about it's been nagging at me."

So I ran through the details again.

"And none of the jewelry has hit the market yet?" she asked.

"Not as far as we know. What are you thinking?"

"Give me a minute."

She remained silent until I pulled the car to the curb in front of the terminal. Then she leaned over for a kiss and told me again how much she'd miss me. I fetched her bag from the back, placed it beside her on the sidewalk, and wrapped my arms around her. When I finally let go, she grabbed the bag and briskly walked away, her thoughts about the robbery seemingly forgotten.

I'd just started the car when someone rapped on the passenger-side door. I turned, saw Yolanda standing there, and lowered the window. She stuck her head inside.

"Mulligan?"

"Um?"

"Has it occurred to you that the jewelry could still be inside the bank?"

After I dropped Yolanda's car at her condo in Providence, Joseph picked me up and drove me home in his truck. As far as I could tell, we weren't followed.

While Joseph horsed around in the snow with Brady and Rondo, I placed another call to Bowditch, got his voice mail again, and left another message. Then I stretched out in bed, closed my eyes, and mulled over Yolanda's question about the bank job. I was still at it a half hour later when I heard Joseph open the door and come inside. Then I heard the dogs' nails skittering on the kitchen floor. They burst into the bedroom, leaped on me, and shook themselves, scattering snow all over the bedspread.

Joseph stuck his head in, said "Sorry, boss," and tossed me a beer. I popped the top, took a gulp, grabbed my cell phone, and called Crowder.

"It's Mulligan. Got a question for you."

"Shoot."

"Were Cargill's jewels loose in the safe deposit box, or did he keep them wrapped in something?"

"No idea."

"Can you ask him?"

"Now, why would you be wanting me to do that?"

"I've got a hunch."

"Gonna tell me about it?"

"Not just yet."

"The man don't like to be bothered with small stuff, pardner. This had better be important."

"I won't know if it is until you ask him. Check it out and call me back."

Two hours later, he did.

"According to Cargill, six pairs of diamond earrings were in clear Mylar bags. The other twenty pieces—mostly bracelets and necklaces—were sealed in bubble wrap."

"Interesting."

"Wanna tell me why?"

"I will once I figure it out."

Just after midnight, the burner on my bedside table rang.

"Mulligan."

"The little freak's been inside my apartment."

"Belinda?"

"Yes."

"Is he there now?"

"No."

"Did you call the police?"

"A patrol officer just left. He looked in all the closets and checked under the bed. Told me I should call again if I needed him and promised to drive by my place a couple of times during the night."

"But you're still scared."

"Damn straight."

"Should I come over?"

"Please."

Ten minutes later, I knocked on her apartment door. She peered through the peephole, unlatched the chain lock, grabbed my arm, and pulled me inside. Then she wrapped her arms around my neck and hugged me. I felt her body shaking.

"Tell me," I said.

"I was out drinking with some girlfriends tonight. When I got home, the front door was unlocked."

"Could you have forgotten to secure it?"

"With Alexander stalking me? No fucking way."

I opened the door, examined the lock, and saw tool marks.

"Find anything out of place?" I asked.

"Hell, yeah. The creep opened my bureau drawers and pulled out all my bras and panties. I think a few of them are missing."

"Show me."

She grabbed my hand and led me into the bedroom. All the bureau drawers yawned open. Several dozen undergarments were strewn on the floor and across the blue chenille bedspread. I watched as she stooped to pick them up, folded them, and returned them to the drawers.

"Can you stay?"

With Cargill gone, the report filed, and a cop promising to check on her, it didn't look like Belinda needed me. And after seeing Yolanda off, it felt wrong to be in another woman's apartment—especially a woman like this one.

"I think you'll be fine, Belinda. You can call me if . . ." But she'd disappeared.

Just as I was about to shout "take it easy" and leave, John Legend began moaning from her sound system. She returned wearing a yellow terry-cloth robe and clutching a bottle of Knob Creek.

"A drink would calm my nerves," she said. "I keep picturing that creep in here, clawing through my things." She put two glasses on the coffee table, plopped down on the couch, and lifted an inquiring eye in my direction.

A drink wouldn't hurt, right? I seated myself at a respectable distance, which Belinda quickly and efficiently closed. Before I knew it, her head was in my lap. I couldn't help thinking of the way Rondo had laid his head in Yolanda's lap once he'd decided it was okay to be in love with her.

"Feeling better?" I asked.

"I'd feel better if you'd touch me."

I pulled my fingers tentatively through her hair. An exasperated sigh told me that wasn't the type of touch she had in mind. She nuzzled her head deeper into my groin and grabbed one of my hands, pushing it toward her breast beneath the robe.

"Not gonna happen, Belinda."

"You know your girlfriend can't see us, right?"

"Doesn't matter."

That exasperated sigh again. After a moment, she popped up, her demeanor changed. Suddenly she was Belinda Veiga, bank officer, again—although her robe gapped in very unprofessional places.

"I hear you're still poking into the robbery case."

"You heard right."

"Even though you're not getting paid?"

"Yes."

"You just can't let it go, can you?"

"It's too damned intriguing."

"Is there anything new?"

"Nothing I can get into with you."

"Why not?"

"I'm sorry, Belinda. I'm just not at liberty to discuss it."

With that, I could actually see her body soften, her eyes smoldering again. "I'm still pretty scared," she whispered. "Think you could at least hold me?"

I gathered her in my arms, and she pressed her face against

my neck. After a few minutes, her breathing slowed, and for a moment I thought she had fallen asleep. But then she murmured.

"The bed would be more comfortable."

"Go ahead, then. I'll sleep on the couch."

"You don't want to join me? I could use some love tonight."

"Love wouldn't have anything to do with it."

If she had a reply to that, I didn't hear it. The whiskey, and a long, hard day, were dragging me under. I'm not sure how much time had passed when I felt her fingers fumbling with my zipper. I gently pushed them away, and she gave up. I heard her stumble off to the bedroom.

Maybe the excitement of the evening had worn her out. Maybe it was the whiskey. Or maybe that woman nine hundred miles away in Chicago was more powerful than I thought.

25

I awoke to the sound of a shower running, got up, and left without saying good-bye. I dashed home to feed Brady and Rondo and then headed straight to the Jamestown police station.

"Bubble wrap?" Ragsdale said.

"That's right."

"What about it?"

"Did you find any in the vault after the robbery?"

"No."

"Check the wastebasket?"

"Yeah. No bubble wrap."

"Then you've got to let me watch the surveillance video from the bank."

"No can do, Mulligan. It's evidence in an open criminal investigation."

"Yeah, but if you bend the rules, maybe I can help you close it."

Ragsdale crossed his arms and stared at me. I stared back. After a minute, he unlocked a desk drawer, slid out a portable hard drive, and plugged it into his computer. I stood behind him as the video began to play.

"Fast-forward to when the perp leaves the vault and walks out of the bank," I said.

"What are you looking for?"

"Bubble wrap."

"Mulligan, I already told you—"

"Humor me," I said. So he did.

"Okay," I said. "Show me the same time sequence from each of the other cameras."

As we watched the perp stroll out of the bank one last time, Ragsdale turned to me and said, "Satisfied?"

"Yes."

"See any bubble wrap?"

"No."

"Are we done?"

"Uh-uh."

"Because?"

"Because according to Ellington Cargill, most of the jewelry pieces were sealed in bubble wrap. If it wasn't left behind in the vault, it should be on the perp."

"And?"

"And it's not."

Ragsdale raised one eyebrow, then started running through the video again.

"Bubble wrap is bulky," I said.

"But none of his pockets are bulging," the chief said. "Could he have sewn some kind of pouch inside his sweatshirt?"

"If it was stuffed with bubble wrap, I think we'd notice."

"Well, I'll be a sonovabitch."

"So what do you think it means?" I asked.

"That we need to shoot some pool. Eight ball helps clear my head."

It was a slow evening at the Narragansett Café. No live music. Just a couple of customers hunched over the bar and an ancient couple gumming a late dinner. Ragsdale racked, and I broke. The balls scattered, and the twelve streaked cleanly into the right corner pocket. I dropped five more, missed a bank shot for the seven, and Ragsdale ran the table.

"Means the drinks are on you," he said.

"If I knew that, I wouldn't have let you win."

"The hell you did. Go again?"

I shook my head no, asked the bartender to draw a Blue Moon and a Sam Adams, and carried them to a corner table.

"So what's your theory?" he asked.

"What's yours?"

"I'm thinking the perp must have a safe deposit box of his own."

"I'm with you so far," I said.

"Once Cargill's and Veiga's eyes were taped," the chief said, "our guy unlocked it with his key and the master Veiga used to open Cargill's box. Then he switched the jewelry from one box to the other, told Cargill and Veiga to count to a hundred, and calmly strolled out of the bank."

"Pretty slick," I said. "There'd be nothing incriminating on him if he got stopped."

"Except the gun," Ragsdale said.

"Probably dumped that in the box, too."

"Even slicker."

"Only one thing wrong with your scenario," I said.

"What?"

"When you open a safe deposit box and pull the metal tray out, it makes a distinctive scraping sound. It's something Belinda must have heard a thousand times. She would have recognized it."

Ragsdale raised an eyebrow. "When I questioned her, she never mentioned it," he said.

"Didn't mention it to me, either."

"Well . . . Maybe she was too rattled to notice."

"Yeah," I said. "That could explain it."

With that, he drained his beer, set the glass on the table, and shoved it toward me. I got up and went to the bar for another round just as Carter Blount, the night manager, wandered out of the kitchen with an angry scar where his left ear used to be.

"Jesus!" I said. "What the hell happened to you?"

"A skinny punk with a gravity knife tried to jack me when I was taking the day's receipts to the bank. Stuck me in the right arm and sliced my ear off before I kicked him in the nuts and knocked the blade out of his hand. I tried to grab him with my good arm, but the prick got clean away."

"They couldn't sew the ear back on?"

"Couldn't find it. Either an animal got it or it went down a storm drain."

"Did you go to the hospital?"

"Nah. I got cut up way worse than this back when I was working as a deckhand on a fishing boat. My sister's husband is a doctor. He stitched me up in his office, gave me a tetanus shot, and I was back to work the next day."

Which explained why my check of area hospitals had come up empty. Another mystery solved, and it was only Monday.

"Shit," Ragsdale said as I clunked our refills on the table and sat across from him. "Now you've got me wondering if Belinda could be involved in this. I always thought she was a good kid."

"Hot, too. I figured she wanted to sleep with me because of my manly physique and rugged good looks. Now I'm wondering if she was just trying to pump me for information."

"Did you?"

"Sleep with her? No."

"Tell her anything?"

"Not that, either."

"Damn," the chief said. "She never tried to seduce *me*."

"Gee. Imagine that."

"Fuck you, Mulligan."

"Do you know if she's got money troubles?" I asked.

"Not that I've heard."

"Well," I said, "a drawer full of diamonds and emeralds is enough to tempt anybody."

"Which includes everybody who worked at the bank," the chief said. "Any one of them could have tipped the gunman off about surveillance-camera angles and bank procedures."

"What's your gut telling you?"

"That maybe it was Carson," he said. "With twins on the way, she must have had money worries."

"What's her husband do?"

"The bastard ran out on her."

"I still don't see it," I said. "If it was her, why would she have brought me in on the case?"

"Wasn't her idea. Corporate ordered her to do it."

"Oh. I didn't know that."

We sipped our beers and thought about that for a while.

"Maybe we've doped this out wrong," I said. "If Belinda was the inside man, the loot could have ended up inside *her* safe deposit box."

"Are you sure she's got one?"

"No."

"Well," the chief said, "I guess I better bring her in and find out."

"If she does, can you get a warrant to open it?"

"Not a chance. At this point, all we've got is conjecture."

I shrugged. "I doubt the jewelry's still in the bank anyway. Whoever was behind this has had nearly four months to get it out."

"Maybe," he said, "but it looks to me like they've been waiting for the heat to cool before they fence it. Can you think of a better place to hide it in the meantime?"

I picked up my beer and took a long pull. "No," I said. "No, I can't."

. . .

Late that night, I bolted awake from a sound sleep and padded into the kitchen. I opened the freezer, lifted the ice tray, and slid out the baggie. Then I snapped on the overhead light, sat at the kitchen table, and stared at the contents.

Somebody was missing a right ear.

Carter Blount had lost his left.

26

A couple of days later, I was playing tug-of-war with the dogs when "Who Are You," my ringtone for unknown callers, began blaring. I pulled out a kitchen drawer, dumped five burner phones onto the counter, and took a minute to figure out which one was ringing.

"Mulligan."

"It's Conner Bowditch returning your call."

"Where are you?"

"In Providence."

"We should talk face-to-face, Conner. Can we meet for lunch?"

"Name the place."

"Rogue Island at noon."

"Where's that?"

"In the Arcade building downtown."

"Sounds expensive."

"Don't sweat it. I'm buying."

Three hours later, I pushed through the door and found Bowditch seated at a table with a glass of beer in front of him and a Sharpie in his hand. A dozen patrons, most of them clutching menus, crowded around him, clamoring for autographs.

"Wait your turn, bud," a guy in a Patriots jersey said as I pushed past him. I shrugged, pulled out a chair, and took a seat at the table.

"Mr. Mulligan?"

"Yes."

"Sorry about this. It'll only be a minute."

"Take your time."

So he did, asking each person's name, writing personal messages for them, and patiently answering a series of inane questions about football. The last of them, a middle-aged woman in a cranberry blouse and tan slacks, stuck out a plump hand and squeezed his left bicep. Then she giggled, turned, and asked him to write his name on her ample bottom. Bowditch hesitated a beat, then scrawled a John Hancock–size signature across the fabric.

"This must happen to you all the time now," I said.

"Yeah. I hated it at first, but I'm getting used to it. Except for the part about signing butts and breasts. That's freaking embarrassing."

With three hundred and thirty pounds of bone and muscle sculpted onto a six-foot, seven-inch frame, Conner Bowditch was the largest human being I'd seen close up since the Syracuse center cracked my hand against the rim in a Big East basketball game. And that was a long time ago.

"I left a lot of messages for you, Conner. What took you so long to get back to me?"

"I apologize for that, Mr. Mulligan. First I was busy with football. Then I was studying for exams. When I'm doing that stuff, I don't like distractions."

"So Meghan told me."

"Truth is, I was pissed off at you, too."

"Because I told her about your gambling?"

"Yes, sir. Wish you hadn't gone and done that. She really read me the riot act."

"I'm about to do the same."

Before I could say more, two men in business suits strolled

in, spotted us, and made a beeline for our table. More autograph seekers. If this kept up, it was going to be difficult to have a conversation.

"Please forgive the intrusion," one of the men said, "but aren't you Liam Mulligan? The guy who used to write all those investigative stories for *The Dispatch*?"

"The one and only."

"It's an honor to meet you, sir. My son is a journalism student at Providence College, and he's been studying your work in class. I was wondering if I could trouble you for your autograph."

Bowditch stared openmouthed as I snatched his Sharpie, pulled out a business card, and wrote my name on the back. As the man thanked us and walked away, the two of us burst out laughing.

"Maybe this wasn't such a good idea," I said. "I doubt anyone's going to ask *me* to sign a butt, but most people who come in here are sure to recognize you. I don't think you're going to want them overhearing the questions I'm going to ask."

"What do you suggest?"

"Let's enjoy our meal and then find a quiet place to talk."

"Okay by me, Mr. Mulligan."

"And knock off the 'mister.' It's just Mulligan."

"Yes, sir."

After we ordered, I turned the conversation to safer subjects.

"What are you doing in town? I thought you'd be back in school by now."

"I'm taking the spring semester off. You wouldn't believe all the stuff I've gotta do to get ready for the draft. Hours in the gym every day to stay in shape. Interviews and workouts with nearly every pro team. The NFL combine next month. Hard to do all that and still keep my grades up."

"And you don't like distractions."

"Like I said. Oh, and I gotta find an agent, too."

"You haven't done that yet?"

Until then, he'd been looking me straight in the eye. Now he hesitated, averted his gaze, and said, "No, sir."

After we finished the meal, Conner signed more autographs while I paid the check. Then we slogged across town on slush-clogged sidewalks, strolled past Johnson & Wales dormitories, massage parlors, head shops, and several boarded-up storefronts, and pushed through the door to Hopes.

Lee, the daytime bartender, spotted Conner, widened his eyes in surprise, turned away to grab a bottle of rye from the shelf, and replenished the shot glasses of two serious drinkers who were slumped over the bar. There was no one else in the place. I ordered our drinks, Killian's for me and a bottle of Poland Spring for Conner, and led him to a table in back.

"Do you have a gambling problem, Conner?"

"Wow. You don't pull your punches, do you?"

"Well?"

"No, sir. I don't believe I do."

"Can you elaborate?"

"I know a lot about sports, you know? So I figured I could place a few bets. Maybe pick up a little spending money."

"How's that been working out for you?"

"Not so good."

"Who have you been betting with?"

"Meghan says you already know."

"Anybody besides Joseph DeLucca?"

"No, sir."

"No bookies in Boston?"

"No."

"No side trips to Vegas?"

"Never been there in my life."

"Internet gambling?"

"Never."

"Have you ever bet on football?"

"No, sir. Just basketball and hockey."

"And baseball?"

"Once in a while, yeah."

"Never bet on games you played in?"

"Oh, God, no! I'd never do that."

"So tell me, Conner. What the hell happened in the Syracuse game?"

"What do you mean?'

"You sucked."

He sighed. "Everybody has a bad game once in a while, Mr. Mulligan."

"You weren't shaving points?"

"Absolutely not," he said, his voice colder now.

"Let me see your phone."

He furrowed his brow, drew it from his pants, and placed it on the table. I picked it up and dropped it in my shirt pocket.

"Hey! I need that."

"Soon as I'm done with it." I slid a brand-new prepaid from my jacket and slapped it in his palm. "In the meantime, use this."

"What do you need my phone for?"

"I'm going to have a computer guy look at it."

"Why?"

"To make sure you haven't used it to place bets on Internet gambling sites. Do you have a computer?"

"A laptop, yeah."

"Where is it?"

"In my car."

"When we're done here, I'm going to need you to give me that, too."

Until then, nothing I'd asked had angered him—at least not outwardly.

"You think I'm lying to you?"

"I'm paid to be thorough."

"I don't like having my integrity questioned, Mr. Mulligan. I could kick your ass for this."

"No you couldn't."

"You sure about that?"

"I'm starting to like you, Conner. It would be a real shame if I had to shoot you. Now let me see your wallet."

"Why?"

"I need to look at your credit cards."

"What for?"

"So I can run them to be sure you haven't used them on Internet gambling sites."

"I haven't. I already told you that."

"I'm inclined to believe you, Connor, but no way the Patriots are just going to take your word for it."

He hesitated, then pulled his wallet from his pants and tossed it on the table. I flipped through it, drew out the lone credit card, and jotted the number on a cocktail napkin.

"Meanwhile, stop gambling. If word gets out that you're in debt to a bookie, some teams might shy away from you on draft day, and that could cost you a lot of money."

"Okay. I get it."

Bowditch had barely touched his water. I got up to fetch another beer. As Lee pulled the bottle from the ice chest, the front door creaked open. In the mirror behind the bar, I saw Michael McNulty stepped inside. Behind him, a pencil-thin Hispanic I took to be Efrain Vargas entered and stamped the slush from his shoes. They both stood by the door for a moment to let their eyes adjust to the dim bar light. I ignored them, grabbed my beer, and returned to our table.

"Recognize the two guys who just walked in?"

Bowditch twisted in his chair to look them over, then said, "Never seen them before."

"You sure?"

"Yes, sir."

The two thugs seated themselves at the bar, and McNulty tossed some bills on it. Lee wandered over to take their orders and clunked bottles of Budweiser in front of them. They each took a sip and spun on their stools to stare at us.

"I get the feeling they know you," I said.

"Most people do."

"The big guy is Michael McNulty, and I think the other one is Efrain Vargas. The names mean anything to you?"

"No. Who are they?"

"A couple of strong-arm types from Boston. After the Patriots hired my firm to do a background check on you, they started tailing me."

"Why would they do that?"

"I don't know. Do you?"

"No, sir. I got no idea."

"I didn't spot them behind me when I drove in this morning," I said. "Makes me wonder how they knew I'd be in town."

"I didn't tell them, Mr. Mulligan, if that's what you're thinking."

"You know what else I wonder, then?"

"What?"

"If maybe they were tailing you."

Bowditch shifted in his chair. The thought seemed to unsettle him.

"What about Romeo and Dante Vacca? Ever heard of them?"

"No, sir,"

"Morris Dunst?"

"Don't know him either." But this time, he looked away when he said it.

"Last I knew, McNulty and Vargas were driving a white Honda Accord. Keep an eye out, Conner. If you spot them following you, call me right away."

"You're saying they're dangerous?"

"Oh, yeah."

"I can handle myself, Mr. Mulligan."

"Don't even think about it," I said. "They're both packing heat."

"How can you tell?"

"By the bulges under their left arms."

"Jesus! What the hell is going on?"

"I was hoping you could tell me."

"No idea," he said, and once again, he looked away. No doubt about it. That was his tell.

Later, as we trudged to the Weybosset Street lot where Conner had left his car, I kept glancing behind us. There was no sign of McNulty and Vargas, but I took scant comfort in that. I figured they knew where Conner or I—or maybe both of us— had parked.

As Conner got behind the wheel of his Chevy Cruze, I asked him again for his laptop. He hesitated before slipping it from under the passenger seat and reluctantly handing it to me.

"Where are you going now?" I asked.

"To pick up Meghan. I promised to take her to a movie at Providence Place."

"And after that?"

"I'll drop her at her dorm and then head home."

"Where's that?"

"I'm staying at my folks' place on the East Side."

"Stay safe, Conner. I'll call when I need to talk to you again."

Once he drove off, I strolled to McCracken's office in the Turks Head Building, filled him in on my conversation with Conner, told him about our brush with McNulty and Vargas, and gave him Conner's phone, laptop, and credit card number.

"My tech guy should be done with this stuff in a day or two," he said. "Soon as I get the results, I'll give you a holler."

As a precaution, I took the long way home, driving west to Fall River, meandering through busy city streets, turning south into Tiverton, and crossing the bridge over the Sakonnet River to Aquidneck Island. By the time I rolled into Newport, I was sure I hadn't been followed. I sped over the Claiborne Pell Bridge to

Jamestown and made it home in time to join Brady and Rondo on the couch for the first period of the Bruins-Canadiens game.

Later, just as P. K. Subban, the Canadiens' all-star defenseman, leveled Brad Marchand with a crosscheck, "Glory Days," my favorite Springsteen song, started playing on one of my cell phones. It was the ringtone for calls from the prepaid I'd given to Conner.

"Mulligan."

"It's Meghan Falco. Conner and I are on the way home from the movies, and he thinks we're being followed."

"A white Honda Accord?"

"Yes. What should we do?"

"Do you have the phone on speaker?"

"I do."

"Conner, I want you to drive Meghan straight to your folks' place, go inside, and lock the doors. Watch the street, and if you see the car lurking outside, call the police."

A half hour later, he called back.

"I think they're gone," he said. "I haven't seen them since we turned onto our street. My dad called the security chief at his construction firm, and he's on his way over; so whatever this is about, we should be okay for now."

27

"What did Belinda Veiga have to say for herself?" I asked.

"She got real indignant," Ragsdale said. "Swore up and down she had nothing to do with the stickup."

We were seated in his office, both of us chewing on cigars while I silently cursed the nanny-state antismoking law he insisted on observing.

"Did you ask her if she has a safe deposit box?"

"Of course I did."

"And?"

"The bank gave her one as a job perk. She let me watch while she opened it. Nothing inside but a light coating of dust. The way she tells it, she's never owned anything valuable enough to put in it."

"So we're back to thinking the stickup guy has a box of his own," I said.

"Unless we've missed something, but darned if I know what it could be."

"Anything new on the dognappings?" I asked.

"We lost another one last night."

"Aw, hell."

"A female lab named Layla. Burned up so bad we'd never have ID'd her without her tags."

"Who'd she belong to?"

"Marlon Jenks."

That stopped me. I stared at the ceiling for a moment, then said, "It could be a coincidence."

"Maybe, but I'm thinking it's retribution for him trying to spoil the fun with his citizen patrol."

Early next morning, Ragsdale rang me up with worse news.

"Brace yourself, Mulligan."

"What now?"

"A couple of Jenks's vigilantes were prowling down by Clarks Village when they spotted what looked like a pile of clothes in the woods off Beaver Tail Road. They got out to check and found a body."

"Any ID?"

"It's only tentative but . . ."

"Spit it out, Chief."

"They're saying it's Belinda Veiga."

I swallowed hard. "What happened to her?"

"Not sure yet. I just got on scene. . . . Christ! There's a lot of blood."

"I'm on my way."

I arrived to find a uniformed officer stringing crime-scene tape through the scrub oaks and brush about thirty yards off the road. Beyond it, Ragsdale and three more uniforms watched a detective snap photos with a digital camera. Outside the police line, two civilians in parkas stamped their feet in the snow.

Ragsdale waved me over. I ducked under the tape and got my first glimpse of the corpse, sprawled facedown in a blood-soaked snowdrift.

"Are those the guys who found her?" I asked.

Ragsdale nodded.

"You sure it's Belinda?"

"So they say. They turned the body over to look at her face

and then rolled it back. I already chewed them out for messing with the scene."

During my years as a reporter, I'd seen putrid human remains dragged from rivers, mobsters blasted against barroom walls, bodies tangled in the wreckage of airplanes, families burned beyond recognition in house fires . . . and the one that had stayed with me the longest, bloody bits of a twelve-year-old boy dangling from trees after he'd been dismembered by a train. But most of them had been strangers. A few had even deserved what they got. This was a woman I'd recently cradled in my arms.

I excused myself, ducked outside the police tape, and deposited my breakfast in the snow. Behind me, I heard a couple of the cops snicker. When my stomach stopped heaving, I wiped my mouth with my sleeve, returned to the body, and squatted on my heels for a closer look.

"Are you okay?" Ragsdale asked.

"Fuck, no."

"Maybe you should sit this one out."

I felt the bile rise again, fought it down, and shook my head. "Is the medical examiner on the way?"

"She should be here in twenty."

"Judging by the amount of blood, I think she was killed right here," I said. "Two holes in her coat and one in her head. From the size of them, I'm guessing they're entrance wounds."

"That's how I see it."

"Could the men who found her have done this?"

"Don't seem likely."

"Check them for weapons?"

"Found a Mossberg double-barrel in their truck, but those aren't shotgun wounds."

"They could have ditched the weapon."

"When we're done here, I'll take them to the station and test their hands for gunshot residue, but I don't expect to find any."

"So what are you thinking, Chief?"

"I'm thinking Alexander Cargill better have himself an

air-tight alibi. Soon as the M.E. establishes time of death, I'll haul Richie Rich's ass in for a chat."

"Mind if I sit in?"

"No can do."

"I could bring my brass knuckles. And some salt to rub in the wounds."

"Knuckle dusters are illegal in Rhode Island, Mulligan, so I'm gonna pretend I didn't hear that. Besides, we don't do things that way anymore." He rubbed his eyes with the heel of his hand and added, "Sometimes I miss the good old days."

Minutes later, the chief and I stepped aside as Glenna Ferguson, an assistant state medical examiner, knelt in the snow and rolled the body.

"Two gunshots to the back and one to the head," she said. "Powder burns on her clothes indicate the shots were fired from no more than three feet away. Judging by the angles of the entry and exit wounds, the killer made her kneel and stood behind her as he fired. The body is in the early stages of rigor mortis, so she's been dead at least four hours."

Ferguson unzipped Belinda's blue Columbia jacket and yanked up her blouse. Then she plucked a scalpel from her kit and sliced an incision in the abdomen. I looked away as she drove a thermometer into the liver. I tried to conjure a memory of the sexy young woman I'd known, but my mind was fixed on the broken thing sprawled in the snow.

"Lividity and body temperature put time of death at four to eight hours ago," Ferguson said. "Find any shell casings?"

"Not yet," Ragsdale said. "We'll sift through the snow after you bag her."

Once she did, there was nothing left for me to see, but I hung around until the body bag was loaded into the medical examiner's wagon. A chill seeped through my shoes as I watched the taillights dim and disappear.

.   .   .

Late that afternoon I shrugged on my Richard Harding Davis persona, wrote an account of the murder for *The Ocean State Rag,* and e-mailed it to Mason. Then I poured myself a stiff one, threw it down, and refilled the tumbler to the brim. I carried it into the sitting room, put Muddy Waters on the sound system, and flopped on the floor with my dogs.

Why the blues again? Why not a sultry crooner or that upbeat pop star everyone was listening to. Bruno Mars? Was that the guy's name? Why was I always drawn to music about hard times at the bottom of a shot glass? The music of the scorned and shattered.

At the end of most every day—even the ones that didn't involve shaking a tail, tracking down thieves, or staring at a broken body—I'd lean back with a glass of something bitter and drown in Koko Taylor's growl, Buddy Guy's soulful riffs, or the vibing wire of Stevie Ray Vaughan's guitar. Just like my dad did before the cancer took him.

He'd come through the door, exhausted from another day of delivering milk, put a scratchy Son Seals album on the turntable, pull out his Comet harmonica, and play along. Like him, I belonged to the downtrodden tribe that turns misery into music—the kind of music that warns us what the world is like and steels us against it.

My old job as an investigative reporter, like my new one as a detective, was to probe the dark hearts we pray against. I'd locked eyes with murderers. Wondered, more than once, if something rotten was eating away at me, turning me into the very thing that I fear. Then the twang of a blues guitar would fill the room, preaching that even in the darkest of times, the idea of light exists—and that the purpose of life is just to live it.

The blues is pain, but it's pain that brings joy. B. B. King said that.

When the music cycled around to "Baby, Please Don't Go" for the second time, I got up, staggered into the kitchen, and poured myself another drink. I held the tumbler up to the light, thought better of it, and tried to pour the whiskey back into the bottle. My hands shook, and half of it ended up on the floor.

I made some coffee and drank two cups, which sobered me up a little. Then I called McCracken to tell him that my prime suspect in the bank heist had turned up dead.

"You're still messing around with that?"

"Yeah."

"Well, forget it. We've got *paying* clients to worry about."

"Hey, a guy needs a hobby."

"Are you drunk?"

"Do I sound drunk?"

"As a skunk."

"Drinking's my other hobby."

"Well, sober up and call me back. I got some news."

An hour later, I did.

"My tech guy's all done with Bowditch's laptop and cell phone. They both came up clean."

"What about the credit card?"

"For five hundred bucks, a Capital One clerk e-mailed me copies of his bills for the last two years. Nothing there to suggest the kid's been using it to gamble."

"Doesn't prove anything," I said. "Maybe he's got another credit card. He could have used somebody else's computer. A roommate's, or one at the school library."

"It's possible," McCracken said, "but I doubt he was thinking that far ahead."

"Did you check the call logs and e-mails?"

"Of course."

"Any record of Bowditch communicating with Morris Dunst?"

"No. Should I have a messenger deliver his things to his dad's place?"

"I'll come tomorrow and pick them up," I said. "I want to return them myself."

.   .   .

The Bowditch clan lived behind a six-foot wrought iron security fence in a massive redbrick colonial just off Blackstone Boulevard in Providence's best neighborhood. I was just a couple of blocks away when Conner's cell phone tinkled. I pulled to the curb and snatched it from the passenger seat.

"Hello."

"Conner?"

"No. I'm a friend of his."

"Why are you answering his phone?"

"He's currently indisposed. I heard the phone ring, so I picked it up."

"He's on the toilet?"

"Uh. . . . Yeah."

"Well, drag him out of there and put him on the line." The voice was a low rumble—like Sam Elliott but with a Boston accent.

"I'm sorry, sir, but I'd need a heavy-duty tow truck for that, and I don't have one handy. Besides, Conner doesn't like distractions when he's squeezing one out."

"Then I'll hold."

"May I tell him who's calling?"

"Morris Dunst."

"And the nature of your call?"

"It's a private matter."

"I think he's gonna be a while. Perhaps it would be best if I have him call you back."

"You do that," he said, and clicked off.

28

"So do you believe me, now?" Bowditch asked.

"About online gambling? I think so, yeah."

"Why do you keep looking out the window?"

"Because McNulty and Vargas are back. They're sitting in their white Honda Accord a half block down the street."

Bowditch tried to rise from the couch, but his father, Malcolm, a fifty-something about two-thirds Conner's size, stretched out a paw, clamped it on his son's shoulder, and pulled him back in place. "Stay away from the windows," he said, "and let Rene do his job."

Rene Vachon, Bowditch Construction's head of security, roused himself from an easy chair and joined me at the window. Vachon wasn't a Mulligan fan. Five years ago, when he was still a Providence vice cop and I was writing for *The Dispatch*, I'd exposed him and a half dozen of his coworkers for padding their paychecks with phony overtime. He still held a grudge, but in front of the Bowditch clan, he was making an effort to be civil.

"Where?" he asked.

I pointed.

"I say we sneak out the back door, circle around behind, and roust them," he said. "Give them a few lumps and maybe they'll tell us what the hell they're after."

"And if they start shooting?"

He didn't have an answer for that.

"Do they intend to harm my son?" Malcolm Bowditch asked.

"If that was their plan," I said, "they probably would have done it already."

"How do you suggest we handle this?" Vachon asked.

"Wait till I leave," I said. "If they follow me, don't do anything. If they don't, call the cops."

"Do you have any idea what's going on, Mr. Mulligan?" the older Bowditch asked.

"I suggest you ask your son."

"I already told you," Conner said. "I got no clue."

"What's your business with Morris Dunst?"

Conner slid his eyes off mine and turned to his father. "He asked me that a couple of days ago, Dad, and it was the first time I heard the name."

"That so?" I said.

"Yes, sir."

"So why's he been calling you?"

"Sir?"

"Your cell rang when I was on my way over here, Conner. When I picked up, the caller identified himself as Dunst and demanded I put you on the line."

"Son?" Malcolm Bowditch said.

"I can't explain it, Dad."

"When I told him you were unavailable, he said you needed to call him back. The number's in your log of incoming calls, but I'm guessing you already know it."

Conner glared at me and vigorously shook his head.

The white Accord was still there when I walked down Bowditch's front walk and opened the gate. I made it a point not to look. I stepped behind the RAV4, scooped a handful of mud from the gutter, and smeared it on the front and rear plates.

As I pulled away from the curb, the Accord fell in behind me.

McNulty and Vargas weren't bothering to disguise the tail now. They wanted me to know they were there. They wanted to intimidate me. Or worse. I reached for my cell and hit speed dial.

"Zerilli's Market."

"Joseph?"

"Yeah."

"Can you get away?"

"If you need me. What's up?"

"The two thugs who've been tailing me off and on since you incapacitated the Vacca brothers are on my ass again."

"Inka what?"

"Since you fucked them up."

"Got it."

"I'm just two or three minutes away. Bring a gun and meet me on the corner of Hope and Burlington. Oh, and pull something over your head. These two haven't seen you yet."

When I braked at the corner, Joseph was standing there in the evening gloom, the hood of a Patriots sweatshirt covering his noggin. I unlocked the passenger door, but he didn't climb in. Instead, he turned and studied the Honda, which had come to a stop about fifteen yards from my bumper. And then he grinned.

He raised the hem of the sweatshirt, jerked a large revolver from his belt, raised it, and pulled the trigger. And then he pulled it some more, the gun cracking five times in quick succession. I turned in my seat in time to see the last two slugs smash through the hood into the Accord's engine block.

Then the car's doors flew open, and McNulty and Vargas burst out. Joseph gave them a little wave and jumped in beside me. I hit the gas and ducked, expecting the rear window to implode with return fire. There was none. A couple of minutes elapsed before my heart stopped racing.

"When did you get the cannon?" I asked.

"Last week."

"What model?"

"Forty-four mag Smith and Wesson."

"The nine mil wasn't enough gun for you?"

"I wanted something with more stopping power," he said. "This was the first chance I had to try it out."

"Next time you decide to pull a stunt like that, I'd appreciate a warning."

"Sorry. I didn't know I was gonna do it till I did it."

"That was fucking crazy, Joseph."

"It worked, didn't it?"

"For now, but they'll be back."

"Yeah, but they're gonna have to steal some new wheels first."

29

"Rack, 'em," Ragsdale said.

"Loose or tight?"

"Tight."

He chalked his cue and broke. The balls streaked across the table, and the eight ricocheted into the right corner pocket.

"Drinks are on you again," he said.

"Lucky bastard."

"It ain't luck, Mulligan. I drop the eight ball at least one break out of ten."

"You've been hustling me."

"Bet your ass. Go again?"

He whipped me three more times, only one of the games close, before we picked up our beers and carried them to a corner table.

"Got your head clear, now?" I asked.

"Clear as it gets, I guess."

"And?"

"Alexander Cargill claims he was at the mansion when Belinda got shot."

"Anyone back up his story?"

"A couple of the servants, yeah, but they'd say anything he wants them to."

"Tell me about the interrogation."

"I asked him to account for his whereabouts the night before. He wanted to know why I was asking. I danced around that for a few minutes, but I couldn't get anything out of him. When I finally told him Belinda was dead, he burst into tears."

"Think it was an act?"

"The tears were real enough. The kid put his hands over his eyes and blubbered."

"But was he crying for Belinda or for himself?"

"Damned if I could tell," the chief said, "but he sure did carry on. Took a couple of minutes before he could compose himself."

"And then I bet he asked for a lawyer."

"He didn't."

"No shit?"

"Surprised the hell out of me, too. All the trouble he's been in, the kid ought to know not to talk to a cop without one of his daddy's shysters present."

"So then what?"

"I got him a cup of coffee, which he didn't drink, and started in with the questions again. He didn't answer at first. Kept asking *me* questions. How did she die? Where she was found? Did she suffer? Who could have done this to her? Then he started in with a song and dance about how much he loved her."

"Maybe he did," I said.

"Obsession and love ain't the same thing, Mulligan."

"Still think he killed her?"

"I don't have enough to hold him, but my gut says yes."

I nodded, went to the bar for another round, and returned to the table.

"When's the last time someone got murdered in Jamestown?" I asked.

"Belinda's the first since I joined the force."

"When was that?"

"Eighteen years ago."

"Huh. . . . Wasn't there something about a serial killer? About fifteen years back, I think."

"Yeah," he said. "Hadden Clark."

"Can you refresh my memory?"

"After Clark got locked up for murder in Maryland, he bragged about burying a couple of bodies on one of our beaches. Two girls he supposedly killed in the 1990s when he was living with his grandfather in Providence. But we dug the place up and didn't find anything."

"Nothing else since then?"

"Well, there was David Swain, the scuba shop owner who got convicted of drowning his wife by ripping her regulator off during a dive. But it happened when they were on vacation in the British Virgin Islands. This is a peaceful town, Mulligan. Hell, the stickup at the bank and the attack on Carter Blount were the first armed robberies we've had here in over a decade."

"Forgive me for saying this," I said, "but maybe you need to bring the state cops in on Belinda."

"I'll think about it."

"Find any shell casings at the scene?"

"Uh-uh. No indication the shooter pawed through the snow looking for them, either. Must have used a revolver."

"Find the slugs?"

"They're still looking."

"Any guess on the caliber?"

"Ferguson says she can't say for certain but that the wounds were consistent with a thirty-eight."

I drained my beer and thought for a moment. "You're probably right to focus on Alexander Cargill, but I gotta tell you, Chief. The timing of this bothers me."

"Because she was killed the day after I questioned her about the bank job?" Ragsdale said.

"Yeah. What if her partner got worried that she might talk? Or decided not to share the profits?"

"Not much there to hang my hat on," Ragsdale said. "We don't even know that she was involved."

30

"It's done," Joseph said. "We're all legal."

"What's the setup look like?"

"Three-year-old five-story building with two-foot-thick concrete walls, steel bars on the windows, and a state-of-the-art security system. We've got the southwest corner on the fourth floor, and there's two other online gambling operations just down the hall. I spent a couple of days watching two techies wire stuff up and plug stuff in. Antigua's a fuckin' paradise, Mulligan. You and me, we ought to pop down there now and again. Catch some rays, get ourselves laid, drink Wadadli, and visit our money."

"What's Wadadli?"

"The local beer. It's fuckin' killer."

With that, he popped the top on a can of Narragansett. I rose from the couch and fed wood to the iron stove I'd recently installed. Outside, the temperature had dropped into the teens, the yard covered with another four inches of fresh snow.

"Got an ATM card for you," Joseph said, "but check the bank balance before you use it. Ain't much money in it yet, but the dough is starting to roll in."

"Send a card to Zerilli?"

"Uh-huh."

"And he's okay with this?"

"Took me a fuckin' hour to explain everything to him over the phone, but yeah, he's fine with it long as he gets his cut."

"Good work, Joseph."

"Nothin' to it. The computer geeks Yolanda set us up with did the heavy lifting."

"What did it cost us?"

"Forty large. Yolanda says we can write it off as a business expense."

I nodded.

"Gonna be some fireworks tomorrow, though," he said.

"Oh?"

"That's when Widget and Fritos will be dropping by for their monthly payoff. I finally get to tell the assholes to go fuck themselves. Don't think they're gonna like it."

The bookie operation at Zerilli's Market had been an open secret. For years, old man Zerilli, and then Joseph, had been paying off the Providence cops to look the other way. The bagmen were a couple of bent detectives, Wargart and Freitas, but Joseph never could get their names right.

"Call me if they give you trouble," I said.

"Sure thing."

Just past three o'clock the following afternoon, he did.

"The bastards got me chained to a table in an interrogation room," Joseph said. "Thanks for pickin' up. You're my one phone call."

"Sit tight and keep your mouth shut. Help's on the way."

It took me nearly two hours to reach Yolanda. "Sorry," she said. "I was in class. Soon as I heard your message, I got ahold of Mark Gardner, one of our junior associates. He'll head over to the police station as soon as he finishes taking a deposition."

Forty-five minutes later, I stepped into a second-floor interrogation room at the Providence PD and found the interested parties seated on steel chairs at a heavy metal table. Wargart, a big lug with fists like hams, and Freitas, a bottle blond with a predatory Cameron Diaz smile, were on one side, their backs to the door. Joseph and a suit I took to be Gardner sat on the other. Joseph's hands were cuffed in front, his left leg still chained to the table. He had an angry purple bruise under his left eye and a ribbon of dried blood curling from a split lip.

The detectives' heads swiveled when they heard the door creak open. "What the fuck are you doing here, Mulligan?" Wargart asked.

"I require Mr. Mulligan's presence," Gardner said. "He is an operative for a detective agency that I have retained to assist on this case." He turned to me and added, "You haven't missed anything. We were just getting started."

I liked Gardner already. Claiming he'd retained me was a clever lie on short notice. Seeing no empty chairs, I leaned against the wall and said, "Care to explain what happened to Joseph's face?"

"He resisted arrest," Wargart said.

"Like hell I did," Joseph said. "If I had, you'd be the one with the fuckin' bruises."

"Please refrain from speaking, Mr. DeLucca," Gardner said. "I'd prefer not to have to remind you of that again."

"Let him talk, counselor," Freitas said. "We can't wait to hear how the scumbag's going to try to lie his way out of this one."

"I suggest you refrain from name calling, Detective," Gardner said. "Mr. DeLucca is a legitimate businessman."

"Oh, is he now?" Wargart said. "And what does that make you, a fucking comedian?"

Gardner calmly opened his briefcase, slid out a manila folder, and placed it on the table.

"What this?" Freitas asked.

"Documents confirming that Mr. DeLucca is the proprietor of an online gambling enterprise operating in conformity with state and federal law."

Freitas opened the folder and rifled through it. "This is all gobbledygook to me," she said.

"Then perhaps *you* should consult an attorney."

"We'll have the prosecutor look it over, Freitas said, "but whatever it means, it won't do your client any good. We know for a fact he's been taking bets illegally in the back room of Zerilli's Market for more than a year."

"Yeah," Wargart said. "Ever since his asshole buddy Dominic Zerilli retired to Florida."

"And how exactly do you know this?" Gardner asked.

The detectives exchanged a glance and chose not to respond.

"Zerilli is a capo for the Rhode Island mob," Wargart finally said. "That makes your client an associate of organized crime."

"That's just guilt by association," Gardner said. "Charge him or release him."

Silence.

"Permit me to speak hypothetically for a moment," Gardner said. "Let's say, for the sake of argument, that you are in possession of evidence that Mr. DeLucca illegally accepted bets for a period of a few months—an accusation, by the way, that he vehemently denies. Given that he has gone to great lengths and considerable expense to establish a *legal* online gambling business, I doubt that the attorney general's office will seek to prosecute. And even if my client should somehow be convicted, he would in all likelihood be sentenced to nothing more than a two-thousand-dollar fine.

"Then again, still speaking hypothetically, let's suppose that Mr. DeLucca could produce compelling evidence of ongoing corruption in the Providence Police Department. I'm confident the attorney general would be inclined to forgo charges against him in return for his cooperation."

Wargart slammed his ham-size fist on the table. "Are you *threatening* us, counselor?"

"Only hypothetically," Gardner said. And for the first time, I saw him smile.

"No one's gonna believe your client's lying ass," Freitas said.

"They will when they see the video," I said. That shut them up. "What? You mean you didn't notice the surveillance camera in the office where you've been *hypothetically* collecting your monthly payoff? I guess it *is* hard to spot. It's hidden in the wall clock."

"You're bluffing," Wargart said.

"Oh, it's there all right," I said. "I installed it myself."

Wargart and Freitas hauled themselves to their feet and stalked out of the room. When they returned a half hour later, they changed the subject.

"All right, DeLucca," Freitas said. "Can you account for your whereabouts at approximately seven fifteen on Monday evening?"

"Don't answer that," Gardner said. "Detective, may I inquire what this is regarding?"

"Shots fired outside Zerilli's Market."

"I see. Was anyone injured in the incident?"

"We're not sure," Wargart said. "A car stolen in Somerville, Massachusetts, a week ago got blasted to all hell, but no one was inside when officers responded."

"I shall require a private moment to consult with my client," Gardner said. The detectives slammed the door on their way out.

"Do you know anything about this?" the lawyer asked Joseph.

I answered for him. "We both do."

"Go ahead," Joseph said. "You tell it better."

After I spilled the story, Gardner instructed us on how to handle it and called the detectives back in.

"Is Mr. DeLucca a suspect in this incident?" Gardner asked.

"At this point," Freitas said, "we consider him a material witness."

"Ask your questions, Detective."

"Where were you at seven fifteen P.M. Monday?"

"I don't recall."

"Were you at your place of business?"

"You mean the market?"

"Yes."

"Can't say. I might have already left for the day."

"Did you hear any gunshots before leaving?"

"No way I could have."

"And why would that be?"

"I was blasting AC/DC on my iTunes. Can't hear a fuckin' thing with my earbuds in."

"You remember what music you were playing?" Wargart asked.

"It was either them or Metallica. I play their shit all the time."

"Did you see a white Honda Accord parked on the street when you exited the store?" Freitas asked.

"Not that I can recall."

"The car was shot up with a large-bore handgun," Wargart said. "A forty-four magnum Smith and Wesson revolver was registered in your name just last week."

"Is that a question?" Gardner said.

"Where's the gun now?" Wargart asked.

"Lost or stolen."

"Have you reported it stolen?"

"Not yet. I just noticed it was missing. I'm hoping it will turn up."

"Bullshit," Wargart said.

"A black Toyota RAV4 was observed fleeing the scene," Freitas said. "You drive one of those, don't you, Mulligan?"

"There are lots of them on the road."

With that, the detectives rose and stomped out of the room again.

"No way they've got the plate number," I said.

"You're sure?"

"Positive."

I pulled out a cell phone and punched in the number for my source at the state crime lab. "It's Mulligan. Did you run ballistics on the slugs from a Honda Accord involved in a shooting on Hope Street Monday night?"

"Yeah. Five slugs from a large caliber handgun, but that's all I can tell you. They shattered when they smashed into the engine block."

"So there's no way to make a comparison?"

"That's right."

"Oh, darn. Thanks, Henry."

"Gee," Joseph said. "I just remembered where I put my Smith and Wesson."

A half hour later, Wargart and Freitas filed back in and wordlessly cut Joseph loose.

"Let's celebrate at Hopes," I said as I followed Joseph and Gardner down the police station's salt-strewn front steps. "The drinks are on me."

"I'm afraid I must decline," Gardner said. "I'm needed back at the office."

"It's already past eight P.M."

"Such is the life of a law firm associate."

Joseph and I both thanked Gardner and shook his hand. He turned away, but then he spun back to face us.

"Mr. Mulligan?"

"Um?"

"Did you really install a video camera in the clock?"

"Of course not."

Gardner gave me a high five and strode down the street with a bounce in his step.

31

I was nursing my second beer and Joseph was on his fourth when Stevie Wonder's "Golden Lady," my ringtone for Yolanda, started playing on the phone I reserved for personal calls.

"Hi, baby."

"Did Gardner get Joseph sprung?"

"He did. Smart guy. You ought to promote him."

"Good to hear. Need anything else?"

"We're set."

"Okay. Gotta run. I'll call late tonight so we can talk dirty."

Joseph drained his bottle and signaled for another. "Today was a fuckin' blast," he said.

"Except for the beating you took."

"Except for that, yeah."

"Think we can both stay out of trouble for a while? I don't need any more drama right now."

"Maybe not," he said.

"Oh-oh. Now what?"

"Have you talked to Arena yet?"

"What about?"

"He's expecting his taste at the end of the month," Joseph said. "Now that we're legal, we got no reason to pay the prick."

"Oh, shit. I hadn't thought of that."

"You should have."

"You're right. I've been distracted lately. Got a lot on my plate."

"Want me to talk to him?"

"Oh, hell, no."

"Why not?"

"It's a delicate situation, Joseph, and you don't do tact."

"I'm supposed to deliver his package on Friday. Can you talk to him before then?"

"I don't think so."

"Then what the fuck am I supposed to do?"

"For now, keep paying him. I'll let you know when I get it worked out."

32

I was sitting on the floor with Brady and Rondo, their tails slapping time to the latest album by Tommy Castro and the Painkillers, when one of my burner phones interrupted with the haunting theme from *The Godfather*, my ringtone for organized crime sources.

"Mulligan."

"Don't say my name, but do you recognize the voice?"

"I do."

"I just got a phone call you might find interesting."

"I'm listening."

"Was from a guy who's in my line of work. He had a question concerning that thing you came to see me about."

"And?"

"It's not something we should talk about on the phone," he said.

"Your place in an hour?"

"I'll be waiting."

I parked at the curb on Allens Avenue, strolled under the three brass balls, and stepped into the pawnshop. The clerk with the sleeve tattoos must have been expecting me, because he didn't say a word as I walked past him and entered the warehouse. The cases of Crown Royal were gone now, replaced with enough Johnny Walker Black to poison every liver from Newport to Woonsocket. The refrigerator in the blue suit was at his post in front of Carmine Grasso's frosted office door.

"There's a handgun in a shoulder holster under my left arm," I said, and assumed the position.

He shoved a paw inside my bomber jacket, extracted the Kel-Tec, shoved it in his waistband, and patted me down. When he was satisfied, he opened the office door and waved me in.

Grasso's knee joints cracked audibly as he rose from behind his ebony desk to shake my hand.

"You're fuckin' late."

"Traffic."

"Where's that big dog of yours?"

"Home crushing a beef bone."

"Too bad. I wish you'd brought him. That's one handsome beast."

He pointed me to a leather easy chair, dropped into a matching one, and plopped his feet on a coffee table fanned with magazines—*Whiskey Advocate, National Jeweler,* and *Guns & Ammo.*

"That fifteen percent finder's fee for the stolen jewelry," he said. "It's still on the table?"

"It is."

His eyes stayed dead, but his lips cracked into what might have been a smile. "The call I told you about? Was from a guy up in Boston who specializes in fencing high-end rocks."

"Max Barber?"

"Good guess."

"And?"

"And he tells me a story. Seems that yesterday, a young guy from Rhode Island comes to his office unannounced. Flashes a few cell phone pictures of what he's got. Asks would Barber be interested in buying. Barber recognizes the loot right off."

"From the press photos of the Cargill heist?"

"I guess so, yeah."

"He told you this why?"

"He says he knows the young guy but hadn't seen him in two or three years. Doesn't know what he's been into lately. Asks if I can vouch for him. I say, 'What's his name?' He says he don't want to do this on the phone. Asks can I take a run up to Boston. I tell him no can do, but that I'll send one of my boys."

"Who?" I asked.

"You."

"I'm not one of your boys, Carmine."

"Yeah, but he don't know that. Already gave him your name."

"If he googles it, he won't like what he finds."

"Just told him 'Mulligan.' Didn't give him your first name."

"Okay, then. Tell him to expect me tomorrow morning."

"Will do. I'll text you the address. And Mulligan?"

"Yeah?"

"If this pans out, make damned sure I get my fuckin' money."

"About that," I said. "I'm thinking we should split it down the middle."

"No fuckin' way. . . . But you oughta get a little sometin' for your trouble. How 'bout a ninety/ten split?"

"Make mine thirty percent, and you've got a deal."

"Twenty."

"Done."

Grasso's laugh was mirthless, the sound of an asthmatic dog. "You seen them three brass balls out front the shop?"

"Sure."

"*You* ain't got three, but you got a pair, Mulligan. I'll give you that."

Then he rose and shook my hand. Guys like Grasso think everyone is crooked. No way he would have trusted me if I hadn't asked for a cut.

Max Barber operated out of a four-story brownstone in Boston's fashionable Back Bay. I circled the block for a half hour before a parking spot opened up, the head of the meter poking through the top of a soot-smeared snowbank. I fed in some quarters and climbed the stone front steps.

There was nothing to indicate that the house was a place of business, just a brass street number hanging discreetly beside a windowless steel door that could be opened from the outside if you rammed it with a Sherman tank. I didn't have one, so I rang the bell.

I heard footsteps and sensed someone peering at me through the peephole. Then the door swung open, and a little bald man with a pencil mustache looked me up and down.

"State your name," he said.

"Mulligan."

"Ah, yes. You were expected. Please step this way."

He led me down a gleaming marble-floored hallway and stopped at the foot of a curving staircase. "Second floor. Third door on your left."

I climbed the stairs, walked down a hall lined with oil paintings, and tried the door. It was locked. I knocked, and a man in a blue pin-striped suit opened it and invited me in. He was built like the refrigerator who guarded Grasso's office. The wiseguys must have a secret factory that spits them out.

"Mulligan?"

"That's my name."

"Carrying?"

"Not just now." I raised my arms so he could pat me down.

"Sit."

I made myself comfortable on a sofa with blue-and-green flowered upholstery, and he sat opposite me in a matching chair. He stared at me. Ten minutes later, he was still doing it.

"So, how about those Patriots?"

Silence.

"I hear we're in for rain this afternoon."

Nothing.

"Want to see some pictures of my dogs?"

Still nothing. Either I hadn't hit on the right subject, or he wasn't much of a conversationalist. I looked around the room for something to read. I didn't see anything.

The Frigidaire stared at me some more. After a half hour, an inner door floated open, and a long cool woman in a black dress, the kind the Hollies had sung about, beckoned me.

"This way, please, Mr. Mulligan."

I stepped in expecting to meet Max Barber. Instead, I found myself in another waiting room. It held a couch, two easy chairs, and a desk with nothing on it but a laptop and a pair of pink-rimmed eyeglasses. The woman pointed me to a chair, slid behind the desk, stuck the glasses on her nose, and began to type.

I fidgeted for fifteen minutes until the phone console on the desk beeped. She picked up, said, "Mr. Barber will see you now," and pointed to an arched doorway behind her.

I entered a fussy room with polished mahogany paneling, a ten-foot ceiling, a slick hardwood floor, and a buff-and-red oriental rug. The furnishings—overstuffed Victorian sofa and chairs, Tiffany-style lamps, and a large cherrywood desk—looked British, antique, and expensive. The desk was placed in front of a bay window that overlooked snow-choked Marlborough Street. It held a laptop, a green-shaded banker's lamp, a clothbound ledger, and a jeweler's loupe.

The man behind the desk looked to be in his fifties, with a slight paunch, piercing blue eyes, and a mane of coiffed silver hair. He shot French cuffs from the sleeves of a tailored gray suit and pursed his lips. He did not get up to shake my hand. He simply pointed to a chair in front of the desk and said, "Please be seated."

I did.

"So, tell me, Mr. Mulligan. How's business down in Providence?"

"Booming. Liquor and electronics come in one door and fly out the other."

"I never liked dealing in such merchandise," he said. "It requires a warehouse, forklifts, trucks, at least a half-dozen employees. An operation like that? It's too easy for the authorities to locate." The accent was Boston. Not working-class Boston, I thought. More Harvard than Southie. But there was something off about it.

"Oh, the cops know where it is," I said. "They come by every month with their hands out."

"If things are as you say, Carmine must be pleased."

"You'd think so, but the man is never satisfied."

"Greed will do that to a man."

"As we both know firsthand."

"Indeed. Did you happen to observe the security cameras in the hallways on your way in?"

I nodded. "Saw the one concealed in the outside light by the front door, too."

"I'd like you to view a bit of video we captured a couple of days ago," he said. He tapped a key on his laptop and spun the screen toward me. "Do you recognize this man?"

"I do."

"What dealings has he had with the organization you represent?"

"None, as far as I know."

"Carmine never purchased anything from him?" The accent sounded practiced, as if he'd learned it for a role in a bad movie about the Kennedys.

"Not that I'm aware of," I said, "but if you like, I can double-check when I get back to Providence."

"What else can you tell me about this man?"

"He manages a boat shop on the island of Jamestown."

"He's just the manager? He doesn't own it?"

"That's right."

"A legitimate business?"

"So it appears."

"Is he known to the police?"

"He doesn't have a criminal record, if that's what you're asking."

"But should he?"

"If he's broken any laws before, I haven't heard about it."

"Do you think he possesses the wherewithal to have planned the job at the bank?"

"I don't know."

"The stones to walk into the vault with a gun?"

"I couldn't say."

"Is it possible that he could be a police informant?"

"I haven't heard anything to suggest that. Truth is, there's not much to inform *about* on Jamestown. It's a quiet little town."

"Until recently," he said.

"Yes."

Barber propped his elbows on the desk and fiddled with the diamond cuff link on his left wrist. "So the bottom line is that you are unable to vouch for his reliability?"

The *l* sound. That's what was off. I casually pulled out my phone, glanced at it as if checking for messages, set it to record, and returned it to my shirt pocket.

"I can't swear that he's reliable," I said, "but I'm not telling you he isn't."

"I see. In that case, I believe I shall have to decline his proposition. He could be attempting to set me up, and I can't afford to take the risk." His *th* was odd, too.

"Maybe so," I said. "But if you *were* going to buy the swag from him, you'd tell me the same thing."

"Mr. Mulligan, our business is concluded."

"Just one last thing. May I ask where you grew up?"

"Why, right here in Boston."

Mr. Barber, I thought, that's the second time you lied to me.

33

I ate an early dinner at JM Curley, a restaurant just off the Boston Common, and then headed home in a rainstorm. As I crossed into Providence on route I-95, I spotted a tail. A silver Toyota Camry this time, two men in the front seats.

Were Barber's people following me? More likely, it was McNulty and Vargas again. I turned east toward Massachusetts, shook them in a tangle of country roads in Seekonk and Rehoboth, and got back to Jamestown in time to give Brady and Rondo their dinner.

Then I sat at the kitchen table, fired up my laptop, and googled experts on accents. There was one at Brown University, a tenured linguistics professor named Chapman with six academic books to his credit and a listed phone number.

I explained that I was a private detective working on a case, that I wasn't at liberty to disclose the details, but that I needed his help. "Can you tell what country someone is from by listening to the way he speaks English?"

"Possibly," he said. "It depends on a number of factors including how old he was when he left his native country and how much effort, if any, he has put into acquiring one of the regional American accents."

"May I have your e-mail address? I'd like to send you a short recording."

"How short?"

"Just four or five sentences."

"That may not be enough of a sample, Mr. Mulligan, but I'm willing to give it a try."

I thanked him and shot off the e-mail. Twenty minutes later, he called back.

"The speaker has made a determined effort to master Boston Brahmin, the regional accent associated with upper-class Bostonians. However, it is apparent to me that he lived elsewhere in his youth, at least into his early teens and perhaps into adulthood. For one thing, he struggles a bit with the short *i* sound, sometimes getting it right and sometimes not. He pronounced the word 'in' correctly, but the word risk sounded a bit like 'reesk.' He also has difficulty with the letter *l*, the sound in 'decline' and 'concluded' formed by pressing his tongue against the roof of his mouth instead of his front teeth. I also noticed that his pronunciation of the word 'that' has a hint of the letter *z* in it, coming out halfway between 'that' and 'zat.' The anomalies are slight, barely detectible to the trained ear, but they are definitely present."

"And what does this tell you?"

"The sounds he struggles with are the ones that are the most difficult for native Russian speakers to master."

"He grew up in Russia?"

"Either there or one of the neighboring states, perhaps Belarus or the Ukraine. I could be more definitive if I had a larger sample to work with."

"Thank you, Professor Chapman. You've been a big help."

I ended the call and phoned McCracken.

"Do you know anybody at Interpol?" I asked.

"No, but I've got a Rhode Island state police source who can reach out to them. What do you need?"

I filled him in and clicked off.

The dog's bowls were empty now, so I opened the back door and let them out. Ten minutes later, I heard them barking and peered out the bedroom window.

At first I couldn't find them in the dark. Then I spotted them jitterbugging in the snow, backlit by the headlights of dark car that had stopped by the side of the road. I didn't like the look of it, so I grabbed a flashlight, flew out the door, and called their names. Rondo ran to me, but as usual Brady ignored my command. As I sprinted down the long driveway, the beam from my flashlight glinting off the snow, the car pulled from the curb and drove away. I pointed the flashlight at it but couldn't catch the make.

My first thought was that I hadn't shaken the tail after all—that McNulty and Vargas now knew where I lived.

I dashed back inside for two Beggin' Strips and used them to lure the dogs into the house. Then I removed my two nine millimeters and my shotgun from the gun safe, placed them on the coffee table in the sitting room, and spent a minute or two staring at the street through the bedroom window. The car did not return.

If it did come back, I could count on Brady and Rondo to hear it first and raise a ruckus, so I returned to the sitting room and checked the loads in my guns. Then I sat on the floor, examined the dogs' paws, and pried out the snow that was wedged between their pads.

Later that night, Joseph called.

"You home?" he asked.

"I am."

"Turn your TV on."

"Why?"

"Something you gotta see on the Channel Ten news tonight."

"What?"

"You'll know when you see it," he said, and hung up.

I tuned in just in time to learn that my old high school pal, Fiona McNerney, had declared her candidacy for a third term as Rhode Island governor. That couldn't have been it. Joseph didn't give a shit about politics. Then the anchorwoman informed me that all of Rhode Island's thirty-nine cities and towns had exhausted their snow-removal budgets for the year. Joseph wouldn't have cared about that either. Next was an "exclusive update" on the dog burnings in Jamestown. They tried to dress it up with a couple of sound bites from Chief Ragsdale, but the report contained nothing new.

Finally, the anchorwoman introduced the reliably unreliable Logan Bedford for a puff piece about a local man who'd started a legal online sports-betting business. To my surprise, Joseph had combed his hair and put on a tie for his twenty seconds of fame.

The anchor ended the broadcast with a warning to stay off the roads. An ice storm was about to hit, and the temperature outside was five below and dropping.

As I zapped the TV off, the phone rang.

"So whadda ya think?" Joseph asked.

"As usual, Logan got half the facts wrong," I said, "but the publicity might do us some good."

"How'd I look?"

"Almost human."

"It took more than a half hour for them to record that sound bite from me."

"Why?"

"'Cause I kept forgetting not to say 'fuck.'"

After we signed off, I got up and let the dogs out to pee. About ten minutes later, they started barking again.

I looked out the window and caught a glimpse of a dark car, its headlights off, stopped by my front fence. In the dim glow of a streetlight, a figure emerged from the driver's-side door and walked to my gate. It was hard to be sure from this distance, but it looked like he might have been trying to open it.

I grabbed my Walther from the coffee table, ran outside wearing nothing but a T-shirt and jeans, and shouted for the dogs. As usual, Rondo came running, and for once Brady did too. I hustled them inside, grabbed the keys to the RAV4, and bolted out the door, not taking the time to grab a jacket. The dark car was gone by the time I reached the front gate. I used the remote to open it and roared down the street.

I drove more than a mile before I spotted taillights about a hundred yards ahead, cruising south on North Main Road. It was nearly midnight now, no other cars on the road. Chances were good that this was the car I'd seen at my gate. I still couldn't catch the make, but it wasn't the Camry that had followed me earlier. I hit the gas to close the gap between us, then thought better of it. I backed off, snapped off my headlights and followed at a distance.

When the car turned right on Frigate Street, I sped up and made the turn in time to catch its taillights as it cut left on Beacon. It was moving slowly now, prowling a residential area of modest family homes. Inside most of them, the lights were off. Outside, the wind picked up, and a freezing rain began to fall. In a minute or two, my windshield wipers clogged with ice.

The car turned left on Garboard Street, then right on Keel Avenue. There, the driver snapped off his headlights, rolled forward a few more yards, and braked at the side of the road. For a minute or two, nothing stirred. Then the driver's door opened, and a man stepped out. He must have switched off his dome light, because the interior of the car stayed dark. I was certain now that he was up to no good. He had something dangling from his left hand. A length of rope, or maybe a dog leash.

He got down on his haunches and stretched out his right hand. There must have been something tempting in it, because a medium-size dog scampered toward him through the snow. The man stuck something in the animal's mouth, attached the rope or leash to the collar, and led the pooch into the car. He didn't turn his lights on again until he rolled out of the neighborhood and turned south on North Main. I kept mine off and followed.

He skirted the island's business district and picked up Southwest Avenue. Five minutes and several turns later, he pulled into a deserted, half-plowed parking lot at Fort Wetherill State Park—the place where Crispy had been set on fire in September. And there, he stopped.

The park, which overlooks the bay's east passage and the entrance to Newport Harbor, had been the site of an earthenwork fortification during the American Revolution. Later, it held a gun battery that guarded Narragansett Bay during both world wars. Now, the gun emplacements and bunkers lay in ruins, the stone walls plastered with graffiti. There was no good reason for anyone to be out here on this bitterly cold stormy night.

I left my car out of sight on Fort Wetherill Road and crept into the parking lot. Twenty yards later, my hair and T-shirt were caked with ice, and my teeth began to chatter. Ahead, I saw the car door open. A small man stepped out and yanked the dog from the car. I got within thirty feet of him before he spun at the sound of my shoes crunching the brittle snow cover.

"Some weather we're having," I said. "You picked a hell of a night to take your dog for a walk in the park."

34

I couldn't make out Alexander Cargill's expression in the dark, but I saw the dog straining at the leash.

"There's a sapling behind you," I said. "Tie the dog to it. Then empty your pockets and place the contents on the hood of your car."

"Fuck you. You're not a cop."

"Too bad for you, Alexander. A cop might rough you up a little for mouthing off. I've got half a mind to shoot you."

He glared at me and didn't move.

The ice was falling harder now, like blades stabbing my skin. I was shivering. My hands and feet felt numb. I raised the hem of my T-shirt and gave Alexander a look at my gun. His eyes widened at the sight of it, and he started to do what he'd been told.

"*Walk* the dog to the tree, Alexander. Drag him again and you'll be one sorry-ass little creep." A half hour ago, he'd stalked Brady and Rondo. It could have been one of them at the end of that leash.

Alexander secured the dog, dug into his pants pockets, and tossed his car keys and wallet onto the car.

"And your jacket pockets?"

"They're empty."

"Turn around and place your hands on the roof."

As he turned, I kicked his legs apart. "Anything sharp in your pockets? A knife? A needle?"

He didn't speak.

I patted him down, felt something hard in the right pocket of his parka, dipped my hand in, and pulled out a can of Ronson lighter fluid.

"What were you planning to do with this, Alexander?"

"I didn't even know it was in there."

"Where'd you get the dog?"

"Adopted him from the pound."

"No you didn't. I was fifty yards behind you when you snatched him."

He turned, then, and laughed at me. "No you weren't. I saw *you* snatch it. I figured you might be the guy who's been setting dogs on fire, so I followed you here."

"That's how you want to play it?"

"Your word against mine, shithead. Believe me, you don't want to go to war with my family's money. What's it to you, anyway? Why the fuck do you care about some stupid dog."

And that's when I hit him—a left hook to the ribs and a right cross to the jaw. He crumbled, his lights out before he hit the ground.

The moment unfolded in slow motion. I sensed what was about to happen and grabbed for him. My useless fingers slid off the collar of his coat. He tipped over backward and landed hard, his skull cracking on the edge of a cinder block–size chunk of ice that had been thrown up by a snowplow. In seconds, there was a lot of blood.

I squatted and felt the side of his neck. I couldn't find a pulse. Was that because my fingers were numb or because he didn't have one? There was no way to know. I bent close and couldn't hear him breathing. More than the cold made me shiver now.

I sucked in a lungful of bitter air to stave off the panic and tried to think. Where was the can of lighter fluid? It had gone flying when I slugged him. Had I left my fingerprints on it? I got down on my hands and knees and groped around in the dark, but I couldn't find it. Had I handled anything else? I didn't think so.

I stood over him and dropped my hand to the butt of my gun. If he lived, he'd have a story to tell the police. A story about being assaulted by a dog-killing psychotic named Mulligan. Maybe the smart thing was to finish him off. But I'd never killed anybody. I didn't know if I had it in me. My hand was so frozen now that I wasn't even sure I'd be able to squeeze the trigger. I don't know how long I stood there, paralyzed, trying to figure out what to do.

But I was not thinking clearly. The shivering was uncontrollable now. It dawned on me that hypothermia must be setting in. Finally, I turned and ran for my car, my Reeboks leaving tracks in the snow. But my legs weren't working right. I'd gone several yards before I realized I was running in the wrong direction.

When I reached the car, I couldn't get the door open. That confused me. I kept staring at it. Finally, I realized that it was frozen shut, coated with a glaze of ice. I kicked it to crack it open.

My hands were so numb that I had trouble inserting the key in the ignition. When I finally did, the engine sputtered and died. My chest tightened with panic. I worked the starter three more times before it caught . . .

As the heater kicked in, my mind gradually began to clear. I'd meant to drive home. What was I doing on the Jamestown Verrazzano Bridge? When I got to the end of it, I pulled off the road. Was Alexander really dead? I fumbled to open the glove box, pulled out a fresh burner phone, and punched in a number.

"Jamestown PD, Officer Crowley speaking."

"There's an injured man lying beside a car in the parking lot at Wetherill State Park. There's a dog with him, too. You need to get somebody out there."

"Your name sir?" he asked, and I hung up.

When I got home, Brady and Rondo greeted me as if nothing had happened. I rubbed them behind the ears, sat on the floor in front of the wood stove, stripped off my icy sweatshirt, and placed it on the coals. Then I pulled off my running shoes and fed them into the fire. I added a couple of sticks of wood, watched the flames rise, and felt the chilblains burning my nose and fingers.

Once I'd thawed out, I took my hammer from the utility closet, placed the phone I'd used on the floor, and smashed it to pieces. Then I gathered the shards and added them to the fire.

Next morning, my fingers were red and swollen and my toes weren't doing much better. I downed two cups of coffee and fed the dogs. Then I fetched a garden trowel from my shed and used it to scoop the ashes into four Ziploc freezer bags. I scraped the snow away from a spot near my driveway, found four baseball-size rocks, and added them to the bags.

I carried them to the water's edge and hurled the evidence of my crime into the bay.

35

That day and the next, I closely monitored the news. Only the "Save Our Dogs" Facebook page carried any mention of the events at Fort Wetherill, reporting that a missing three-year-old dog named Augie had been recovered there and returned to its owner. Either Chief Ragsdale was keeping the lid on or Cargill had made a miraculous recovery and scooted before the cops showed up. I didn't believe in miracles.

On Friday afternoon, the swelling and redness had subsided, so I decided to pay Ragsdale a visit. I entered his office, placed two Cuban cigars on his desk, and sat.

"Can I help you with something?" he asked.

"Dmitry Souza."

"What about him?"

"What's his story?"

He raised an eyebrow. "You're not here about Alexander Cargill?"

"Why would I be?"

"You don't know?"

"Know what?"

"The kid's in intensive care with a fractured skull. The family asked me not to release anything, but I thought you might have heard."

"Jesus! How bad is it?"

"Real bad. The doc who operated on him at Rhode Island Hospital says he might never wake up. Might be best if he doesn't, because there's a lot of brain damage. His father can't accept that, so he's having the kid air-lifted to Johns Hopkins."

"How did this happen?"

"It's not clear. Maybe an accident. Maybe an assault."

"Can you run it down for me?"

"At twelve thirty-eight A.M. Tuesday, an anonymous caller reported seeing an injured man in a parking lot. The responding officer found Cargill lying faceup beside his car. The lot was a river of icy ruts, so at first we figured he slipped and hit his head. But at the hospital they found a fresh bruise on his jaw."

"Maybe he banged his face on the car when he fell."

"I thought of that, but I don't believe that's how it went down."

"What aren't you telling me?"

"A dog that had gone missing from Keel Avenue late Monday night was tied to a tree a few yards away. And when we looked under the car, we found a full can of Ronson lighter fluid."

"I saw Clara Martin's post about a dog found at Fort Wetherill."

"That would be the one."

I pretended to think about that for a minute. "You're saying Alexander Cargill's our dog killer?"

"Yup."

"But he offered a big reward for the person responsible."

"Good cover story."

"Is it possible he stumbled on the real dog killer and got beaten up?"

"Not likely. The weather was brutal that night. No way he was just driving around down there."

"Maybe he spotted a suspicious car and followed it into the park."

"That's how his father wants to spin it. Says his kid must have intervened to save the dog and paid a price for being a Good Samaritan."

"But?"

"But we found dog hair inside his car. The state crime lab says it was shed by several different animals, but most of it was a match for the dog we found tied to the tree."

"I'll be darned."

"One more thing. His wallet and keys were on the hood, as if somebody made him empty his pockets."

"So you're thinking somebody else was there."

"Looks like. My best guess is that one of Jenks's vigilantes caught him as he was about to set fire to the dog and slugged him. Jenks had two cars on the road that night, two men in each car."

"Question them yet?"

"Went at them hard, but they all vouch for each other. Of course they would do that, whether they were there or not."

"Any fingerprints on the Ronson can?"

"Nothing usable."

I tried not to look relieved. "Any tire tracks or footprints?"

"The first responders tromped all over the scene, so we couldn't make any sense of what we found. Besides, the freezing rain that fell that night mucked everything up."

Turns out, I hadn't needed to burn my shoes after all.

Ragsdale picked up one of the cigars I'd brought him and ran it under his nose, giving us both a moment to collect our thoughts.

"Now that we know what Alexander is capable of," he said, "I'm more convinced than ever that he killed Belinda Veiga."

"Probably," I said, "but I've got another suspect that might be worth a look."

"Who?"

"Souza."

"Dmitry? No fucking way. He was Belinda's best friend."

"And her partner in crime," I said.

Ragsdale folded his arms across his chest. "You've uncovered something new on the jewelry heist?"

"I have."

"Spill it."

"You first. A few weeks ago, you told me you've known Dmitry all his life. What's his story?"

"It's a doozy."

"I'm listening."

The chief gave me a hard look.

"Indulge me," I said. "I promise it will be worth your while."

The chief stared at the ceiling, as if searching for a memory up there. "Winter of 1994," he said, "a Russian factory ship with a crew of a hundred and sixteen spent four months anchored in the west passage within swimming distance of the island. The crew bought herring from local fishermen and processed it for the Russian market. Only the officers were allowed to come ashore, so folks got to feeling sorry for all those seamen stuck on that cold, stinky ship. One day, town council president Ted Pease and a crew of sixteen locals loaded a hundred and fifty steaks and some cases of soda on a boat, ferried them out to the ship, and spent five hours partying with the sailors."

"I remember hearing something about that."

"Yeah? Well, here's the part you didn't hear," Ragsdale said. "One of the officers took a shine to a local girl named Cheryl Souza. A couple of months after the ship pulled anchor and steamed home to Saint Petersburg, she found out she was pregnant."

"Hence, Dmitri," I said.

"Exactly. She named him after his father, but the jerk never got in touch with her after he left. Cheryl was pretty resentful about that."

Ragsdale was right. The story was a good one.

"Now your turn," he said.

"Last Friday, Souza approached a Boston fence named Max Barber and offered to sell him the Cargill jewelry."

"You've got to be shitting me."

"I'm not."

"You know this how?"

"If I tell you, it's got to stay between us."

"Go on."

I gave him most of it, holding back only Grasso's name and my suspicion about the identity of Dmitry's father.

"Where do you think the jewelry is now?" Ragsdale asked.

"Could be anywhere," I said. "Under Dmitry's bed. Buried in his yard. Hidden somewhere in the boat shop he manages. Or he might have sold it to Barber by now."

"But you said Barber is a cautious guy."

"Yeah. He wants to be sure Dmitry isn't setting him up. He's probably still checking the kid out."

"Your best guess?"

"That Dmitry still has it. Bet you a box of Cubans he's got a safe deposit box at Pell Savings and Trust."

"Let's find out," Ragsdale said.

The visitor's chairs in the bank manager's cramped office were gone now. In their place were two bassinets that held sleeping baby girls. As Ragsdale and I stepped in, Mildred Carson put an index finger to her lips and went "*shhhh.*" She rose and nudged us back into the lobby.

"Back to work already?" I asked.

"I was going to take another week, but corporate asked me to cut my leave short after Belinda was killed. Her office is still empty, so we can talk there."

Once we were seated, Ragsdale got right to the point. "I need to know if Dmitry Souza has a safe deposit box here."

"Why?"

"I can't go into that right now."

Carson frowned. "Does this have something to do with the jewelry robbery?"

"It does."

"Well, I wish I could be more cooperative, Chief, but the information you are requesting is private. I'm not allowed to disclose it unless you have a warrant."

"And I can't get a warrant for the box unless I know he has one," Ragsdale said.

"Then I'm afraid we are at an impasse," Carson said.

After leaving the bank, I strolled down the street to the Narragansett Café. I'd nearly finished my lunch when Carson came through the door, chose a table, and hailed the waitress. I drained my beer and headed back to the bank.

The guard, Owen McGowan, was at his post near the front door. I whispered in his ear, letting him know what I was there for. He gave me a discreet thumbs-up.

The metal box holding the safe deposit sign-in cards was on top of a file cabinet a few feet from the vault. The tellers and loan officers were busy with customers. No one paid me any mind as I strolled over, flipped the box open, rifled through the cards, and then slipped out the side door.

"Max Barber is one bad hombre," McCracken said.

"Tell me something I don't know."

"According to Interpol, he was born Dmitry Bagrov in the Russian city of Krasnogorsk in 1961. His mother was a nurse; his father, a jeweler. He earned a degree in engineering at a Moscow university and joined the Soviet navy, serving as a political officer on destroyers. Political officers were Communist Party members assigned to keep an eye on ship captains to make sure they remained loyal. When the Soviet Union dissolved in chaos in 1991, the navy discharged him. Not clear why. He found work as the first officer of a fishing vessel, but that didn't last.

"In the midnineties, he surfaced in Moscow as a part of a

criminal gang his father built during the country's wild-west day—before Putin took over and implemented his perverted version of law and order. They bought up Russian Orthodox Church icons and czar-era antiques at rock-bottom prices in the Russian countryside and pulled a series of jewelry and art heists in Moscow and Saint Petersburg. Sometimes drilling through walls in the middle of the night, sometimes bursting in with guns blazing. His father was shot down in a gunfight with a rival gang in 1999. After that, Dmitry Bagrov vanished.

"Interpol figured he was probably dead, but three years ago they learned that he'd slipped out of Russia, made his way to Hungary, immigrated to the United States under a false identity, and set up shop in Boston. Interpol suspects he's a conduit to the West for stolen art, jewelry, and antiquities coming out of Russia and several of the former Soviet republics. But they don't have any hard evidence."

After we hung up, I searched the *Providence Dispatch*'s Web site and found three old stories about the Russian fishing vessel that had anchored off Jamestown in 1994. One of them included a photo of the ship's officers.

Cheryl Souza lived with six cats and a nervous canary in a peeling white cottage a half mile from the Jamestown business district. It was apparent that she'd been a beauty once, but the early onset of osteoporosis had left her stooped and fragile. She invited me to sit on a worn damask sofa, stepped into her kitchen, and returned with two cups of tea on a hammered aluminum tray.

"Did you know that Dmitry's father is living in Boston now and that he's going by the name Max Barber?" I asked.

"Why, yes, I did."

"Have you seen him?

"Just once. He dropped by for a visit three or four years ago, and I told him he wasn't welcome. I'm afraid I was rather rude."

"Did you tell him about Dmitry?"

"I didn't mean to, but he spotted a photo of the boy. That one on the mantel with him in his Little League uniform. He noticed the family resemblance straightaway."

"Did he want to meet his son?"

"He did, but I told him no. After his ship returned to Russia, he never bothered to get in touch. I felt that he'd used me. I told him we didn't need him waltzing back into our lives after all these years. But he asked around town and learned that Dmitry works at the boat shop."

"So he went to see him?"

"Yes, he did."

"How did that go?"

"May I ask why you are inquiring about our private affairs?"

"I believe Dmitry's father is the leader of a criminal gang. I just want to be sure your son isn't getting involved with him."

"Oh, my!"

"What?"

"He's been sending me money every month. Not a lot, but it's enough to cover the rent. I thought that was kind of him considering how I acted when he came to see me. I'm not comfortable taking his money; but the last few years, I haven't been able to work because of my health. So I've been cashing the checks."

"I understand."

"Dmitry met him once—for a get-acquainted dinner at the White Horse Tavern in Newport. But as far as I know, he hasn't seen his father for a couple of years."

"That's probably for the best," I said. "Thank you for your time. I can let myself out."

But when I got to the door, I turned back to her. "Mrs. Souza?"

"Yes?"

"You should keep cashing those checks."

.   .   .

Dmitry Souza was busy with a customer when I entered the boat shop, so I strolled the isles, making a show of examining the merchandise. I was looking over a shelf of marine lights when he approached and asked if I needed help.

"I could use a handheld searchlight for my Sundowner."

"There are several brands to choose from," he said, "but I recommend the Leland strobe light." He reached up and pulled a box down from a shelf. "It's got a visibility of up to three miles and a rugged housing that'll bounce if you drop it on the deck and float if it falls in the water."

I took a moment to read the specs on the box before saying, "I'll take it."

After he rang me up, I asked if there was a place where we could talk privately.

"What about?'

"Max Barber."

"Who?"

"Maybe I should have said Dmitry Bagrov."

"I have no idea what you're talking about."

"Sure you do. He's your father."

He looked around to make sure we were alone, then said, "Did he send you?"

"No."

"Who are you?"

"My name is Mulligan."

"Are you a cop?"

"I'm a private detective."

He gave me a searching look. "Oh, I think I remember you. Didn't I see you dancing with Belinda at the Narragansett Café one night?"

"Yeah. Back in the good old days. Before you killed her."

"What! You think *I* did that?"

"Didn't you?"

"Of course not. That bastard Alexander Cargill did."

"That's what Chief Ragsdale thinks, but I'm not so sure."

He beckoned me to follow, led me into a cramped office behind the counter, and firmly shut the door. He stepped behind a cluttered desk and dropped into a torn vinyl office chair. The only other chair was occupied by some oily outboard motor parts, so I remained standing.

"I would never have hurt Belinda. She was my best friend."

"And your partner in crime," I said. "You pulled the bank job together."

"Bullshit," he said, and nervously twirled his beard with his fingers.

"I know you offered to sell the swag to your father."

"Where the hell did you hear that?"

"Private-eye trade secret."

"Well, it's not true." His fingers dug at his beard again.

"Did you kill Belinda because you were afraid she'd talk, or did you just get greedy and decide to cut her out permanently?"

Silence.

"Where's the jewelry now?"

He didn't speak.

"It could be here," I said. "There's plenty of nooks and crannies to hide it in the shop. But I'm betting it never left the bank. I think it's in your safe deposit box."

He drew in a sharp breath and then slowly shook his head. "Can you prove any of this?"

"Nope."

"But you think you've got it all figured out, don't you." Again with the beard.

"Not all of it," I said. "Who tipped you off that Cargill was going to the bank that day?"

Nothing.

"Did you pay off one of the household staff? Did Alexander let something slip when he was trying to sweet-talk Belinda? Or was it Cargill's bodyguard, Yuri Bukov?"

Still nothing.

"Bukov hasn't been seen for months," I said. "Did you kill him, too?"

"I never killed anybody."

"What did you do with the gun?"

"I don't have a gun. I don't even know how to shoot one."

"Well, whatever you did, you're going to get away with it. Unless . . ."

"Unless what?"

"Unless you open your safe deposit box. Do that, and you'll be spending the next ten years in Supermax."

He was still twirling his beard when I turned and walked out the door with my new searchlight under my arm. Outside, I called Ragsdale and asked him to set up a meet.

36

Mildred Carson and Owen McGowan were already there when I stepped into Ragsdale's office. A couple of minutes later, Ford Crowder and Harvey Booth, the insurance investigator, strolled in together.

"What's the purpose of today's hoedown, Chief?" Crowder asked.

"Ask Mulligan. He called the meeting."

All eyes turned to me.

"I know who stuck up Pell Savings and Trust," I said, "and I know where Ellington Cargill's jewelry is."

"Well, now," Crowder said. "Ain't *you* the cat's meow."

"I've been meaning to ask you, Ford. How much of your simple-country-boy routine is an act?"

He grinned. "Reckon I been ladling it on too thick?"

"Sounds like you're auditioning for *Duck Dynasty*," Ragsdale said.

"Or *Hillbilly Handfishin'*," Booth added.

"For crissakes," Carson said. "Can you guys knock it off and get to the point? Some of us have to work for a living."

"Dmitry Souza was the gunman," I said. "And his best friend, Belinda Veiga, was his accomplice. After they blindfolded Ellington Cargill, they snapped a few cell phone pictures of the jewelry and moved it from his box to one Souza had rented just a few days before."

"How did you know Souza has a box at my bank?" Carson asked.

"Because you just told me," I lied.

"Ha!" Crowder said. "That was slicker than deer guts on a glass doorknob."

"Last Thursday," I said, "Souza drove up to Boston and showed the photos to Max Barber. Far as I know, they haven't stuck a deal yet. Souza's box hasn't been opened since the robbery."

"You're saying the jewelry is still in there?" Booth asked.

"I am."

"How'd you learn all this, pardner?" Crowder asked.

"Confidential sources."

"That ain't good enough."

"It'll have to have to be."

"Chief?" Booth said. "Can you shed some light on this?"

"'Fraid not."

"Well, can you get a warrant for the box?"

"Absent exigent circumstances," Ragsdale said, "there's no way we get a look inside that box unless Mulligan provides a detailed statement."

"Which I'm in no position to do," I said.

"Why is it that you can't be more cooperative?" Booth asked.

"Those confidential sources?" I said. "They're violent people with a long reach. If I violate their trust, they won't think twice about killing me."

"Well then," Crowder said, "why don't we take turns watching the bank till Souza comes back to fetch the loot?"

"He won't," I said.

"Why not?" Crowder asked.

"Because he knows we're on to him."

"How?"

"When I was puzzling this thing out, I questioned him and his mother."

"Now, why in the hell did you go and do that?"

"Long story," I said.

"What's the short version?"

"Something the chief said made me suspect that Barber was Souza's absent biological father, but I didn't know for sure until I talked to them. Confirming that was a key to figuring everything out."

"I got a shorter version for you," Crowder said.

"Which is?"

"You screwed the pooch."

"Did Barber help his son plan the robbery?" Booth asked.

"He didn't," I said, "but don't ask me how I know that."

"So what do you suggest we do now, Chief?" Booth asked.

"All *I* can do is bring Souza in and bluff him. I'll say I've got him dead to rights and try to squeeze a confession out of him."

"Hot dang!" Crowder said. "That oughtta be as easy as pushin' a watermelon through a garden hose."

"Oh, for crissakes, Crowder," I said. "Will you please cut that shit out?"

Crowder leaned forward and looked me straight in the eyes. "Know what I'm startin' to think, pardner?"

"That you wish you were rockin' on a back porch pickin' a banjo?"

"I'm thinkin' maybe you set this whole thing up."

"What are you implying?" Carson asked.

"Mulligan's got no love for the Cargills," Crowder said. "And I reckon he ain't all that sweet on fences and outlaws who pull guns in banks either. Long as the jewelry stays in the box, Souza can't sell it to Barber, Ellington Cargill can't get it back, and everybody is fucked."

And Grasso won't get a big payday for ratting out Barber,

either, I thought, but what I said was, "You gotta admit there's a nice symmetry to it."

"Well, I'll be damned," Booth said.

McGowan, who'd been silent until now, cleared his throat. "One thing maybe none of you thought of yet. What if Souza gives his key to a bank employee and pays him off to get the jewelry out of the box?"

"I'll make sure that doesn't happen," Carson said. "It takes two keys to open a safe deposit box. From now on, the bank's master keys will be secured in the vault, and only Mr. McGowan and I will have access to them."

"Which is fine and dandy unless he pays one of *you* off," Crowder said.

Carson bristled. "You'll just have to trust us on that, Mr. Crowder."

"Okay, then," Ragsdale said.

"What about your end, Booth?" Crowder said. "Is your company gonna pay off on Cargill's claim?"

"I'll have to consult with the home office," Booth said, "but probably not. As long as we think we know where the jewelry is, there's a chance it can be recovered. So the case file will remain open."

Crowder hooted. "Like I been saying. Everybody gets fucked."

With that, everyone but Ragsdale and I got to their feet.

"You've got to admit Mulligan did a hell of a job sniffing all this out," Booth said as he led Crowder out the door.

"Shucks," Crowder said. "Even a blind hog finds an acorn every now and again."

After they were gone, Ragsdale jerked open a drawer and pulled out a bottle of Jack Daniel's. He sloshed some into two tumblers and slid one across the desk to me. For a moment, we drank together in silence. Then he drew two Perdomos from his humidor, clipped the ends, and tossed one to me.

"Screw it," he said, "We both could use a good smoke." He reached across the desk to light mine and then set fire to his.

"Didn't figure you for a scofflaw," I said.

"Today only. We can't go making a habit of it."

"That Crowder is a piece of work," I said.

"But was he right about you?"

I just shrugged.

"I'll take that as a yes."

"Take it any way you want."

"Notice how his country bullshit got thicker after you called him on it?"

"Yeah. He was having a good ol' time pissing me off."

"I thought it was pretty funny."

"Maybe he should tour with Larry the Cable Guy."

"Get 'er done," Ragsdale said.

"Don't you start with me," I said. "So, tell me. When are you going to bring Souza in?"

"First thing tomorrow."

"I'd like to be there."

"Can't do it."

"No way he's going to talk anyway."

"You're probably right."

"There's still one thing we don't know about how the robbery went down," I said.

"How Souza and Belinda knew why Cargill was going to the bank that day," Ragsdale said.

"I'm thinking they got it from the bodyguard," I said.

"Cargill says he never told Bukov why he was going to the bank."

"But Bukov could have overheard him talking about it."

"I guess it's possible."

"Awful suspicious, the way Bukov skipped town so soon after the robbery," I said.

"And he's Russian," Ragsdale said. "Damn Ruskies are all over this thing."

"You still think Alexander Cargill killed Belinda?"

"I do," he said.

"So do I." Or maybe, given what I'd done, I just hoped it had been him.

"But you have doubts," the chief said.

"Well . . . I still wonder if it could have been Souza."

"Unless Alexander wakes up from his coma and decides to confess," the chief said, "we'll never know for sure."

Two days later, Ragsdale called me with the news. Alexander Cargill had succumbed to his juries in the neurological unit at Johns Hopkins without ever regaining consciousness.

That afternoon, Richard Harding Davis's account of Cargill's death was the lead in *The Ocean State Rag*. The story took no position on whether he had been the dognapper, as the police suspected, or the Good Samaritan of his father's imagination.

The story raised the possibility that the death was accidental but reported that the police were investigating it as a homicide. So far, the story added, there were no viable suspects.

After I watched Logan Bedford plagiarize the piece for Channel 10's eleven o'clock news, I put Joe Bonamassa's new blues album on the sound system and cracked open a bottle of Locke's single malt. Then I sprawled on the floor with my dogs and drank straight from the bottle. Brady and Rondo nuzzled me, sensing that something was wrong.

Alexander had been such a twisted little bastard. A stalker. Probably a murderer. Definitely a psychopath who'd found joy in setting family pets on fire and watching them burn. If he'd managed to get my gate open on that stormy night, Brady and Rondo might be in the ground instead of snuggling by my side. I wasn't sorry he was dead, but I wished I hadn't killed him. I was going to have to live with that for the rest of my life.

The title cut, "Different Shades of Blue," was playing now. The song was a wrenching tale of lost love, but one line spoke to me.

"You carry the pain around, and that's what gets you through."

37

A week later, I was washing the breakfast dishes when Joseph called.

"Guess who just popped into the market?"

"I give up."

"Conner Bowditch."

"What? Why?"

"To buy a six-pack."

"You're telling me this because?"

"Because when he drove off, a car pulled from the curb, made a U-turn, and followed him down the street."

"McNulty and Vargas?"

"Not them. Some old coot in a silver Subaru Legacy."

"Get the plate?"

"No."

"Okay. I'm on it."

I clicked off and punched in Conner's number.

"Hello?"

"It's Mulligan."

"Can't talk now. I'm driving."

"Put the phone on speaker and drop it in your lap."

"Okay."

"Check your mirror. Is there a silver Subaru on your tail?"

"Uh . . . yeah. How did you—"

"Never mind that. Is your bodyguard with you?"

"Vachon is back at my dad's place."

"Okay. Don't try to shake the tail, Conner. Just drive home, go inside, and lock the doors. I'll be there as fast as I can."

Fifty minutes later, I turned onto Bowditch's street and spotted the silver Subaru parked at the curb a half block from the house. I called Conner and asked him to keep everyone inside. Then I climbed out and strolled toward the car, my pistol out of sight behind my right leg.

The driver, his gaze locked on the Bowditch place, startled when I rapped my knuckles on the driver's-side window. Then he lowered the glass and said, "Can I help you with something?"

"Open the door and get out of the car."

"I don't think so," he said, and reached for his key to crank the ignition. When I stuck my pistol in his face, he thought better of it and did as he'd been told.

"Assume the position."

He placed his hands flat on the roof of the car, and I patted him down.

"Got a weapon in the car? I asked.

"No, sir."

"Turn around."

He looked me up and down, then frowned and asked, "You a cop?"

"Gee," I said. "Why does everybody keep asking me that?"

"If this is a stickup, I've only got twenty dollars on me."

"Nice watch, though," I said.

"Don't hurt me. Just take it."

"I'll pass."

"So what do you want with me?'

"The question is, what do you want with Conner Bowditch?"

"Who?"

"Drop the act. I know you've been following him."

He didn't say anything to that.

"What's your name?"

"Crabtree."

"First name?"

"Elliot."

"Who are you working for?"

"I'm not working for anybody."

"Why were you following Bowditch?"

"Maybe I just want his autograph."

"Give me your wallet."

"Robbing me after all, huh?"

"Shut up and hand it over."

According to his driver's license, Elliot Crabtree was fifty-nine years old and lived in Tarrytown, New York. I returned the license to the wallet, dropped it in the snow, turned my back on him, and walked to the house, where Conner, his father, and Vachon were watching me through the front window.

Behind me, I heard the Subaru start up and drive away.

"Who was he?" Conner asked.

"His name's Elliot Crabtree," I said. "Know him?"

"I don't think so."

"Give me a minute." I dropped into an easy chair across from the couch where Conner was sitting beside his father. Vachon was still at the window, studying the street. I used my cell to google Elliot Crabtree and turned up dozens of them. On a hunch, I added the word "football" to narrow the search and found him.

"He's a scout for the New York Jets," I said.

"So he's harmless," Vachon said.

"Sure," I said. "As long as Conner keeps his nose clean."

38

Marcus Eliason, the Patriots' assistant director of player personnel, and Ellis Cruze, the team's chief of security, were already seated on McCracken's leather couch when I stepped into his office.

"You're five minutes late," McCracken said. "We were about to start without you."

"Sorry, boss. I had trouble finding a parking spot."

"So what have you learned?" Eliason asked.

"First off," McCracken said, "Conner Bowditch has stopped gambling."

"You're sure about that?" Eliason said.

"Sure as we can be," McCracken said. "We warned him that it could affect his draft status, and he seems to have taken it to heart."

"Still no indication he ever bet on BC games?"

"None that we can find," McCracken said. "The Providence bookie assures us that Bowditch only bet on other sports. I haven't turned up anything to suggest that he's done business with the Boston bookmakers, and he's apparently never set foot in Vegas."

"What about online gambling?" Cruze asked.

"Conner voluntarily gave us his Visa account number and

let us examine his cell phone and laptop," McCracken said. "We found no evidence that he's placed bets over the Internet."

"Okay, then," Eliason said. "Is there anything else we should be concerned about?"

"Everybody who knows Conner claims that he's Mister Perfect," I said, "but somehow, he's gotten himself into big trouble, and he keeps lying to us about it."

"Something besides the gambling?" Cruze asked.

"We don't know what it is yet," McCracken said.

"What do you know?"

"That as soon as we started asking around about him, we got pushback."

"Meaning?" Cruze asked.

So McCracken filled them in on our encounters with the hired thugs, leaving out the part about Joseph snapping some trigger fingers.

"Jesus!" Cruze said. "Do you have any idea who they're working for?"

"No," McCracken said, "but we're going to find out."

"Ticktock," Eliason said. "You've got a little over two months to get to the bottom of this. We can't afford another mistake like Aaron Hernandez. If we don't get answers by draft day, we'll have to take the kid off our board."

With that, our guests got up and turned for the door.

"One last thing," I said. "Have either of you ever run across a guy named Morris Dunst?"

Eliason and Cruze exchanged looks and then both shook their heads.

"Who is he?" Cruze asked.

"A Boston lawyer."

"What's he got to do with this?"

"Maybe nothing," I said. "It's just a name that happened to come up."

After they were gone, McCracken turned to me and said, "I think it's time we paid a visit to your Mr. Dunst."

39

Late February turned unseasonably warm, melting the mounds of soot-smeared snow that had lined the Boston streets since Christmas. The sudden flood overwhelmed the city's storm drains. Outside the office building where Dunst and Moran occupied the fourth floor, Milk Street was a river. McCracken and I sat in his Acura and watched fast-food wrappers, old newspapers, and Styrofoam cups bob in the current.

"This isn't getting us anywhere," McCracken said. "Maybe we should drop in on him and ask some questions."

"Let's give it a little more time," I said.

"Christ, Mulligan, we've been sitting out here for three days already."

"Um."

"I could use another cup of coffee."

"There's a Starbucks a couple of blocks south on Federal Street."

"Want me to bring you back something?"

"I'm good."

A stakeout requires patience and concentration. Let yourself slip into a daydream or get distracted by a pretty thing in a tight pair of jeans, and you could miss whatever it was that you'd spent days looking for. What we were hoping to spot on this busy city street, I had no idea. I just hoped that we'd recognize it when we saw it.

McCracken had just dropped back into the driver's seat with a coffee in his fist when a tall young man in a maroon-and-gold Boston College sweatshirt sloshed down the sidewalk.

"Recognize him?" McCracken asked.

"Yeah."

The guy looked up at the office building as if he were checking the street address and then pushed through the door. We climbed out and followed him in.

We found him in the marble-walled lobby, standing in front of a bank of elevators. A door rolled open and three men in business suits stepped out. The young man got on the elevator alone, and the door closed. McCracken and I watched the numbers that lit up as the elevator rose. It stopped on the fourth floor.

We were still loitering in the lobby forty minutes later when B.C. sweatshirt stepped off the elevator and turned for the front door.

"Lance Gabriel?"

"Yeah."

"My name is Bruce McCracken and this is my associate, Liam Mulligan. We represent the New England Patriots. I'm wondering if we can buy you a cup of coffee."

"The Patriots? Sure thing."

Five minutes later, we were sipping Starbucks at a table by a window that looked out on soggy Federal Street.

"You had yourself a fine season this year," McCracken said.

"Thanks."

"Except for the three passes you dropped in the Syracuse game," I said. "One of them bounced right off your chest."

"It happens," he said. "Everybody has a bad game once in a while."

Word for word, that was what Bowditch had said when I'd asked about his shoddy performance against Syracuse.

"You played fullback for two seasons before switching to tight end," I said. "Where do you see yourself lining up as a pro?"

"Tight end. Most definitely."

"Why?"

"I got all the tools, man. Good hands. The power to punish linebackers in the running game. And I run the forty in 4.53 seconds."

"Think you'll still be on the board in the third round?" McCracken asked.

"I wouldn't count on it. From what I hear, I'm likely to be gone by the middle of the second."

"Well, you'd be a hell of an asset if we could pair you with Rob Gronkowski," I said. "But out of curiosity, who were you visiting on Milk Street today?"

"My agent."

"Oh? Who would that be?"

"Morris Dunst."

"Dunst? I thought he specialized in business litigation. You're telling me he's an agent now?"

"Yes, sir."

"Well, he's got no experience with it," I said. "As one of the top tight ends in the draft, you could have your pick of big-time sports agents, Lance. What made you sign with Dunst?"

"Uh. . . . A friend recommended him."

"Who?"

"Coach Creighton."

"Forrest Creighton? The receivers coach?"

"Yes, sir."

After we finished with Gabriel, I reached Creighton in his Chestnut Hill office and asked if he could spare a few minutes.

We were nursing glasses of beer at a table in Mary Ann's, a college hangout on Beacon Street, when a graying fifty-something in a B.C. ball cap strode into the place. He grabbed a Bud Light at the bar, saw me wave, ambled over, and pulled out a chair.

"So you two work for the Patriots?"

"In a manner of speaking," McCracken said.

"What's that supposed to mean?"

"We're private detectives. The team hired us to help them vet a player they're considering drafting."

"Which player?" Creighton asked.

"Conner Bowditch."

"Figures. Everybody wants Bowditch. So what do you need from me?"

"Tell us what you know about a Boston lawyer named Morris Dunst."

"He's an asshole."

"Can you elaborate?" McCracken asked.

"He started coming around during spring practice, button-holing our best players and trying to sweet-talk them into signing agent contracts."

"Signing while they were still playing college ball would be a violation of NCAA rules," I said.

"I told him that. The greasy bastard didn't give a shit. I had to throw him off our practice field three or four times last fall. After that, he started hanging around the bars where the players go to blow off steam. We warned all our guys to stay clear of him."

"As I understand it," McCracken said, "the NFL Players Association has certified eight hundred people to act as player agents."

"That's right. A few of them are shysters, but most of them do a good job of representing their clients' interests. There's no need for anybody to sign with a sleazeball who's got no experience in the business."

"So I take it you didn't advise Lance Gabriel to sign with Dunst," I said.

"Of course not."

"He says you did."

"*What*? Why in hell would Lance tell you something like that?"

"No idea."

"He didn't, did he?" Creighton asked.

"Didn't what?" I asked.

"Didn't sign with him."

"I'm afraid he did."

"Aw, hell." He shook his head sadly, then said, "What about Bowditch? Don't tell me he signed with the asshole, too."

"I'm not sure," I said. "Conner claims he never heard of Dunst, but I think the kid's lying to me."

"Jesus! If some of my boys made this mistake, is there any chance you can get them out of it?"

"Not our job," McCracken said.

"True," I said, "but there might be something we can do."

40

I stepped into the Narragansett Café and found Ford Crowder waiting for me at the bar. He was sipping a cocktail from a dainty stemmed glass with a pearl onion floating in it.

I straddled the adjoining stool and said, "Really? I figured you for Maker's Mark and a beer back."

"You figured wrong. I got *you* figured for Irish whiskey straight up and a Sam Adams."

"You figured right."

"Jameson?"

"I prefer Locke's, but they don't serve it here."

"Bushmills, then?"

"That'll do."

He waved the barkeep over, placed my order, and put it on his tab.

"Ragsdale's stab at hornswoggling Souza into a confession went nowhere," he said.

"I heard. That why you asked for a meet? To tell me something I already know?"

"Nope."

"What, then?"

"Ellington Cargill's back in town."

"So?"

"He wants to hire you."

"Hire *me*? What the hell for?"

"The man wants to tell you himself. He's waitin' on us at the mansion."

"I'll pass."

"He'll tear me a new one if'en I don't show up with you."

"Not my problem."

"Look, pardner. Can you do me a good turn and just hear the man out?"

No way I wanted to work for Cargill, but curiosity was getting the best of me. "Okay, Crowder. Soon as I finish my drink."

"But after you hear his proposition, I want you to turn him down."

"And why would that be?"

"Because I don't like you. After the stunt you pulled with the safe deposit box, I don't trust you none, either."

"But he does?"

"I ain't told him about what you done."

"Why not?"

" 'Cause if I did, he'd find a way to blame it on me."

The butler ushered us into a mahogany-paneled room that he called the library, but I didn't see any books. Instead, the walls were hung with modern art. To my eye, it was indistinguishable from the finger paintings that are proudly displayed in every kindergarten—except for one small detail. Instead of being stuck up with masking tape, the childish smears were mounted in gold-leaf frames.

Ellington Cargill was seated in a throne-like chair, a crystal carafe beside him on an end table and a half-empty goblet in his hand. He did not get up to greet us. He did not offer to shake hands. He just waved us into an upholstered couch across from him and asked if we'd care for some wine. Crowder and I both declined.

"Thank you for coming, Mr. Mulligan."

"Sure thing."

"Has Mr. Crowder informed you about the purpose of our meeting?"

"Not in any detail."

"Well, then, let's proceed. I propose to retain you to investigate the murder of my son."

Oh, fuck, I thought. For a second, I was afraid I'd said it out loud. I took a moment to compose myself and asked, "Why me?"

"Because I have been informed that McCracken and Associates is the most respected private investigative firm in Rhode Island. And because you singlehandedly deduced the whereabouts of the stolen jewelry, a feat that proved to be beyond the capabilities of both the local authorities and my security staff."

"I see."

"If I may, sir," Crowder broke in, "I still don't think this course of action is advisable. Chief Ragsdale has asked the Rhode Island State Police to assist him in the investigation, and I and my three best men are devoting all of our time to it."

I noticed that Crowder dropped the shitkicker act when addressing his boss.

"I have made my decision, Mr. Crowder."

"Yes, sir."

"Are you amenable, Mr. Mulligan?"

"I'm sorry, but no."

Cargill's eyebrows shot up in surprise. "Oh? And why would that be?"

"I'm busy."

"On?"

"I'm in the middle of a complex investigation for an important client, and it's going to keep me tied up for several months."

"More important than me? Surely not, Mr. Mulligan."

"Client confidentially prevents me from being more explicit, Mr. Cargill. All I can say is that it's a very big case."

Cargill lifted his glass and sipped. Then he reached into his suit pocket and withdrew a check. "Crowder, please take this and hand it to Mr. Mulligan."

Crowder sprang from the sofa, glanced at the check, blanched at the sum, and did as he'd been told.

"I am prepared to pay you three thousand dollars a day for your services," Cargill said. "The retainer you have in your hand is an advance to cover the first month of our arrangement. I trust it will be sufficient to get you started."

I glanced at the check and saw that it was made out for ninety thousand dollars.

"One more thing, Mr. Mulligan. I am offering a reward of a quarter of a million dollars for information leading to the arrest and conviction of the killer. If you are successful in your investigation, you might be able to claim that as a bonus."

"I thought we agreed you'd turn him down," Crowder said as we walked across the paving stones to our cars.

"Really? I don't recall agreeing to anything."

"Well, I don't like it, but I can't say I blame you none," Crowder said. "That was way too much cabbage for a workin' man to walk away from. I reckon you're as happy as a puppy with two peckers."

It *was* too much to walk away from. If I'd declined Cargill's offer, Crowder would have wondered why. With Alexander's blood on my hands, I couldn't risk having the security expert poking into my business.

Still, accepting the money wasn't enough. Now I was going to have to make a show of pretending to earn it.

"A whole box of Cubans this time?" Ragsdale said. "You must be after a bigger favor than usual."

"I am."

He pried the top off the box, drew out a San Cristóbal de la Habana, and sniffed it.

"Okay," he said. "Spill it."

"I'd like to see your interview notes on the Alexander Cargill murder."

"No can do."

"Come on, Chief. Nobody has to know."

"Gunning for that big reward the prick's father is offering?"

"Something like that."

"Well, I can't help you."

"Ellington Cargill hired me to investigate his son's death," I said. "I'm sure he'd appreciate your cooperation."

"Really?"

"Yeah. Should I have him give you a call? See if you'll bend the rules again for the richest guy in town?"

"That won't be necessary."

He slid open a drawer, pulled out a file, and shoved it across the desk to me.

"Who have you questioned?" I asked.

"I started with Jenks and the members of his vigilante committee who were out prowling that night. They're all sticking to their stories."

"Who else?"

"I talked to Belinda Veiga's father and her friends on the off chance that one of them decided to go after Alexander for stalking her. But that didn't go anywhere."

"Was one of the friends Souza?"

"Yeah. Turns out, he's got a solid alibi for the night Alexander was killed. Other than them, I couldn't think of anybody with either motive or opportunity."

"Maybe it was just a random act of violence," I said.

"If that's what it was, we're probably never going to find the killer."

"No physical evidence besides the dog hair in Alexander's car?"

"Nope."

"The state police haven't been any help?"

"They sent down a detective named Eddie Spikes. He nosed around for a few days, interviewed everyone I'd already talked to, came up empty, and left town. Said I should give him a call if anything turns up."

"So you're nowhere."

He nodded. "Take a seat in the hall and look the file over. But don't make any copies, and bring it back when you're done."

So that's what I did. When I returned, he said something that took me by surprise.

"So, Mulligan, how are you enjoying life in Jamestown?"

"You know where I live?"

"Uh-huh."

"You've been following me?"

"Oh, no. Nothing like that."

"How, then?"

"I was driving along East Shore Road one evening when I saw your RAV4 turn into a driveway. Thought maybe you were visiting somebody; but a week or two later, I passed by and saw a Bernese mountain dog in the yard."

"Aw, shit."

"Sorry. Didn't know it was some big fucking secret."

"Well," I said, "I don't like to advertise it."

"Because you make enemies in your line of work?"

"Yeah."

"I won't tell anybody," he said. "I promise."

41

"Mr. Dunst will see you now."

We tossed aside the magazines we'd been skimming for the last half hour—*The American Lawyer* for McCracken and an out-of-date *Sports Illustrated* for me—and entered an inner office.

Dunst rose to greet us with a handshake. He was one of those guys who works your arm as if it were a water pump and then holds the grip long enough to make you uncomfortable. I put him at five-ten, one-eighty with long brown hair slicked straight back and tied off in a ponytail. His suit was a navy chalk stripe and looked expensive.

The office was uglied up in postmodern, lots of blue and yellow plastic furniture molded into shapes they never taught you about in geometry class. The desk resembled a span of wings salvaged from a Klingon battle cruiser. I wondered if it had a cloaking device.

A huge flat-screen suspended from a sea-green wall was tuned to ESPN with the sound turned off. On either side of it, auto-graphed photos of college football players were mounted in yellow plastic frames.

"Your clients?" McCracken asked.

"Yes," Dunst said.

"I recognize Bowditch and Gabriel. Who are the other two?"

"Therman Hendricks, a UConn linebacker, and Marvis Styles, a safety at UMass."

"Are those the only players you have under contract?"

"At the moment, yes, but I'm in discussions with several others. But I'm forgetting my manners. Please sit down and make yourselves comfortable."

Seeing nothing that *looked* comfortable, I planted my butt on a yellow blob. A minute later, my back began to ache.

"Can I offer you a refreshment? Coffee? Water? Or perhaps you'd prefer something stronger."

"We're fine," McCracken said.

Dunst wedged himself into something I'd mistaken for a planter and crossed his legs, displaying a pair of garish argyle socks. Behind his head, his diploma from Suffolk University Law School hung in a walnut burl frame.

"So, then," he said, "I understand you represent the New England Patriots. What is it that I can do for you today?"

"For starters," McCracken said, "we're curious how you managed to land Conner Bowditch. He could have signed with Jimmy Sexton, Jason Fletcher, Joel Segal or any of the other big names in the business. Why did he choose a business lawyer with no experience as an agent?"

"I assume he liked my pitch," Dunst said. "But maybe you should ask him."

"I did," I said. "He claims he never heard of you."

"I can't imagine why he'd tell you that," Dunst said, "but I can assure you he's a client."

"Do you have anything to confirm that?"

He rose, went to his desk, opened and drawer, returned with several stapled sheets of paper, and handed them to me.

The first page was labeled "NFL Players Association Standard Representation Agreement." I flipped through it and saw that it guaranteed Dunst three percent of Bowditch's earnings. With the kid's first NFL contract expected to be eighteen million a year for four years, plus a twelve-million-dollar signing bonus, Dunst stood to make a cool two and a half million. I checked the last page and found Dunst's and Bowditch's scrawls on the signature lines.

I smirked, tore the contract in half, and stuffed it in my jeans.

"Why on earth did you do that?" Dunst said.

"Because I don't like you."

"Well, it was just a copy. The originals are stored in a secure place."

"Go get them," I said. "And while you're at it, fetch the original contracts for the other three players too."

"I don't know what the hell your problem is," Dunst said, "but I must ask you two gentlemen to leave my office immediately."

"We're not gentlemen," I said. "You know exactly who we are. You've had your hired thugs tailing us for weeks."

"I have absolutely no idea what you're referring to."

"The Vacca brothers weren't up to the job," I said, "so now you've sicced Michael McNulty and Efrain Vargas on us. If you're trying to intimidate us, it's not working."

"I don't know anyone named McNulty or Vargas."

"I suggest you call them off," McCracken said. "If you don't, better make sure they've signed up for Obamacare."

"I don't appreciate your threats and unfounded accusations. Get out, or I'll be forced to call security." As we headed for the door, Dunst snarled his parting shot: "And don't come back."

"Oh, you'll be seeing us again, counselor," I said. "We're not finished with you yet."

"So now what?" I asked as McCracken pulled the Acura onto the jammed Southeast Expressway and inched south.

"Now we wait for McNulty and Vargas to show up."

"Think they'll have more in mind than just tailing us this time?"

"Depends on their marching orders. But considering what's at stake . . ."

I finished his thought: "We just gave Dunst two and a half million reasons to take us off the board. I guess I better call Joseph."

42

Early next morning, I boarded my dogs at the Jamestown Animal Clinic and drove to Providence. There, McCracken and I sat in his office sipping hot coffee and cleaning our guns. Every few minutes, I went to the window and studied the street.

"Think they'll try something here?" I asked.

"No way," McCracken said. "Too many witnesses. And they'll want to avoid the security cameras in the lobby."

"So we pick the spot." I said.

I finished cleaning my Kel-Tec, dropped it on the desk beside my Walther, fired up the desktop, called up Google Maps, and found a street view of Wetherill State Park.

McCracken moseyed over and studied the screen.

"Know the place?" I asked.

"Yeah. The perfect spot for a picnic. . . . Or a gunfight."

Just after noon, Joseph strode in carrying four large pizzas in one hand and a case of 'Gansett in the other. He had his forty-four magnum stuck in his waistband and a nine mil in a shoulder holster.

We downed a few slices and then sat together to review the plan.

"So, what do you think?" I asked.

"Should work," Joseph said. "Unless . . ."

"Unless what?"

"There's more than two thugs in Boston, Mulligan. What if they bring help this time?"

I thought about it a moment, pulled out my cell, and placed a call.

"Anything else we'll need?" the guy on the line asked after I laid it out for him.

"Yeah," I said. "Bring an ambulance."

We spent the next two days ordering takeout, sleeping in the office, and taking turns looking out the windows. Late Thursday afternoon, Joseph spotted McNulty lurking in the entrance to the Bank of America building across the street.

It was time.

At six P.M., we rechecked our guns and stuffed extra ammunition into our pockets. Then we rode the elevator down, dashed across a sidewalk teeming with pedestrians, and climbed into the Acura. McCracken navigated the congested city streets, turned onto the interstate, and headed south through the heavy commuter traffic.

Fifty minutes later, we cruised across the Jamestown Verrazzano Bridge that spanned Narragansett Bay's west passage. It was dusk now, the overcast sky burning red in the west.

"Spot a tail yet?" Joseph asked.

McCracken glanced in the rearview. "Can't be sure, but there's a black SUV four car lengths back. It's been on us for a dozen miles now."

"How many men?" Joseph asked.

"Can't tell. The windshield is tinted."

As we pulled off the bridge, McCracken floored it, not wanting to risk a confrontation until we reached our chosen terrain. We screeched to a stop at the butt end of the Fort

Wetherill parking lot and spilled out of the car. Twenty minutes later, we were waiting in the dark, McCracken and I crouching behind a boulder and Joseph lying prone behind a tree.

"Still think they're coming?" I whispered.

"Yeah," McCracken said. "They're just being cautious. They know they've got us cornered, but they also know we picked the place."

Another ten minutes crawled by before I sensed something moving in the gloom. Four men, spread out in military formation, were skulking toward us through the lot. When they drew within forty yards, I saw that they were carrying shotguns.

They inched closer, just thirty yards away now. And then, from somewhere off to our right, a shout: "Jamestown Police. Drop your weapons."

"Cops my ass," one of the thugs hollered. He swung his shotgun in the direction of the voice and fired.

Thirty seconds later, it was over.

Chief Ragsdale and five of his officers cautiously emerged from the park's World War I–era bunkers and approached four bodies that were sprawled awkwardly on the pavement. The cops shined flashlights on them, kicked the shoguns aside, and then checked for pulses.

When that was done, McCracken, Joseph, and I stepped out of the shadows.

"Recognize them?" Ragsdale asked.

"This one's McNulty," I said, "and the one over there is Vargas. I've never seen the other two before."

"Did any of you fire?"

The three of us said no.

"Well, I gotta make sure. Please surrender your weapons to Officer Clark."

So that's what we did.

Ragsdale stood amidst the carnage and sadly shook his head.

"Well, we won't be needing that ambulance after all. Maybe we could have avoided all this bloodshed if we'd pinned them in with our cruisers before they got to the park."

"If you'd done that, you couldn't have held them for long," I said. "And once you cut them loose, they'd have come gunning for us again."

Next morning I woke up late, collected Brady and Rondo from the kennel, and spent an hour romping with them in the yard. Then I sat at the kitchen table and pounded out Richard Harding Davis's account of the shootout in Wetherill State Park. The story credited Chief Ragsdale and his men with foiling an attempt to ambush two private detectives and a Providence businessman but said the motive for the attack was unclear. The targets had declined to comment.

43

The big question looming in the Bowditch affair was why he'd signed with Dunst in the first place. The lawyer must have had something to hold over him—maybe something that would make the kid poison in the NFL draft. Whatever it was, the Patriots were paying us a lot of money to figure it out.

Before I could start digging into that, Crowder called and demanded to know what I'd been doing to earn Cargill's money. So I drove to the hardware store to have a chat with Jenks.

"I've already gone over this three fuckin' times with Chief Ragsdale," he said. "Then I had to tell it all over again to that redneck, Crowder. After that, I got grilled by a state cop. You're telling me I gotta repeat it to *you,* now?"

"If you don't mind."

"Well, I do."

"I'll try to make it quick," I said. "Are you sure only four of your vigilantes were on the road the night Alexander was killed?"

"Only two teams were scheduled, and they spent most of the night parked at the East Ferry Wharf drinking coffee out of Thermos bottles. Nobody in his right mind would have been on the road that night 'less they absolutely had to. The weather was wicked bad."

"Where were you?"

"At home."

"Doing what?"

"Hell, I don't know. Watching TV, I guess."

"Can anybody vouch for that?"

"Just Angie."

"Your wife?"

"Yeah."

"You must have been pretty pissed off about what happened to your dog."

"I still am."

"Angry enough to go looking for the dognapper that night?"

"Bet your ass. But that's not what I did."

He hacked violently into a handkerchief. Then he fingered a soft pack out of his shirt pocket, shook out a Marlboro, and set fire to it. That didn't seem like a good idea to me, but it was none of my business.

"He's lucky it *wasn't* me who cornered him," Jenks said. "I would have burned the bastard alive, just like he done to my Layla."

For the next few days, I reluctantly continued the charade. I questioned the vigilantes who were on duty when Alexander was killed and talked to Belinda Veiga's friends and family members. All of them repeated the stories they'd told to the police.

Nobody had a clue who'd killed Alexander Cargill—except, of course, for the son of a bitch who did it.

44

McCracken and I strode up the walk to the redbrick colonial and rang the bell. Conner Bowditch's father, Malcolm, opened the door with a worried look on his face.

"They're waiting on you in the living room," he said. "Come on in."

Conner and his fiancée, Meghan, were seated on the couch. The security man, Rene Vachon, was on his feet by the window. Malcolm dropped into an easy chair. McCracken and I decided to remain standing.

"I take it you all read about the dustup we had in Wetherill State Park last week," I said.

Nods all around.

"Two of the skells were the same ones who'd been dogging Conner," Vachon said. "Did this have something to do with his gambling debt?"

"No."

"But it *did* have something to do with my son?" Malcolm said.

I nodded. "The four men who died trying to kill us were sent by a Boston lawyer named Morris Dunst. Want to tell everyone what he is to you, Conner?"

His voice was small when he answered. "He's my agent."

"What?" Malcolm said. "I thought we agreed you were going to sign with Joel Segal."

The contract I'd torn in half in Dunst's office, now mended with cellophane tape, was in my jacket pocket. I drew it out and handed it to Malcolm.

"You actually signed this, son?" Malcolm asked.

"Yes, sir."

"When?"

"It's dated January twentieth," I said, "but that's a lie, isn't it, Conner. I think you signed it sometime during the football season, but Dunst faked the date."

"To circumvent NCAA rules?" Malcolm said.

"Yeah," Conner said. "I'm sorry, Dad."

"Dunst specializes in business law, but he has no experience representing professional athletes," McCracken said. "According to Forrest Creighton, the B.C. receivers coach, Dunst started hanging around the practice facility last spring trying to badger the team's best players into agent contracts. The coaches threw him out several times, told all the players that he was trouble, and warned them to stay clear of him. We since found out he'd been up to the same thing at UConn and UMass. And we know, now, that he's not just unscrupulous. He's a very bad guy."

"Son," Malcolm said, "every top agent in the country has been hounding you. Why in the *hell* did you sign with this asshole?"

Conner shook his head and stared at the floor.

"That's what we came to find out," I said.

"Son?" Malcolm said.

Under his father's withering gaze, Conner Bowditch seemed to shrink to normal size. He shook his head again and didn't speak.

"No?" I said. "Okay then. Let me take a stab at it. I think it all started when Dunst asked you to shave points. Maybe he offered you some easy money. Maybe he found out about your gambling, told you that it could hurt your draft status, and threatened to expose you unless you went along with it. Whatever it was, you agreed.

"To make the scheme work, Dunst needed an offensive player, too. That's where Lance Gabriel came in. I figure the target was the Syracuse game, because both of you played like shit that afternoon. Once Dunst had his hooks into you, he threatened to anonymously blow the whistle on the point shaving unless you signed with him. So both of you did."

"Jesus Christ!" Malcolm said. "Is any of this true, son?"

Conner just kept staring at the floor. Meghan reached over and grabbed his hand.

"Please, baby. You've gotten yourself mixed up in something, and it nearly got Mr. Mulligan and Mr. McCracken killed. Whatever it is, you can't just sit there and not say anything."

Conner raised his eyes and drew a deep breath. "Mulligan's got *some* of it right."

"Okay," I said. "What's your version?"

"Dunst kept bugging me all season. Buttonholing me outside the stadium after home games. Calling me on the phone. Pounding on my apartment door. Barging into Mary Ann's when I was drinking with my boys. Always waving a contract at me and urging me to sign. When I kept saying no, he offered me stuff. Money. Women. A new car. Honest to God, Dad, I turned it all down. Finally—in early November, I think it was—he came by my place late one night. But this time he brought a couple of thugs with him. When I tried to shut the door on them, they pointed guns at me and forced their way in."

"Who were they?" I asked.

"I don't know."

I punched up mug shots of the Vaccas on my cell phone and handed it to Conner.

"Yeah," he said. "That looks like them."

"So then what happened?"

"Dunst said that if I didn't sign the contract, he'd tell the thugs to hurt Meghan. Said they'd take turns raping her, slit her throat, and leave her dead body on my doorstep."

Meghan emitted a small cry and dropped her head onto Conner's chest.

"The thugs grinned when Dunst was saying it, like they were hoping I *wouldn't* sign," Conner said. "Jesus, Dad. What choice did I have?"

"You could have told me," Malcolm said. "We could have called the police. I could have assigned Rene to protect Meghan."

"Dunst warned me not to try anything like that. He said there was no way I could protect everyone I loved. That if they couldn't get to Meghan, they'd go after you, or Mom, or my sisters. Or maybe Coach Shroyer."

"What about the point shaving?" McCracken asked.

"That was the two thugs' idea," Conner said. "I don't think Dunst had anything to do with it."

"Go on," McCracken said.

"A couple of weeks after I signed the contract, the thugs came back and said they weren't done with me yet. That if I didn't agree to shave points against Syracuse, they'd still go after Meghan. I figured they must have threatened somebody on offense, too, but I had no idea who until Lance dropped three easy passes in the second half."

"Conner," I said, "you could have saved all of us a lot of trouble if you'd come clean with me the first time we talked."

For a moment, no one spoke. I glanced at Malcolm. He looked stricken. Then he shook his head and said, "Well, I guess I better call the police."

"No," I said.

"No?"

"If you do, all the sordid details are going to come out. Conner's gambling. The point shaving. It won't matter *why* he shaved points. Just that he did. The media will crucify him. There's no proof that Meghan was threatened, so everyone will think Conner placed a big bet on Syracuse."

"He'll fall like a rock in the draft," McCracken said. "In fact, he probably won't get drafted at all."

"So what are we supposed to do?"

"Sit tight and let McCracken and me fix this," I said.

"You think you can?"

"It's what we do."

45

"Mulligan?"

"Yeah?"

"It's Ragsdale. Where are you?"

"In my car."

"Going where?"

"Providence."

"Well, turn the hell around."

"Why?"

"I need to see you in my office."

"What for?"

A pause, and then, "I know who killed Alexander Cargill."

Oh, shit! Several seconds dragged by before I sputtered a reply. "You do? Who was it?"

"Not over the phone."

How the hell had he figured it out? There were no finger-prints on the Ronson can. The shoes and sweatshirt I'd worn that night had been reduced to ashes. The phone I'd used to call the police was in pieces at the bottom of the bay. I was sure there hadn't been any witnesses in the park that night. Obviously I'd missed something. But what?

If Ragsdale believed my story, I might be charged with involuntary manslaughter instead of murder, but that still carried a sentence of ten to thirty years in prison.

I thought about running, but I'd never get far without money. And Ragsdale knew where I lived. If I went for the cash in my floor safe, I'd be sure to find the cops waiting for me. I continued north for a half dozen miles, pondering my options. Once I realized I didn't have any, I turned around and pointed the Mustang toward Jamestown to face the consequences.

I stepped into the police station and walked past several uniformed officers. None of them drew their weapons. None of them told me I was under arrest. As I headed down the hallway to the chief's office, my panic subsided a little. If Ragsdale had found me out, would he have called and asked me to come in? More likely, he'd have tried to take me by surprise. Still, my hand shook as I rapped on his door.

"It's open."

I stepped inside and found Ragsdale behind his desk, fiddling with a pair of handcuffs. Suddenly, I felt sure they were meant for me.

"Did you drive back from Providence," he asked, "or did you run all the way?"

"What do you mean?"

"You sweated right through your shirt."

I shrugged, collapsed into an office chair, and tried to slow my breathing.

Ragsdale rattled the handcuffs and then dropped them on the desk. "I took these bracelets off of Marlon Jenks a half hour ago," he said, "just before I locked him in a holding cell."

"*What?*"

"He always was kind of a hothead," Ragsdale said, "but I never figured him for a killer."

"You think *Jenks* killed Alexander?"

"I know he did."

"What makes you say that?"

"He confessed." The chief picked up a sheet of paper and

waved it at me. "After I arrested him at the hardware store this afternoon, he sat in the interrogation room and wrote the whole story down for me."

"Can I see that?" I asked.

Ragsdale slid the confession across the desk. My hand shook as I reached for it. Just a one-page scrawl on lined paper torn from a legal pad. One sentence leaped out at me: "When I saw him with that dog, I thought about what he'd done to my Layla, and I just lost it."

"I don't know about this, Chief. It's awfully thin. He doesn't mention any of the details you held back. Nothing about the wallet and car keys on the trunk of Alexander's car. Nothing about the can of lighter fluid. In fact, he doesn't seem to know anything that hasn't already made the news."

"He says he doesn't remember much," Ragsdale said. "Claims he was in a daze after he slugged the kid and whacked his skull on the ice."

"Can I talk to him?"

"No, and neither can I. After he wrote this down, he lawyered up."

"Start at the beginning," I said. "What made you arrest him in the first place?"

"His wife came in this morning and said he told her the whole story a couple of weeks ago. According to her, the guilt's been eating both of them up ever since. So she finally decided they had to come clean."

"When's the arraignment?"

"Ten tomorrow morning."

With that, I congratulated Ragsdale for clearing the case and drove straight to Providence to talk things over with my best friend.

The flowers I'd placed on Rosie's grave the last time I visited had long since withered. I felt bad that I hadn't stopped off to pick

266 | Bruce DeSilva

up some fresh ones. I flopped down in the grass, wrapped my arms around the headstone, and gave her a hug.

"I'm sorry I didn't bring the Manny Ramirez jersey with me today, Rosie. It's hanging in my closet at home, and I was in too much of a rush to go get it. . . ."

"Hell, yes, there's something wrong."

And then I told her what I'd done.

"He was a bad guy, Rosie. The world is better off without him in it. I'm in the clear as long as I keep my mouth shut, but there's no way I can live with this. . . ."

"Because somebody else just confessed to the crime. . . ."

"No, I don't have any idea why he did that, but I've got to get him free of it. He has a wife and two kids, Rosie. I can't let them pay the price for something I did. I just wish there was a way that didn't involve me spending the next decade or more in prison. . . ."

"Yeah. I'd miss our talks too."

"It's not a good time for you to get involved in this," McCracken said. "We've still got a lot of work ahead of us on the Bowditch mess."

"I know, but I can't let Jenks go to prison for something he didn't do."

"What makes you so sure he's not the killer?"

"It's more than just a feeling," I said.

He waited for me to say more. When I didn't, he got up, went to his office bar, poured me a glass of Irish whiskey, and placed it in my hand. Then he sat back behind his desk and asked me to run it down for him.

I gave him everything—except for the name of the real killer.

"Okay," McCracken said. "There are a lot of reasons why an innocent man would confess to a murder. To protect someone else. Because he craves notoriety. But in this case, I'm betting it has something to do with that quarter-million-dollar reward."

"That's what I'm thinking."

"The money will go to his wife?"

"She turned him in, so guess so, yeah."

"Still, it seems odd," McCracken said. "A lot of people go a quarter million in hock to stay *out* of prison." He sat quietly for a moment and rubbed his jaw. "Is Jenks an old man?"

"Just forty-five."

"So he'll die in prison or be a codger when he gets out."

"That's right."

"Then there must be something else going on in his life that makes money for prison a good deal."

"Maybe so."

"Any idea what it could be?"

"Not yet," I said.

"If I were you," he said, I'd try to find out if he's got debts that are too big to get clear of."

46

Giuseppe Arena agreed to see me at his summer place in Newport, a sprawling Nantucket-style cottage with weathered cedar shingles, a wraparound porch, and a glorious view of the sea. I drove Mister Ed up the winding crushed-shell drive and parked under a sprawling oak that was just beginning to leaf. The doorbell was answered by a maid who informed me in Spanish-accented English that the man of the house was waiting for me around back.

I found him stretched out in a snow-white chaise longue beside a swimming pool that was still covered for winter on this toasty April afternoon. His bodyguard, a Coke machine in a pinstriped suit, stood with arms crossed a few yards away. He didn't say "Have a Coke and a smile."

"Mulligan is usually packing, boss. Should I pat him down?"

"No need, Santo. He's a friend of ours."

Arena was the *capo famiglia* of the Patriarca crime family—still called that even though the legendary Raymond Loreda Salvatore Patriarca had fled Rhode Island jurisdiction thirty years ago to run the rackets in Hades. When I'd last seen Arena about a year ago, he was a spry seventy-year-old with roped forearms and a healthy-looking tan. Now he looked frail, the pale skin on his face as thin and crinkled as tissue paper. He had a gray wool blanket pulled up to his neck, a clear plastic tube in his nose, and an oxygen tank resting beside him.

"Beautiful day," I said.

"A bit chilly," he said, "but they say the salt air is good for what ails me." His voice was at once hoarse and wet, like water seeping through a clogged sewer pipe.

"Emphysema?"

"Yeah. It's been getting worse, so they got me tethered to this fucking tank several hours a day now."

"Sorry to hear that."

"Ah, what can you do? Gettin' old is a bitch. So how you been, Mulligan? Grasso tells me you got yourself a dog now."

"Two of them," I said. I pulled out a cell phone and showed him some pictures.

"Handsome beasts," he said.

"That they are."

"Can I offer you something? Bottled water? Coffee? A glass of wine?"

"I'm good."

"So," he said, "did you bring the package?"

"I didn't."

"*No?* Why the fuck not?"

"You must have heard by now that we've gone legal," I said.

"So Grasso's been telling me. Think I saw somethin' about it on the news a while back, too."

"That means we don't need your protection anymore," I said.

"The hell it does."

I didn't say anything to that.

Arena coughed, ripped the tube out of his nose, and coughed some more. "You got some fuckin' balls coming here to tell me this."

I didn't say anything to that, either.

"Planning to cut Zerilli out, too?" he asked.

"No way. It's still his business. I just run it for him."

"And he's okay with you trying to break away from this thing of ours?"

"I haven't told him about that part yet."

"Well, let me explain the facts of life to you, Mulligan. Going legit don't mean shit. Lots of legal businesses pay us for protection."

"Like the strip club owners you've been shaking down?"

"Among other things, yeah."

"They pay because they're afraid of you," I said. "I'm not."

"No? And to think I had you pegged as a smart guy."

"Boss?" the Coke machine said. "Want I should work him over a little? Teach the fucker some manners."

"Not just yet, Santo."

"Not ever," I said.

Santo smirked and pulled open his suit jacket, giving me a look at the pistol in his shoulder holster. I reached behind me, stuck my hand under my shirt tail, and rested it on the semiauto in the small of my back.

"Jesus!" Arena said. "Cool the fuck down, both of youse. There ain't gonna be no gunplay. Not here at my fuckin' house." He coughed again and slid the tube back in his nose.

"Mulligan," Arena said, "take out whatever you got in your waistband, put it down, and step away from it. Santo, you do the same thing."

"You sure, boss?"

"Stop pretending you can think for yourself, and do what I tell you."

Santo grimaced, opened his jacket again, and drew out his pistol, holding the butt between his thumb and forefinger. I pulled mine out the same way. Together, we both bent at the knees, laid our weapons on the pool apron, and slowly backed away from them. Never taking his eyes off of me, Santo pulled up a lawn chair and sat beside his boss. I grabbed a matching one and sat across from them.

"I did you a good turn six years ago, Giuseppe," I said.

"When you came to me with proof that Dio and Giordano were behind the arson-for-profit scam that burned up a lot of citizens in Mount Hope," he said.

"And informed you that your lawyer, Brady Coyle, was in on it," I said. "That he was setting you up for a fall on a labor-racketeering charge to get you out of the way because he knew you'd never have sanctioned what they were doing."

"I remember. I also seem to recall that those three mokes ended up getting whacked."

"They did."

"Might be a lesson for you in that, Mulligan."

"I get your point."

"But you figure I owe you a favor?"

"I do."

"I don't negotiate at the point of a gun, Mulligan."

"Neither do I."

"So what do you propose?" Arena asked.

"From here on out, I'll give you half of what you've been getting every month. But in return, I need you to do something for me."

"You mean not send somebody to shoot you?"

"That, too," I said. And then I told him what I had in mind.

47

The Old State House was already thirty-five years old when the Declaration of Independence was first read from its front steps in 1776. Today, the two-and-a-half-story redbrick Georgian edifice still stands at the head of Washington Square in Newport. I strolled past it, admiring the simple elegance of colonial architect Richard Munday's design, and climbed the steps of the graceless Florence K. Murray Judicial Complex. Inside, I entered the district court clerk's office and dug through recent civil filings.

Marlon Jenks was being sued. According to the complaint, a pair of "new" Husqvarna ride-on power mowers he'd sold to a Wakefield lawn service company were actually rebuilt models. Jenks had denied the complaint, and the case was still pending. But the amount at stake was less than five grand. A little more checking showed that neither Jenks nor his hardware store had ever filed for bankruptcy.

I drove home, fired up my laptop, checked the three leading credit rating services, and found that his scores were over seven hundred on all of them. If he'd been having money trouble, I couldn't find any sign of it.

That afternoon, I drove back to Jamestown and popped into the hardware store. Jenks's wife, Angie, was behind the counter, ringing up a sale. His teenage sons, Jake and Dougie, were there too, helping out after school by stocking the shelves. On impulse, I grabbed a pointed shovel, a bag of fertilizer, and five azalea bushes and then waited in line behind two other customers to pay for my purchases.

Afterward, I went back to my place and planted the azaleas beside my back porch. Then I took Brady and Rondo for a run around the property, thought about Marlon Jenks sitting in a holding cell, and wondered what I should do next.

That evening, Buzz Starkey, one of ESPN's army of NFL reporters, went on the air to trumpet an exclusive: Conner Bowditch was gay—and, as a consequence, he was certain to plunge like a leaky submarine in the upcoming college draft.

The story, attributed to an unnamed pro scout, was accompanied by a low-quality, thirty-second video of Bowditch emerging from a Providence gay bar with his arm draped over the shoulder of a little man Starkey referred to only as "the star's longtime companion." I recognized him right off as Bowditch's old high school pal, Ricky Santos. The story had the insidious mixture of facts and innuendo that many people would find convincing.

An hour after it aired, Bowditch called me in a panic.

"It's a lie," he said, "but people are going to believe it. Hell, even Meghan is looking at me funny and asking me if it's true. I got reporters phoning me every five minutes with questions about what they call my *lifestyle*. They've started stalking my teammates and my dad already, too. Christ! It's less than two weeks before the draft, Mr. Mulligan. There's probably not enough time to erase people's doubts about this. It's gonna cost me millions."

"Calm down, Conner, and maybe I can help you straighten this out. Tell me what you were doing at that bar."

He audibly sucked in a breath and started in. "Sunday night, I met Ricky for a drink at the Stable on Washington Street and—"

Suddenly, a woman shrieked in the background.

"Dammit," Conner growled. "It's not a meat market, Meghan. It's a classy place."

"So I hear," I said.

"We sat at the bar, knocked back a few, and talked about stuff," Conner said. "How his studies was going. Where I hoped to play next year. Which team was likely to draft me. Every once in a while, a guy came up and asked for my autograph. After a couple of hours, we finished our beers and went home. I mean, I went back to my parents' house, and he went back to his place. It was all totally innocent."

"But someone wants to make it look like it wasn't," I said.

"Yeah," Conner said. "And I think I know who."

48

McCracken put his phone on speaker, swung his feet onto his desk, and blew a smoke ring. "Good morning, Mr. Eliason. How can we help you today?"

"Jesus Christ!" Eliason growled. "How can you *help* me? Is that what you fuckin' said? We're paying you two donkeys a ton of money to vet Bowditch, and I gotta find out from Buzz fuckin' *Starkey* that the kid's a closeted gay?"

"So what if he is?" I said.

"Are you *shittin'* me?"

"I'm not."

"I thought you guys claimed to know football," Eliason said.

We didn't say anything to that.

"What? You think we're all fuckin' bigots up here now?"

We didn't say anything to that, either.

"Well, we're not," he said. "I got no problem with the gays. Neither does Coach Belichick. Hell, Robert Kraft is on record that he'd welcome an openly gay player on the Patriots."

"Then why are you making a big deal out of this?" McCracken said.

Now it was Eliason who didn't have anything to say.

"Well, here's what I think," McCracken said. "The macho culture of NFL locker rooms is intolerant of gay athletes. A bunch of NFL players have made homophobic comments.

Jonathan Vilma of the Saints actually tweeted that he's afraid gay teammates might *look* at him in the shower."

"You never heard any of that crap from a member of the Patriots," Eliason said.

"True," I said, "but I bet some of the guys in your locker room think that way. A gay player would be a distraction, and we all know how much Belichick hates distractions."

"Look," Eliason said, "we're trying to win football games here. Got our sights on another Super Bowl trophy. You expect us to risk that just to make a *statement*? You think we should make Bowditch our Jackie Robinson just so Robert Kraft can go down in history as the next Branch Rickey?"

"I think that would be nice," I said.

"Well, it's not gonna happen."

"Thanks for clearing that up," I said. "You're right. It's not going to happen. But not for the reason you think."

"What the hell are you talking about?"

"Bowditch isn't gay."

"He's not?"

"That's right."

"Are you sure?" Eliason said. "I mean, Starkey's an asshole, but he usually gets his facts straight."

"Not this time," McCracken said.

"How do you know?"

"Remember us telling you that one of the Jets' scouts, Elliot Crabtree, has been dogging Bowditch?" McCracken said.

"Yeah."

"He concocted the story and got Starkey to fall for it."

"What the hell would he do that for?"

"The Jets will be picking seventh," McCracken said. "If the story causes Bowditch to fall in the draft . . .

"Which it will," I butted in.

"Then they can grab him," McCracken said.

"Sonovabitch!" Eliason said. "You're sure Crabtree is behind this?"

"Absolutely," I said.

"How do you know?"

"He was lurking outside the club when Bowditch strolled out with his arm around a film student named Ricky Santos. They both saw him point his cell phone at them."

"Which is where the video came from?"

"Uh-huh."

"What the hell was Bowditch doing in a gay bar in the first place?" Eliason asked.

"Having a drink with an old friend."

"But why *there*?"

"The Stable is Santos's favorite spot."

"This Santos kid is gay?"

"Definitely."

"Then how can you be sure that Bowditch isn't gay, too?"

"I guess you can never be absolutely sure about that with anybody," McCracken said. "Nobody had a clue about Dennis Hastert until the former Speaker of the House got caught paying hush money to keep a fifty-year-old dalliance with a male student quiet. But we've talked to everybody who knows Bowditch. If he's in the closet, we can't find any hint of it."

"Okay, then," Eliason said.

"And if it turns out that he *is* gay, so what?" I said.

"Aw, Christ. Let's not chew on that bone that again. We've got a deal on the table with Jacksonville for the third pick in the draft. If we make it, we can grab Bowditch. The question is, should we pull the trigger?"

"Probably," I said.

"*Probably*? That's not good enough. We'd be giving up a hell of a lot for the kid. We can't afford to make a mistake."

"Well, we've still got a few loose ends to tie up," McCracken said.

"So you're saying I should hold off?"

"Up to you," McCracken said.

"Ticktock," Eliason said. "The Jaguars are itching to trade

down, but if we hesitate, they might move the pick to somebody else. And the draft—the fucking *dread line*—is less than two weeks away."

"Understood."

"So," McCracken said after we signed off, "think we were right in not telling Eliason about the point shaving?"

"Yeah," I said. "And not telling him who Conner's agent is, too. I doubt the Patriots would want to negotiate a deal with that prick."

"We're going to have to tell him eventually."

"Sure, but we've still got a couple of weeks to make things right. I think it's time we paid Morris Dunst another visit."

"Today's as good a time as any," McCracken said.

"Tomorrow would be better."

"Why?"

"I need to see Mark Gardner at Yolanda's law firm first."

49

According to the little brass plate on her desk, Dunst's receptionist, or administrative assistant, or office manager, or executive support associate, or whatever the hell the language vandals were calling the job this week, was named Doris Platt. The fresh flowers on her leather desk blotter and the message on the bouquet of helium balloons bobbing over her head told me that this was her birthday.

"I'm afraid I don't have you gentlemen down for this morning," Ms. Platt said. "Did you have an appointment?"

"No," I said.

"Is Attorney Dunst expecting you?"

"Not right this minute, but I'm pretty sure he knew he'd be seeing us again."

"I'm sorry, but he's currently out of the office."

"Oh, really?" McCracken said.

"Yes."

He circled her desk, cracked the inner door, peeked inside, and then pulled it closed.

"As I told you, he's not in," she said, her voice colder now.

"Will he be returning anytime soon?" I asked.

"I believe it could be several hours."

"We'll wait."

We grabbed seats in the waiting area and started flipping through dated magazines again.

"Perhaps you'd be more comfortable in a bar or coffee shop," Ms. Platt said, the set of her shoulders hinting that she was growing uneasy with our presence.

"Maybe we could wait in his office," I said. "That would give us a chance to rifle his files and check his desk for firearms."

Ms. Platt's forced smile said she wasn't sure if I was kidding. "There are a couple of nearby places I can recommend," she said.

"That's okay," McCracken said. "I don't think we'll have much trouble finding a bar in Boston."

"Well, then, give me your business card," she said. "I'll give you a call if he is able to squeeze you in today."

Five minutes later, we were sitting in McCracken's Acura at the corner of Milk and Devonshire, where we had an unobstructed view of both entrances to the building. We were still waiting there at six P.M. when Platt emerged from the front entrance, frowned at a sky that was threatening rain, and strolled down the street to a bus stop.

"What do you think?" McCracken asked.

"Could be he got held up on lawyer business," I said. "More likely she called him, and he decided to duck us."

"Want to hang around till dark and then black-bag his office? I checked out the locks on our way out. I could pick them in less than five minutes."

I took a few seconds to think about it and then shook my head. "It's not worth the risk. Chances are he's got the contracts locked in a safe. A Schlage door lock isn't much of a challenge for you, but you're no safecracker."

"The contracts might not even be there," McCracken said. "He could be keeping them at home. Or in a safe deposit box."

"True."

"But if we toss the office, we might learn something."

"Forget it," I said. "We know all we need to know about Morris fucking Dunst."

"So we come back again tomorrow," McCracken said.

That evening, we dined on shellfish and Samuel Adams Summer Ale at the Union Oyster House near Faneuil Hall. After the entree dishes were cleared away, we chatted over cups of Irish coffee.

"So," McCracken said, "how are you making out with that Jenks thing?"

I ran it down for him.

"What are you going to do next?" he asked.

"No idea."

He rubbed his jaw and considered my problem. "If I were you, I'd try to get a peek inside his medicine cabinet."

After dinner, we checked into the Boston Harbor Hotel. McCracken planned to charge the extravagance to the Patriots as a business expense.

Seven A.M. found us parked at Milk and Devonshire again, taking turns reading *The Boston Globe* and watching the building. By four in the afternoon, Dunst still hadn't appeared, so I pulled out my cell phone and called his office.

"Dunst and Moran. How may I direct your call?"

"Mr. Dunst, please."

"May I ask who is calling?"

"Elliot Crabtree. I'm with the New York Jets, and I'd like a word with Mr. Dunst about one of the players he represents."

"I'm sorry, but he's not in the office today."

"When do you expect him?"

"He's out of town conferring with clients. I don't expect him back for at least a week."

I thanked her and signed off.

"Well," McCracken said, "we may as well give the Patriots our final report. We can always deal with Dunst after the draft if it comes to that."

I nodded and called Eliason's number.

"Okay," he said. "Drop by my office in Foxboro next week."

"Next week? I thought you were in a rush."

"No need to hurry now," he said. "The Jaguars just traded the third pick to the Texans, who've got their eye on the star wide receiver from Florida State. We're still stuck at the bottom of the first round, so unless we can work something out with Houston, which ain't likely, the fucking Jets will grab Bowditch with the seventh pick. No way he'll be suiting up as a Patriot."

50

Next morning, there was nothing dead waiting for me on my porch. Five days later, Cat the Ripper still hadn't appeared with his daily offering. Maybe he'd tired of tangling with Rondo and had found another dumping spot for his kills.

I spent the week playing with my dogs, putting the Sundowner in the water, and puttering around in the yard. I turned up a plot of earth in the field in front of the house, planted some tomatoes and green peppers, and strung a wire fence to discourage the rabbits. Raised in the city, I'd never tried gardening before. There was something oddly peaceful about putting things in the ground and watching them grow.

Early Saturday evening, I drove to Clinton Avenue, strolled up a front walk lined with tulips and daffodils, and rapped on the door of a gray-shingled ranch house. Angie Jenks opened the door with a spatula in her hand and a "King of the Grill" apron tied around her ample waist.

"Can I help you?"

"My name is Mulligan. I'm a private detective, and I'd like to talk to you about your husband's case."

"What case? He confessed."

"I'd still like a word."

She opened her mouth to speak, hesitated, and looked me up and down.

"I think I recognize you," she said. "Didn't you buy some tomato plants at the store this week?"

"Some pepper plants and wire fencing too."

"I appreciate your business, but there's really nothing to talk about."

"Ellington Cargill hired me to look into the death of his son," I said. "He wants to be sure that everything's on the up and up before he releases the reward money."

She hesitated again, then said, "I've got chicken and hamburgers on the grill. Walk around back, and I'll give you a few minutes."

The spicy smell of good barbecue hit me before I turned the corner of the house and found the Jenks boys, Jake and Dougie, sprawled in the grass beside an aboveground pool. They were playing with a beagle puppy, a replacement for the pooch Alexander Cargill had killed. Angie was at the grill, turning burgers with a spatula. She plunged her hand into an ice chest, extracted a can of Budweiser, and placed it in my hand.

"I've only got enough chicken for the boys," she said, "but I can spare a burger or two."

"Thanks, but I'm fine." I cracked open the beer and asked, "How are you holding up?"

"As well as can be expected, I guess."

"Why do you think your husband confessed?"

"Because he couldn't live with the guilt," she said, keeping her voice low so her children couldn't overhear.

"You're sure he did it?"

"Aren't you?"

"No."

She turned from her work and stared at me. "And why would that be?"

"I read his confession. He didn't seem to know any of the details the police withheld from the press."

"I wouldn't know anything about that."

I took a pull of my beer and didn't speak, hoping she'd feel the need to fill the silence.

"Marlon is going to be sentenced next week. It's over, Mr. Mulligan. Can you please leave my family in peace?"

"Okay, then. I'm sorry for your troubles, Mrs. Jenks." I finished the beer and dropped the empty into a trash can. "Do you mind if I use your bathroom before I go?"

"Sure thing." She pointed at the rear entrance and said, "It's the second door on your left."

Inside, I turned on the water to muffle my snooping and opened the medicine cabinet. Toothpaste, ibuprofen, Band-Aids, nasal spray, Maalox, sanitary napkins . . . but nothing out of the ordinary. I gently closed the cabinet, padded down the hall, opened the first door I came to, and peered into a bedroom furnished with unmade bunk beds, the floor a tangle of boys' clothing and sports equipment. The door across the hall opened onto the master bedroom. I stepped inside and started with the drawer in the bedside table. Nothing but a Bible and a pair of reading glasses. Next, I tried the top drawer of a tall men's bureau. Tucked beneath the socks, I found five vials. I plucked them out, shook them, and discovered that they were nearly empty. The labels told me they'd been prescribed two months ago. Each was for a different drug I didn't recognize. I pulled out a pad and jotted down the particulars, including the name of the prescribing doctor. Then I returned the vials to the drawer, tiptoed to the bathroom, flushed, and stepped back into the yard.

Dr. Chase C. Utley plucked reading glasses from his nose, tossed them on his desk, and said, "I'm sorry, but there's nothing I can tell you."

"The fact that we're sitting in the Newport Hospital Comprehensive Cancer Center already tells me something," I said.

"Perhaps."

"You're an oncologist?"

"I am."

I pulled a notebook from my shirt pocket, tore out a page, and pushed it across the desk. "And you prescribed these drugs for Marlon Jenks?"

"I can't confirm that."

"I saw your name on the vials, Doctor."

"Nevertheless."

"Is Jenks dying?"

He frowned and shook his head.

"Look," I said. "I think Jenks confessed to a murder he didn't commit. I'm trying to figure out why he would have done that."

Utley steepled his fingers on his desktop and thought for a moment.

"As I am sure you are aware, confidentiality laws prevent me from disclosing anything about a patient, Mr. Mulligan. However, I am free to cite publicly available statistics. Sadly, the median survival rate for patients with stage-four lung cancer is eight months."

When I got home, I let Brady and Rondo outside to run. A few minutes later, I heard them barking. I found them pawing at something under the cluster of white pines on the west side of the property.

"What is it, boys?"

And then I saw it, the headless corpse of a big tabby. At first, I thought he must have fallen victim to one of the island's ravenous coyotes. But when I kneeled in the pine needles for a closer look, I saw that the body was as flat as a deflated balloon. Something had crawled in through the neck and hollowed it out.

Brady cocked his head, puzzled by the scent of death. Rondo whimpered as if in mourning for a worthy adversary.

I fetched an old blanket and a pointed shovel, wrapped what was left of the big cat, and buried him beside the pines. Then

I went inside, called the animal shelter, and told Tracy what I'd found.

"What could do that to an animal?" I asked.

"It definitely wasn't a coyote," she said. "They don't kill like that."

"Then what?"

"A fisher cat."

"What's that?"

"A predator related to the American martin."

"I'm still drawing a blank."

"It looks like a big weasel," she said.

"I've never seen anything like that around here."

"They're out there," she said, "but they're stealthy. Very hard to spot."

"Could they hurt my dogs?"

"Small dogs, sure, but not your boys. Fisher cats are too smart to challenge anything that big."

After we signed off, I removed a large chunk of slate from the stone wall beside my shed and placed it on the grave, marking the spot. Killing had been Cat the Ripper's nature, so I'd never held it against him. It was in the nature of fisher cats, too. But what about Alexander Cargill? And Michael "Mickey Scars" McNulty? And Efrain Vargas? Were they killers by nature? For that matter, what about me?

None of us, I decided, could use that as an excuse.

51

I entered Ragsdale's office unannounced and tossed a couple of Cubans on his desk.

"What is it this time?" he said.

"I think you know."

"Jesus! I hope you're not here about Jenks again, I *told* you to stay the hell away from that."

"You did," I said, "but I suck at following directions."

"Goddammit, Mulligan. Leave well enough alone."

"Why? Are you so hard up to close the case that you're willing to let an innocent man go down for murder?"

"Screw you. Get the hell out of my office, or I'll arrest you for interfering with a police investigation."

"Marlon Jenks is dying," I said.

"No shit."

"How long have you known?"

"Long enough."

"How much time has he got?"

"A month, maybe. Two at the most."

"And that makes this okay with you?"

"Look," he said, "maybe Marlon is guilty, and maybe he isn't. If he didn't kill Alexander Cargill, we'll never know who did. There are no witnesses, and there's not a shred of physical evidence. Except for the confession, I've got zilch."

"So?"

"So now Angie's stuck with trying to keep the hardware store afloat while she raises two boys on her own. They're smart kids, Mulligan. She'll be wanting to send them to college in a few years."

"Which is where that fat reward comes in," I said.

He nodded.

"Yeah," I said. "I figured it was something like that."

"So, are we good?"

I wasn't feeling all that good about it, but I had to admit he had a point. "We are," I said.

Then I stuck out my hand, and he shook it.

I found Ellington Cargill where I'd first met him, sitting by his Lake Erie–size pool with a stemmed glass in hand. A half-full pitcher of martinis stood beside him on that same bamboo table.

His trophy wife was stretched out on a chaise longue, her nose buried in a Timothy Hallinan mystery novel. Sadly, she wasn't half-naked this time, her figure sheathed in something sleek and silky on this cool early April evening. Beyond her, the sun was dropping below the ocean. She pushed her sunglasses down her nose, gave me the once-over, saw nothing of interest, and returned to her reading.

Cargill waved me into a chair across from him, poured me a glass, and slid it across the table. I drew a manila envelope from my jacket and placed it beside the pitcher.

"I finished the job you hired me for, Mr. Cargill," I said. "This is the full report on my investigation."

"What's the bottom line?"

"I'm satisfied that Marlon Jenks's confession is genuine."

"Why did he do it?"

"He was angry that Alexander killed his dog."

"I still don't believe my son was capable of that."

"I understand," I said. "If it helps, you should go right on thinking that."

"You think I'm wrong?"

"It doesn't matter what I think."

His upper lip quivered, and for a moment I thought he was going to weep. Then he sucked in a breath and pulled himself together.

"As I'm sure you've heard, Jenks's wife is the one who turned him in," I said. "I trust you'll be honoring the reward you offered."

"I'll have the check cut in the morning."

I nodded and placed a letter-size envelope on the table.

"What's that?"

"It took only a few days' work for me to figure things out," I said. "At the three-grand-a-day rate we agreed on, my fee comes to fifteen thousand dollars, so I'm returning the balance of your advance."

He nodded, picked up his martini, and dismissed me with a wave of his hand.

On the drive home, I stopped at the Jamestown post office and dropped another envelope into the outside mail box. The letter was addressed to the Animal Rescue League of Southern Rhode Island. Inside was a check for fifteen thousand dollars.

Blood money.

52

Two days before we were scheduled to meet with the Patriots, McCracken and I paid Conner Bowditch and his dad a visit at their house on the East Side.

"You were right, Conner," I said. "Elliot Crabtree planted the story with ESPN so you'd fall in the draft. That way, the Jets can grab you with the seventh pick."

"Then I won't sign with the bastards," Conner said.

"Hold on now, son," his father said. "Mr. Mulligan, do you think the Jets management was in on this, or did Crabtree do it on his own?"

"No idea," I said.

"Can you find out?"

"I don't see how we could," McCracken said.

"It doesn't matter, Dad," Conner said. "After what Crabtree pulled, there's no way I'm ever putting on that fucking green uniform."

"Still want to play for Belichick?" I asked.

"Oh, hell, yeah."

"Why?"

"Are you kidding me? He's the best coach in the league. Maybe the best football coach ever. Before he's done, he's going to add to all those Super Bowl rings he's got, Mr. Mulligan.

I want one on my finger too, and playing for him is the best way to make that happen."

"The way things stand, the Patriots won't be picking high enough to draft you," I said. "But I might be able to fix that."

"How?"

"By pulling the same kind of trick on the Jets that they pulled on the rest of the league. Would you be okay with that?"

"It would serve them right."

"Even if costs you a few million dollars on your rookie contract?"

"Even then. Besides, if I have to sign for less up front, you can bet I'll make up for it in my second deal."

"Exactly what have you got in mind, Mr. Mulligan?" Conner's dad asked.

On Tuesday morning, it took McCracken and me well over an hour to spill everything we'd learned about Conner Bowditch in the past six months. When we were done, Eliason and Ellis Cruze had questions.

"You're *sure* the kid doesn't have a gambling problem?" Cruz asked.

"We are," McCracken said.

"And that he's not gay?" Eliason said.

"That, too," I said.

"I'm still bothered by the point-shaving thing," Cruze said.

"I get that," I said. "But like I told you, the kid was coerced. He was just trying to protect the people he loves."

"What if it comes out?"

"It won't," McCracken said. "The only people who know about it are Bowditch, Lance Gabriel, and the Vacca brothers. All four of them have good reasons to keep their mouths shut."

"Besides," I said, "if it ever does come out, Bowditch is going to come off as more of a victim than a bad guy."

"What about Dunst?" Eliason said. "No way we're going to sit across the negotiating table from him."

"You won't have to," McCracken said.

"You're going to get Bowditch out of that?" Cruze said.

"We are."

"How?"

"You don't want to know," McCracken said.

Cruze and Eliason exchanged glances.

"Well," Eliason said, "the Jets are going to draft him, so none of this matters anyway."

"Maybe they won't," I said.

"What do you mean?"

"What if we could fix it so he falls to the Patriots?"

"How?"

"You *really* don't want to know that," McCracken said.

Eliason gave us both a long look. "After Spygate and Deflategate, the Patriots can't afford another scandal," he said. "Whatever you've got in mind, it can't blow back on us."

"It won't," McCracken said.

"How can you be sure?" Cruze asked.

"You'll just have to trust us on that," I said.

"Would you be breaking any laws?" Cruze asked. "We couldn't condone that."

"Not any important ones," I said. "But if we're going to do this, you're going to have to do a couple of things for us."

"Like what?" Eliason asked.

"With what we've got in mind, Bowditch could fall all the way to you at the end of the first round," I said, "but the kid doesn't deserve that. It would cost him too much money. Any chance you could still trade up?"

"How high?"

"Somewhere in the top ten?"

"We might be able to do that," Eliason said. "One or two teams are still looking to trade down."

"Okay, then."

"You said a couple of things," Cruze said. "What's the other one?"

"You need a cornerback," I said, "and there's this kick-ass player at Oregon State."

"You mean Chuck Crawford, kid who came out as gay last year?"

"Yeah. They say he's got first-round talent."

"He does," Eliason said.

"Most likely, he'll still be on the board when you pick in the third round," I said. "If he is, you have to promise that you'll take him."

"Really?" Eliason said. "You're gonna climb back on *that* soapbox again?"

"That's the deal. Take it or leave it."

"I don't know," Eliason said. "I'll have to run this up the ladder."

"Don't take too long," I said. "Ticktock. The dread line is two days away."

Three hours later, McCracken and I were sipping whiskey in his office when Eliason called. "Belichick took this to the owner," he said. "Who knew? Turns out, when Kraft said he would welcome a gay player, he actually meant it."

"What about trading up?" I asked.

"We're working on a deal for the eighth spot, but the Buccaneers want to hold off until draft day to see if they get a better offer."

"Okay, then," I said. "In the next forty-eight hours, you're going to hear some really bad stuff about Bowditch. Don't believe a word of it."

53

"Channel Ten News, Logan Bedford speaking."

"Hello, Logan. I'm Richard Harding Davis."

"The reporter for *The Ocean State Rag*?"

"Yes, indeedy."

"I love your work."

"I'm a huge fan of yours too," I lied.

"So what's up?"

"I've got a big story for you."

"You do?"

"That's why I'm calling."

"Why give it to me?"

"My editor has declined to print it."

"Why would he do that?"

"Because he's close with Conner Bowditch's father."

"You've got something on Conner?"

"I do."

"Haven't you heard?" Bedford said. "Everybody already knows he's gay. The story's gone national."

"That's the least of it. The kid's dirty, Logan."

"I'm listening."

"My boss will fire me if he finds out I leaked this, but if you promise to keep my name out of it, I'll give you everything I've got."

"Done."

"If you're taping this call, turn the recorder off."

"I'm not."

"You sure, Logan? Because under Rhode Island law, it's illegal to tape a call unless both parties agree to it. If you cross me on this, I'll make trouble for you."

"I'm sure."

So I spun my tale for him.

"Jesus!" he said. "Can you *prove* all of this?"

"As soon as we hang up, I'm going to e-mail you a video of Bowditch walking into Zerilli's Market."

"That's where he's been placing his bets?"

"He's been gambling there for years. If you call Detective Wargart at the Providence PD, he'll confirm that it was a mobbed-up bookie joint before it went legal. DeLucca loved the puff piece you did on him, so he's willing to talk to you about Bowditch. He's waiting for your call at the store right now."

"Great!"

"But he's camera shy on this one, Logan. Doesn't want to be tape-recorded either, so you'll have to make do with notes."

"I can do that. What's the phone number at the market?"

"Look it up," I said. "I'm not going to do *all* of your work for you."

Next morning, McCracken had beer and deli sandwiches delivered to the office. He'd ordered enough to bloat the Patriots offensive line because we were expecting Joseph. Shortly before noon, the big lug strolled in, grabbed a pastrami in one hand and a ham and cheese in the other, and dropped into a chair across from the flat-screen. McCracken got up from behind his desk, tossed Joseph a beer, and snapped on the TV.

"Conner Bowditch, the Classical High School football hero and Boston College All American who'd been expected to be taken early in tomorrow's NFL draft, was recently outed as a gay man," the anchorwoman said. "But as it turns out, that's the least of his troubles. Stay tuned for our exclusive I-Team report. You'll be shocked!"

"Did you follow the script we gave you?" McCracken asked as a commercial for the Foxwoods Resort Casino flashed on the screen.

"Yeah," Joseph said.

"You didn't let him bring a camera into the store?"

"Fuck, no."

"And you're sure he didn't have a tape recorder on him?"

"I showed him my magnum and made him empty his pockets. Then I frisked the asshole to make sure."

We turned back to the TV now as the foxlike face of Logan Bedford leered from the screen, the camera angle gradually widening to show that he was standing in front of Zerilli's Market.

"According to the Providence police," he said, "the establishment behind me is more than a neighborhood market. For decades, an illegal bookmaking racket operated out of an office in back. Recently, it went legal, transforming itself into an online gambling business that conforms to state and federal law. However, Providence detective sergeant Jay Wargart says that it remains under the control of Dominic 'Whoosh' Zerilli, a reputed lieutenant in the Patriarca crime family.

"Thousands of Providence residents have gambled on sports here over the years. The Channel Ten I-Team has learned exclusively that one of the regulars was Conner Bowditch, the former Classical High School and Boston College football star.

"The video now appearing on your screen," he went on, "shows Bowditch entering the establishment yesterday afternoon. I asked Joseph DeLucca, who runs the gambling business for Zerilli, what Bowditch was doing there. 'The same thing everyone does,' DeLucca told me. 'He came in to place a bet.'

"Mr. DeLucca declined to appear on camera, but he told all in an exclusive interview. He said Bowditch first began coming into the store when he was in high school to place small bets on professional basketball, baseball, and football games. But last fall, in anticipation of a big payday after tomorrow's NFL draft, he started gambling big-time. 'Unfortunately for him, he's a lot better at football than he is at gambling,' DeLucca told me, adding, and I quote, 'The kid's into me for more than thirty grand.'

"I asked DeLucca what Bowditch had lost all that money on. 'Mostly college football,' he said. I asked if the player had ever gambled on the Boston College games that he played in. De-Lucca said that he had. Then I asked if he'd ever bet *against* his own team." Logan stared into the camera and paused for dramatic effect.

"DeLucca was hesitant to answer that question," he said. "But finally, he said, and I quote, 'Yea. Five bleeping times.'

"This morning, I contacted the NFL commissioner's office and was told that the league had no official comment on this matter. However, it seems certain that today's shocking disclosure will cause Bowditch's stock to continue to fall in tomorrow's draft. In fact, one NFL official told me privately, the finest football player ever to come out of Rhode Island probably won't get drafted at all. That big payday Conner Bowditch has been counting on to pay off his gambling debt? It won't be coming.

"This is Logan Bedford reporting for the Channel Ten I-team. Back to you, Beverly."

With that, McCracken flipped the channel to ESPN, and we settled down to enjoy our lunch.

"Any regrets about sandbagging Bedford?" McCracken asked.

"Hell, no," I said. "The prick had it coming. He's been plagiarizing my work for years."

Less than an hour later, Sports Center went live with the news: "According to the Associated Press, a Providence, Rhode Island, television station has just reported that . . ." ESPN ended the story with word that the Jets, who were rumored to be considering drafting Bowditch with the seventh pick despite the reports about his sexual preference, were now seeking to trade out of the first round.

"Think the Patriots can work a deal with them?" McCracken asked.

"No fuckin' way," Joseph said.

"He's right," I said. "The rivalry is too bitter for that. The Jets will never deal with the Patriots."

54

Early Thursday evening, I was playing tug-of-war with Brady and Rondo when Joseph's pickup truck rolled down the driveway and braked beside the house. As usual, he hadn't come empty-handed. I helped him lug eight large pizzas and four cartons of beer into the kitchen.

We were well along with our drinking when McCracken came in the door carrying a bottle of Irish whiskey and two grocery bags stuffed with Italian grinders and crab salad sandwiches from the island's East Ferry Deli.

An hour before the NFL draft was set to begin, I fetched my Leland strobe light, switched it on, and placed it at the end of my dock. Twenty minutes later, a seventeen-foot bowrider tied up beside my Sundowner. Malcolm Bowditch jumped out and switched off my signal light. Then he and his son strolled in my back door with two grocery bags of Philly steak sandwiches and a carton of Moët & Chandon Imperial champagne.

"Jesus! I said. "We've got enough food and drink to give the whole NFL the runs."

"You shittin' me?" Joseph said. "I was thinkin' we probably ain't got enough."

"Did the press try to follow you?" I asked Malcolm.

"Yeah. A dozen reporters were camped outside the house

when we pulled out of the driveway. They jumped in their vehicles and chased us all the way to Wickford Harbor."

"Was Logan Bedford one of them?"

"He was. He kept shouting questions as we boarded the boat. When we shoved off, he looked pretty pissed."

"I'll bet."

He sighed. "You know, this isn't how I pictured this day. I figured we'd be celebrating in the green room at the draft."

"You were uninvited?" McCracken asked.

"Yeah. The commissioner's office called about an hour after Logan Bedford's story broke and told us we weren't welcome."

"This is better, Dad," Conner said, and we straggled into the living room to watch ESPN. "I wouldn't have known anybody there anyway. This way, we get to celebrate with friends."

"Where's Meghan?" I asked.

He just shrugged.

"Conner sat down with her yesterday and tried to explain what was going on," Marlon said, "but she's not buying it."

"She called me a liar," Conner said. "Hell, she still thinks I might be gay."

"Don't sweat it, Conner," I said. "She'll know the truth soon enough."

"I don't really care anymore. We're done."

From the look on his face, I wasn't so sure. But if it *was* over, I figured he was better off.

"Any word on the Patriots trading up?" Marlon asked.

"Nothing yet," I said. "I tried reaching out to Eliason this afternoon, but he was too busy in the Patriots' war room to take my call."

"Pipe down," McCracken said. "It's about to start."

We stopped yakking and locked our eyes on the TV as Roger Goodell strode to the podium: "With the first pick in the NFL draft, the Cleveland Browns . . ."

With each team using most of the ten minutes allowed to

make its selection, the evening dragged. An hour passed before the Jets, apparently unable to deal out of the first round, made their choice. Now, with still no word of a trade with the Patriots, the Tampa Bay Buccaneers were on the clock.

Conner's cell phone rang. He clicked it on, and a smile spread across his face. "Thanks so much, Coach," he said. "I'm gonna make you proud." Then he signed off, got to his feet, and exchanged high fives with all of us. Including the dogs.

Up on the podium, Goodell was handed a card with the name of the player who had been drafted eighth. He studied it, scowled, and covered the microphone with his hand. Then he turned to the league official who'd delivered it and muttered something.

"What the hell is he doing?" Malcolm asked. "Can anybody read his lips?"

"Yeah," McCracken said. "I think he asked, 'Is this some kind of sick joke?'"

Goodell turned back to the microphone. "Ladies and gentlemen, we are going to pause the proceedings for a few minutes. Please bear with us." Then he stalked off the stage.

ESPN announcer Chris Berman had a puzzled look on his face. "Something's up," he said. "Whatever it is, we'll have to just wait and see." And then he broke for commercial.

Two minutes later, he was back. "While we were gone, Commissioner Goodell huddled with Tampa Bay Buccaneers general manager Jason Licht. Now he's exchanging words with Patriots head coach and GM Bill Belichick."

"The commissioner doesn't look happy," Mel Kiper Jr. said.

"That's putting it mildly," Berman said. "But Belichick looks like he just swallowed the canary."

Another five minutes dragged by before Goodell returned to the podium. "There has been a trade. With the eighth pick in the NFL draft, acquired from the Tampa Bay Buccaneers, the New England Patriots select Boston College defensive tackle Conner Bowditch."

And hell broke loose. In Chicago, thousands of fans at the live event booed and shook their fists. Some hurled paper drinking cups as the TV cameras panned the crowd. And in Jamestown, Rhode Island, five people watching on TV were sprayed with expensive champagne. Brady and Rondo dove behind the couch to escape the mayhem. After a moment, they ventured out and lapped at the puddles.

Back on the TV, the ESPN analysts were shaking their heads in astonishment.

"What the heck is Bill Belichick thinking?" Kiper snapped. "After yesterday's disclosure that Bowditch gambled on Boston College games, it's hard to imagine him ever playing a single down in the NFL. No question he'll be banned from the league. He could even end up facing criminal charges."

Only Berman offered a word of caution. "Maybe the Patriots know something the rest of us don't. It wouldn't be the first time."

An hour later, with the Giants on the clock, an ESPN floor reporter finally managed to corral Belichick and shove a microphone in his face.

"Every football fan in America is asking the same question," the reporter said. "How could you waste a top-ten pick on Conner Bowditch?"

"We saw an opportunity to select the best player in the draft and jumped at it," Belichick said.

"But aren't you concerned about his gambling?"

"We saw an opportunity to select the best player in the draft and jumped at it," the notoriously terse coach repeated. As the reporter pressed for more, Belichick turned his back and stalked off.

With that, I got up from the couch, sat down at the kitchen table, fired up my laptop, and filed Richard Harding Davis's final story.

· · ·

The first round was nearly over, the Arizona Cardinals on the clock, when Berman broke in with some news. "According to the Associated Press, a respected Rhode Island online news organization is reporting that the gambling accusations recently leveled against Conner Bowditch are all untrue."

"You've got to be kidding!" Kiper said. "How could they know that?"

"According to the story, the Providence, Rhode Island, bookie cited as the source for the original report has sworn out an affidavit declaring that Bowditch never placed a single bet with him. In fact, the bookie insists he never spoke to the Providence television station that first broke the gambling story."

"What about the video of Bowditch entering the market where the bookie conducts business?" Kiper asked.

"According to the bookie," Berman said, "the kid just came in to buy a six-pack. . . . Oh, and the story says the reports about Bowditch being gay are also false. It's a long story, too much for me to digest right now, but at first glance, it looks pretty convincing. Lots of details and named sources."

"I'll be damned," Kiper said. "I've got a feeling there's some funny business going on here."

"Maybe," Berman said. "Or maybe the TV reporter just got it wrong."

Fifteen minutes later, as the draft coverage was wrapping up, Kiper returned with something new.

"According to league sources, the Jets are accusing the Patriots of planting the gambling story in an effort to manipulate the draft. The Patriots deny it and are accusing the Jets of planting the story about Bowditch being gay. One thing we can be sure of. This thing isn't over. The commissioner's office will have to conduct a full investigation."

"What a mess," Berman said. "This could be another black eye for the league. And the New England Patriots, a team whose reputation has already been sullied by Spygate and Deflategate, are right in the middle of things again."

. . .

"I know I'm in the minority on this," I said, "but I've always thought that Spygate and Deflategate were blown out of proportion."

"Me too," McCracken said. "In Spygate, the Patriots were caught taping the Jets' defensive signals, but what was so secret about them? They were being flashed openly in front of nearly seventy thousand people."

"Yeah," I said. "Anybody there could have captured them with a cell phone."

"And I'm still not convinced the Patriots deliberately deflated footballs in the AFC championship game," McCracken said. "But if they did, so what?"

"Well, it *was* cheating," Conner Bowditch said.

"It was just gamesmanship," McCracken said. "The kind of thing that's always been a part of every sport. In baseball, stealing signs isn't even against the rules. Doctoring baseballs is, but it's considered cool if you can get away with it. It got Gaylord Perry into the Hall of Fame."

"Maybe so," Conner said, "but I still think it's wrong."

"I don't see any of it as a big deal," I said. "But manipulating the draft by planting false news stories is a serious matter. *That* one is on me."

On day 2 of the NFL draft, the Patriots made good on their promise. When their turn came in the third round, they chose Chuck Crawford, the openly gay safety from Oregon State.

Ten minutes later, my sister, Meg, and her wife called from their farmhouse in New Hampshire.

"I've always loved the Patriots," Meg said. "But I'm so proud of Bill Belichick and Robert Kraft today."

"Yeah," I said. "Me, too."

55

It was nearly nine by the time Dunst climbed out of a taxi, sprinted through the rain, and ducked into the Milk Street office building. We gave him ten minutes to get settled and then headed up.

"I'm sorry, but Mr. Dunst isn't in," his secretary, Doris Platt, said. "I'm not expecting him at all today."

McCracken glared at her and held it until she averted her eyes. Then he turned to the inner door, tried the latch, and discovered that it was locked. He shrugged, pulled out his wallet, removed a hundred-dollar bill, and placed it on Doris's desk.

"What's that for?" she asked.

"To cover the damage," McCracken said. Then he raised his foot and kicked in the door.

Inside, we found Dunst sitting behind his Klingon-inspired desk. Under the circumstances, he looked remarkably unruffled. As we tried to make ourselves comfortable on the weird office furniture, Doris materialized in the splintered door frame.

"Shall I phone the police, Mr. Dunst?"

"No, Doris. You know who to call."

"Yes, sir. Right away."

"So, Morris," McCracken said. "Disappointed to see us again?"

"Not at all," the lawyer said. "It's always a pleasure to meet with representatives of the New England Patriots."

"Somehow, I doubt that," McCracken asked. "Next time you sic a hit team on us, try to remember that it takes more than four thugs with shotguns to get the job done."

"I'll keep that in mind."

"Enough with the pleasantries," I said. "You know why we're here."

"I do, but I'm afraid I am unable to accommodate you."

I pulled my jacket aside and gave him a look at what I was carrying in my shoulder holster. "Hand over the contracts, and we'll give you a kiss and be on our way."

We were still jawing fifteen minutes later when the Vacca brothers, their trigger fingers healed now, burst in with revolvers in their hands. Dunst's lips curled into a smile as the two thugs spread out on either side of the door and slouched against the walls.

"I'd be happy to make the introductions," Dunst said, "but I believe you've already met."

"We have," McCracken said. "As I recall, these two jerkoffs didn't enjoy it much the last time."

"Be that as it may," Dunst said, "your business here is concluded."

"I don't think so," I said.

"I assure you that it is," Dunst said. "I advise you to leave immediately and never return. If you resist, I shall ask these two gentlemen to remove you. Should that prove to be necessary, I can't be responsible for where they take you or what they do to you when they get there. Considering their reputations, I cannot imagine that it will be pleasant for you."

He grinned again, enjoying this. I grinned right back at him, slipped a finger into my jeans, slid out a burner phone, and hit speed dial.

"I'm with Dunst now," I said. "He's being uncooperative,

so it's time you two talked." I put the phone on speaker and placed it on the desk.

"Good morning, Mr. Dunst," said that voice, the one like water seeping through a clogged sewer pipe.

"Who the hell are you?"

"Giuseppe Arena."

And just like that, Dunst's grin vanished.

"Does my name mean something to you?"

"Yes, sir. . . . I, uh. . . . I am well aware of your reputation."

"Excellent. That ought to simplify things. Mulligan is a friend of mine. I would consider it a great favor to me if you would accommodate his request."

"Then I shall give it serious consideration."

A wheeze and a cough. And then, "Listen, Dunst. If you do as he asks, I might throw a little legal work your way. But if you refuse . . ." He fell silent then, leaving the consequences to the lawyer's imagination.

From somewhere deep inside, Dunst summoned up a modicum of courage. "I don't like being threatened, Mr. Arena."

"Of course not. No one does. Besides, action is more effective than threats, don't you think? People who fuck with my friends never see the bullet coming." And then he coughed again and hung up.

I snatched the phone from the desk and returned it to my pocket. "Enough talk," I said. "Give me the damned contracts."

"Screw you, Mulligan. How do I know that was really Arena?"

Shit. I hadn't thought of that.

"Boys, get these assholes out of my office," Dunst said. "I don't give a crap what you do with them as long as I never see them again."

Dante and Romeo Vacca exchanged glances, shrugged, and kept slouching against the wall.

"Now, if you don't mind," Dunst said.

"I don't think so," Dante said.

"*What?*"

The brothers looked at each other and shrugged again.

"Do as I tell you," Dunst said. "You work for me."

"We work for the highest bidder," Romeo said. "Arena pays better."

A bead of sweat popped from Dunst's brow and trickled down his cheek. "Whatever he's paying you, I'll double it."

"No can do," Dante said.

"Why the hell not?"

"Because if they cross Arena," I said, "he won't have any qualms about wiping them from the face of the earth."

I let that hang in the air for a moment, then said, "I'll take those contracts now."

Dunst's shoulders slumped. For several long seconds, he didn't move. Then he rose on wobbly legs, went to his framed photo of Bowditch, and removed it from the wall. Behind it was a small Paragon-brand safe. He punched some numbers into the keypad, cracked the door, removed a sheath of legal papers, and shoved them at me.

"The originals?" McCracken asked.

"Looks like," I said, "but I bet he's got copies squirreled away somewhere."

Dunst, back behind his desk now, tried to keep a poker face, but the corners of his mouth twitched in a suppressed smile. I didn't suppress mine. I just reached into my jacket, pulled out the documents Mark Gardner had prepared for me, and tossed them on the desk.

"Slap your autograph on these," I said.

"What are they?"

"Letters releasing Bowditch, Gabriel, and the other two players you signed from any obligations they might have with you."

"And if I refuse?"

"The Vaccas will persuade you. Considering their reputations," I added, echoing Dunst's words, "I cannot imagine that it will be pleasant for you."

He swallowed hard, picked up a pen, and started signing.

"You're out of the agent business, Dunst," McCracken said as I gathered the documents from the desk. "If you sign any more players, we'll be back. You can count on it. "

"That was more fun than a lap dance," McCracken said on the drive back to Providence.

"Except for one thing," I said.

"Having the Vacca brothers on *our* side?"

"Yeah. Just being on the same planet with them creeps me out."

"If you tell Arena about their sexual proclivities, he might put a hit out on them," McCracken said. "Old goombahs like him have a hard-on for perverts."

"He might," I said, "but I don't need any more blood on my hands."

"Huh? What the hell are you talking about?"

56

As it happened, the NFL wasn't the only organization with concerns about what came to be known as Connergate. The NCAA, Boston College, ESPN, *Sports Illustrated*, *The Boston Globe*, *The New York Times*, the Associated Press, and the Rhode Island State Police also conducted investigations.

By early August, Conner Bowditch had been cleared of the football gambling accusations. As for suspicions that the Patriots and the Jets had manipulated the draft, the investigations led nowhere.

Roger Goodell's last hope was that Richard Harding Davis, the only newsman who had gotten the Bowditch story right, might be able to shed some light on the situation. But the reporter was nowhere to be found. Edward Anthony Mason III, owner and editor of *The Ocean State Rag*, reported that Davis had abruptly resigned, leaving no forwarding address. NFL investigators and reporters for a half-dozen news organizations made a valiant effort to track him down but were unable to find any trace of him.

It was almost as if he had never existed.

As for Logan Bedford, Channel 10 suspended him without pay. But by midsummer, after Conner Bowditch assured the station that he had no intention of filing a libel suit, the jerk was back to spouting nonsense and half-truths on the air.

. . .

The day the Patriots' training camp opened, Yolanda packed a picnic basket, and we took the dogs for a cruise on the bay. We were halfway to Prudence Island when a stiff wind came up, making the Sundowner bounce like a carnival ride in the chop. Brady stuck his nose in the air and seemed to enjoy the rough ride. Rondo retched and deposited his breakfast on the deck.

"The poor baby's seasick," Yolanda said, so I pointed the boat for home.

There, we spread a blanket on the grass, ate seafood sandwiches garnished with tomatoes from my garden, and watched the sailboats tack in the breeze. When we finished our drinks, Russian River for Yolanda and Killian's Irish Red for me, we wandered inside, stripped off our bathing suits, and made love.

An hour later I collapsed on top of the sweaty sheets, feeling blissful but spent. Yolanda raised her head from my chest and planted a kiss on my forehead.

"Still want to move in together?" she asked.

"Sure do."

"I'm thinking we should keep both places," she said. "We can summer here and stay at my condo in the city when the roads turn bad."

I managed not to scream "yippee!" and said, "Sounds like a plan."

"I could use a cool drink," she said. "Can I get you anything?"

"A whiskey on the rocks would be great."

"Okay, baby. I'll be right back."

She sprang naked from the bed, and, despite my exhaustion, I felt something stirring. She padded out of the bedroom, and a moment later I heard her shriek.

I thought about getting up to see what was wrong, but it was just a little shriek—the sound a startled woman might make if a field mouse dashed across the kitchen floor.

Suddenly she was standing in the doorway, a Ziploc bag pinched between her thumb and forefinger.

"Mulligan?"

"Um?"

"Why do you have a human ear in your freezer?"

ACKNOWLEDGMENTS

I am indebted to John Austin Murphy, a Jamestown, Rhode Island, attorney, for regaling me with Conanicut Island lore, including the story of the Russian factory ship—although as far as I know, none of the sailors really got any locals pregnant. Thanks also to my good friend and former *Providence Journal* and Associated Press colleague, Randall Richard, for taking me on a tour of the island from its north shore to Beavertail lighthouse in the south. And a tip of the hat to Tammy Walter, executive director of the Animal Rescue League of Southern Rhode Island, for providing details about her facility—and for the good works she and her staff perform every day. During the summer of 2014, when I was struggling with the plot, fellow crime novelist Timothy Hallinan offered a suggestion that became a crucial element in this story. My wife, Patricia Smith, the finest poet working in English, edited every line of this novel, adding musical notes to my sometimes toneless prose. My agent, Susanna Einstein, is the best story doctor I know, and Claire Eddy, my editor at Forge, is both a supportive ear and a gentle but demanding taskmaster. Every writer should have such friends. The idea for this book was conceived at the Atlantic Center for the Arts in New Smyrna Beach, Florida. Portions of it were written at the 2014 Sprachsalz International Literary Festival in

Hall, Austria, and during the Sierra Nevada College MFA program's 2014 summer residency in Doolin, Ireland, where Patricia and I taught a fiction class together. My gentle Bernese mountain dog, Brady, and my big goofy mutt, Rondo, served as models for two of the novel's characters and kept me company during the long slog of writing this novel. As Mulligan and I both know, nothing keeps your head straight like the love of a great dog.